"WHAT'S BUGGING YOU?" HE MUTTERED AS IF HE HAD no idea.

Summer shot him a killing glare. "Don't play dumb with me, Cooper Garrett," she snapped. "We agreed to try to bail you out of further social obligations, and you did just the opposite. Now I have the added pressure of trying to pretend we're a couple when we're not. You could easily have gotten out of going to that benefit."

"Maybe I didn't want to get out of it."

Summer eyed him as he stepped closer, forcing her into a corner. She drew back, but there was no escape. She suddenly felt claustrophobic. "What possible reason could you have for wanting to carry on this ridiculous charade?" she demanded.

"I've already told you," he said, his voice so low and husky, she felt the hair on her arms rise. "I wanted you from the minute I saw you. I've decided I'm going to have you no matter what."

"And I've already told you—"

His lips descended, cutting off the rest of her statement. The kiss was hungry and devouring, hot, setting her mouth aflame and making her forget all the reasons she should be protesting. When he finally raised his head, she felt weak and confused.

"I'm willing to play this your way," he whispered against her slightly parted lips. "I'll court you like a gentleman if that's what it takes. But don't make me wait too long, Summer, because I'm not a patient man when it comes to getting what I want."

WHAT ARE *LOVESWEPT* ROMANCES?

They are stories of true romance and touching emotion. We believe those two very important ingredients are constants in our highly sensual and very believable stories in the LOVE-SWEPT line. Our goal is to give you, the reader, stories of consistently high quality that may sometimes make you laugh, sometimes make you cry, but are always fresh and creative and contain many delightful surprises within their pages.

Most romance fans read an enormous number of books. Those they truly love, they keep. Others may be traded with friends and soon forgotten. We hope that each LOVESWEPT romance will be a treasure—a "keeper." We will always try to publish

LOVE STORIES YOU'LL NEVER FORGET
BY AUTHORS YOU'LL ALWAYS REMEMBER

The Editors

Loveswept ® 815

TALL, DARK, AND BAD

CHARLOTTE HUGHES

BANTAM BOOKS
NEW YORK · TORONTO · LONDON · SYDNEY · AUCKLAND

TALL, DARK, AND BAD

A Bantam Book / December 1996

ISBN 0-553-44524-3

Published simultaneously in the United States and Canada

Bantam Books are published by Bantam Books, a division of Bantam Dou-
bleday Dell Publishing Group, Inc. Its trademark, consisting of the words
"Bantam Books" and the portrayal of a rooster, is Registered in U.S. Patent
and Trademark Office and in other countries. Marca Registrada. Bantam
Books, 1540 Broadway, New York, New York 10036.

To those readers who've written letters and sent cards telling me how much they enjoy my "bad boy" heroes. Here's another man you'd think twice before taking home to meet your mama. Just remember, the "badder" they are, the harder they fall. And to my dear friends Bob and Betty Hudson and Suzanne Owens, a special thanks for the cute Dumpster story.

Warmest wishes, C. H.

ONE

"Henrietta, you gave me quite a scare," Dr. Cook said.

Seventy-year-old Henrietta Pettigrew gazed back at the young doctor from her hospital bed.

"So, the old ticker is still working?" she asked, giving him a humorous smile.

"You've got a few miles left on you, dear lady. Angina is quite common in women your age. Not that I think you're old," he added quickly. "These attacks can be frightening, though. And painful at times. I'd like to keep you overnight, just to make sure you're okay."

"Oh, pooh, Avery, is that really necessary? You know what my schedule is like."

"Precisely." Avery sat on the edge of Henrietta's bed. "You might have to slow down on some of your charity work. Stress is a big contributor to this condition. Why not delegate some of the work and free up your time for a little R and R?"

"My work means everything to me, Avery. Much is expected of those who have been as blessed as I have."

He took her hand and squeezed it. "I've never met anyone who felt so guilty about being rich. But if your work makes you happy, I certainly don't want to take that from you. I've seen too many retired patients wither away from simple boredom. All I ask is that you take time out for yourself."

He released her hand, stood, and scribbled something on his clipboard. Clearly, he'd stepped back into his doctor mode. "You'll have to modify your diet and start a light exercise program. I'll write you a prescription for nitroglycerin pills in case you have another attack. Just stick one under your tongue, and the tightness in your chest will go away in about a minute."

"But it's not life-threatening?"

"Not if you do as I say."

Henrietta pondered it. "Please don't mention this to my granddaughter," she said. "I want Summer to think it's . . . uh . . . a little more serious."

Avery arched one brow. "That's not a very nice thing to do to someone who loves you as much as that granddaughter of yours does. I've never seen anyone so devoted."

"It's for her own good," Henrietta said. "The girl is bound and determined to be an old maid. I want to see her happily married before I go. I can't stand the thought of her being all alone in this world."

Avery looked stern. "First of all, you're not *going* anywhere. Your angina can be successfully treated if you follow my instructions. Secondly, I hardly think Summer can be accused of being a spinster at twenty-five."

"Twenty-six and a half," Henrietta corrected Avery, then sighed. "She's a workaholic. Never leaves the office except to go home and collapse at the end of the day. I want her to find a man and settle down. A man who'll be good to her, look after her when I'm gone. If I can convince her I'm dying, maybe she'll start looking just to please me."

"You know I can't lie to her, Henrietta. If Summer

questions me, the best I can do is tell her you don't want me discussing your case."

"That's all I ask," she said.

Avery leaned over and kissed her on the forehead. "You got it, dear."

Summer Pettigrew was in the middle of pitching an advertising campaign for a large tire company, when her secretary buzzed her, interrupting her train of thought. "Excuse me, gentlemen," she said, reaching for her phone. "Yes, Joyce?"

"I'm sorry, Summer," her secretary said from the other end of the line. "I just got a call from your grandmother's housekeeper. Henrietta's been rushed to the emergency room."

Summer heard her own gasp, felt as though she'd just had a blow to the chest. She remembered feeling the same sensation as a kid after falling out of a tree. "Is it serious?" she asked quietly.

"The housekeeper thinks it was a heart attack."

"Thanks." Summer hung up the telephone and faced her clients, trying to maintain her composure. Working in a male-dominated advertising firm since college had taught her many lessons; keeping her emotions in check was just one. She was the consummate professional. Her makeup was flawless; her suits, although on the cutting edge of fashion, had the no-frills look of a woman ready to do business. She seldom allowed herself to become rattled, even with the most difficult client, but when it came to her grandmother, all her defenses crumbled and her insides turned to mush.

"Please forgive the interruption, gentlemen, but I have to leave on an emergency." She glanced at her co-worker, Warren Spencer, the office wolf who'd made his rounds through the secretarial pool before turning his affections her way. She'd thwarted his attempts, but it hadn't stopped him from trying. "Mr. Spencer has been involved with this project from the beginning," she said, "so I'll leave you in his capable hands."

"Here are *our* notes," Summer said, handing him the steno pad that would assist him with the presentation. "As you know, they're very detailed." He looked grateful as she grabbed her briefcase and hurried out.

Summer arrived at the hospital twenty minutes later, parked her sporty Mazda, and literally jogged to the main entrance. She paused at the information desk, where she learned a Mrs. Henrietta Pettigrew had just been moved to a private room. Summer grabbed an elevator and rode to the third floor, where she found a nurse looking over a patient's chart.

"I'm Summer Pettigrew," she said breathlessly. "My grandmother—"

"Room three twenty-one," the woman said, nodding toward a corridor.

"Is it her heart?" Summer asked.

"There was a problem, yes, but you'll have to discuss the particulars with her doctor. All I can tell you is her condition is stable, and that Dr. Cook decided to admit her for observation."

"Do you know where I can find Dr. Cook?"

"I believe he's headed back to his office." She scribbled a number on a sheet of paper and handed it to Summer. "You can try to reach him there if you like."

Summer thanked her, then hurried down the hall, pausing outside the door long enough to catch her breath. It would not do for her grandmother to see her looking so worried. Finally, she fixed a smile on her face and stepped inside the room.

"Grandmother?" she called out tentatively. She heard a whisper of sheets.

"Oh, Summer, I'm so glad you came," Henrietta said, her voice thin and reedy.

Summer crossed the small room and gazed down at the woman. Was it her imagination, or did her grandmother appear more frail than she had only a week before? She took Henrietta's hand, noting how bony and cold it felt in her own. "How are you feeling?" she asked.

Henrietta sighed wearily. "A bit tired, I suppose. My old ticker isn't as strong as it used to be."

Summer had never known her grandmother to complain about her health, even though she knew her arthritis gave her fits when the weather turned cold and damp. As she gazed down at the woman, she couldn't help but wonder why she wasn't in the CCU, where she could be watched more closely. "What does the doctor say?"

"He's putting me on a special diet and exercise plan," Henrietta said, rolling her eyes. "Such foolishness at my age. These young doctors think they can keep you alive forever."

"Was it an actual heart attack?" she asked, then held her breath for an answer.

"Just a wee one. But don't you start worrying. We have to leave these things in the hands of the Lord. Avery is giving me a prescription for nitroglycerin in case I have another . . . uh . . . attack."

"Oh, Granny." Summer's eyes teared. "You have to do as Dr. Cook says. I couldn't bear to lose you."

Henrietta's own eyes misted. "You haven't called me that since you were in grade school," she said softly. She squeezed Summer's hands lovingly. "I'm not afraid of dying, dear. Actually, I look forward to seeing your grandfather and all my old friends who've already passed."

"Please don't talk like that," Summer said, a lump the size of a goose egg forming in her throat.

"What frightens me," the woman continued, "is leaving you all alone in this world. You should be married by now, Summer. I should have great-grandchildren." She paused. "Perhaps *that* would give me a reason to fight." Henrietta sighed heavily, as though it had come from her very soul. "The old house is as quiet as a mausoleum. Some days I don't even want to climb out of bed."

"I had no idea you felt that way," Summer said, guilt-ridden. She'd become so caught up in her work that she hadn't realized how unhappy her grandmother was. How could she have been so thoughtless?

Henrietta gazed off into space as though trying to envision something in her mind. "It should be filled with children's laughter."

Summer looked down at the woman who'd raised her, eyes swimming with tears. Henrietta had taken Summer in when she was only a few weeks old, after her hippie parents had decided to escape the establishment and move to a commune in California. Fortunately, she had been raised with all the advantages, including unconditional love, and Henrietta had never asked for anything in return. Summer decided it was time to repay that generosity even if it meant being dishonest in order to make the woman feel better.

"I *have* found someone I care deeply about, Grandmother," she said, deciding the small white lie might go a long way in restoring her health. "I didn't want to tell you about him until I knew for sure he was the one."

Henrietta arched one gray brow. "You're in love with him?"

Summer fidgeted with her hands and gazed at a spot directly over her grandmother's head. "I'm fairly certain. And I think he loves me."

"Then I must meet this young man."

Summer nodded. "Perhaps when you're better—"

"How about Friday night?"

"F-Friday night," the girl stammered. "But you just had a heart attack. How do we even know you'll be out of the hospital by then?"

Henrietta waved her off. "It was a mild one, thank goodness. The doctor's releasing me tomorrow. By Friday I should be fine. As long as I don't exert myself or allow myself to become stressed."

"Stressed?"

"You know, *upset*." Even as she said it, Henrietta experienced sharp pangs of guilt. She had never lied to her granddaughter, and it pained her to do so now. Nevertheless, she knew it couldn't be helped. She had to see the girl married off to a good man if it was the last thing she did.

"I don't know, Grandmother. I think this is rushing things a bit."

"Don't be silly. I'll keep it simple, just a few of my closest friends. Besides, Mrs. Bradshaw will handle everything. Now, why don't you run along. I need my rest." Henrietta closed her eyes, letting Summer know the matter was settled.

An hour later Summer barged into Warren's office. "How'd it go?"

He leaned back in his chair and gave her a hundred-watt smile. "I'm pretty sure we got the account. Gridlock Tires is supposed to get back to us once they've made a decision."

Summer had worked so hard on the account that she was certain they would get it. "I'm sorry for running out on you."

"Hey, that's what I'm here for. One of these days

you're going to realize how much you need me." His look sobered. "Thanks for leaving the notes. I don't know why you put up with me. How's your grandmother?"

"She supposedly had a mild heart attack, but I couldn't locate her doctor either by phone or when I stopped by his office. The nurses wouldn't tell me anything either. But she talked about dying and how she wanted to see me happily married before she goes." Summer sank onto a chair in front of his desk and rubbed her temples where she could feel the beginning of a headache. "So I went and did something totally stupid. I told her I was seeing someone and it's serious."

He looked shocked. "You are?"

She sighed her frustration. "Wake up, Warren, you know I haven't dated in more months than I can remember. Except for grabbing dinner with you now and then, but that doesn't count."

"You really know how to feed a man's ego."

"I'm afraid I have a big favor to ask," she said.

"Name it."

"Grandmother's having a dinner party Friday night in honor of the new man in my life. Unfortunately, there is no new man in my life. I need you to be there and pretend you're madly in love with me."

"I *am* madly in love with you."

"Yeah, right. Me and a dozen other women."

"So, what's in it for me?" he asked.

Summer pondered it. "How about dinner and a play? My treat," she added.

"And afterward?"

"Don't push it, Warren. Besides, what would you want with an old gal like me when you've got that young receptionist making goo-goo eyes at you every time you pass by her desk?"

He stood and straightened his tie. "Well, then I'd

best go check my phone messages and see what comes of it."

Summer knew she wouldn't get a thing out of him for the rest of the day. "Just don't forget we have a couple of more accounts to discuss. And make sure you keep Friday night open for me."

Summer arrived at her grandmother's estate at precisely eight o'clock the following Friday. The Pettigrew mansion was set back a good quarter of a mile from the main road, separated by a serpentine drive flanked by pines, live oaks, and azalea bushes. Cloaked in ivy and surrounded by formal gardens and tall boxwood hedges, the house was almost hidden from curiosity seekers who liked to drive through the prestigious neighborhood on Sunday afternoons and see how old money lived.

Summer pulled into the wide circular drive in front of the house and groaned aloud when she spied a BMW, a Mercedes, two Cadillacs, and a Bentley. Leave it to Henrietta to turn a simple dinner into an elaborate affair. Not that Summer was surprised. Her grandmother would want to show off the new man in her granddaughter's life, no matter what the risk to her health.

Summer climbed out of her car and smoothed the wrinkles from the black silk jump suit she wore. The crested gold buttons and braiding on the sleeves were dressy without being ostentatious, one of the seven deadly sins as far as Henrietta Pettigrew was concerned. She draped a white wool swing coat across her shoulders, knowing the early March temperatures had a way of dipping as the night wore on.

She'd arranged her hair in an artful beehive that Grace Kelly had made popular in the fifties and was now the rage in Atlanta. It had looked sophisticated in *Cosmo* and *Vanity Fair*, but as Summer crossed the drive and made her way up the grand front steps, she suspected people still saw her as little Summer Medley, the illegitimate infant who'd been abandoned shortly after her birth and raised by her grandmother.

Despite having her own key, Summer rang the doorbell, and a moment later it was answered by the housekeeper. Emma Bradshaw was a crisp, no-nonsense woman who wore matching skirts and sweaters, thick support hose, and clunky shoes. She had appeared in the Pettigrew household when Summer was ten years old and liked to climb trees.

"Young ladies do *not* climb trees, missy," she'd said one afternoon as she pulled Summer inside by the scruff of her neck and ordered her upstairs for a bath. "Is this how you repay your grandmother's generosity? By running about the place looking like a ragamuffin?" The comment had jolted Summer to the soles of her feet, and as she'd gazed at her dirty, snaggle-toothed reflection in her bedroom mirror a few minutes later, she'd realized for the first time what a sacrifice her granny had made by taking her in. To think she might have embarrassed the woman was more than she could endure. She made a solemn vow to try harder. She would make Granny proud.

Summer had fulfilled that promise. Not only had she consistently made the honor roll in school, she'd graduated Dartmouth College with honors. She was the first woman ever to be hired at Worth Advertising, and she'd never once been involved in the sort of scandal her grandmother's contemporaries gossiped about.

"Good evening, Miss Summer," the housekeeper said formally, taking her coat. "Your grandmother and her guests are in the drawing room." The woman stepped aside so Summer could pass.

"Oh, there you are, my dear," Henrietta said as Summer stepped into the room, bringing the men to their feet. She recognized the guests and spoke to them briefly before kissing her grandmother's cheek. "You look much better," she said, noting Henrietta's color had returned. She'd visited twice since her release from the hospital and called several times a day to make sure the woman was okay. Finally, her grandmother had accused her of being a pest.

"Where's your young man?" Henrietta asked.

"He's supposed to meet me here," Summer said. "He should arrive any minute."

Mrs. Bradshaw spoke from the doorway. "May I get you something, miss?"

"A diet soft drink if you have it," Summer replied. The woman nodded and disappeared.

The guests chatted among themselves, talking politics and current affairs. Mrs. Bradshaw appeared with the soft drink and asked Henrietta to buzz her when she was ready for the cook to serve dinner. A brief lull in the conversation caused her to glance down at her wristwatch. It was eight-thirty; where the heck was Warren?

By nine Summer noticed she wasn't the only one glancing at her watch. The hors d'oeuvres were gone and several guests needed refills on their drinks.

"I hope nothing has happened to your young man," Henrietta said. "Would anybody care for another cocktail?"

Mrs. Bradshaw suddenly appeared in the doorway. "You have a telephone call, miss," she told Summer.

"I'll grab it in the den," she said, excusing herself, trying to ignore the curious stares. Summer snatched up the phone, and Warren spoke from the other end.

"Where *are* you?" she asked. "You were supposed to be here more than an hour ago."

"I've been in a car accident," he said, his voice strained. "I'm in the emergency room."

"Oh, my! Is it bad?"

"I think I may have a couple of broken bones."

"I'll come right away."

"No, listen. I called my cousin. He's coming in my place. He should be there any minute."

"Your cousin?"

"Name's Cooper Garrett. He's a bit of a wild card, but he'll do in a pinch."

A wild card? Summer gripped the phone tighter. "Warren, I don't think—"

"I've got to go, Summer. They're taking me to X ray. Cooper knows the game plan and should be able to pull it off." There was a loud click. Summer put the phone down and wondered what to do next.

"Is anything wrong, dear?" Henrietta asked when Summer returned to the drawing room and took her seat.

"Cooper's running late, but he'll be here shortly."

"Cooper?" Henrietta said as though testing the name on her tongue. "Is that his first name or his last?"

"First. His full name is Cooper Garrett."

"I don't believe I know the name," she said, "but then, you've been so secretive about the man. Is he from Atlanta?"

Summer didn't have the first clue, of course, but as she muddled through her answer, there was a roar at the front of the house, and a moment later the doorbell pealed out. "That must be Cooper now," she said, forcing a brightness to her voice she didn't feel.

Once again Mrs. Bradshaw appeared in the doorway, this time wearing the same look she'd worn when she'd discovered Henrietta's Maltese had given birth on a priceless Louis XIV sofa. "Mr. Cooper has arrived," she said, her voice ripe with disapproval.

Cooper Garrett entered the drawing room, drawing gasps from everyone, including Summer, who was thankful to be sitting. His hair was long and blue-black, tied back with some sort of leather strap. He was obviously in the process of growing a beard, because the stubble on his jaw suggested he hadn't shaved in days. He wore jeans, a gray T-shirt, and a black leather bomber jacket. His dark eyes glittered as he scanned the room and lighted on Summer. The smile he offered had a feral but intimate quality to it. "Hi, babe. Sorry I'm late. Trouble with my motorcycle."

At first Summer was too stunned to do anything more than stare at the man. She could feel her mouth hanging open in a most unbecoming manner. She closed it and watched him cross the room, moving toward her steadily, his gaze locked with hers. She felt like a small animal trapped in the headlights of an oncoming car, and it took everything in her power to keep from shrinking away at his approach.

His cocky swagger made her think of Bruce Springsteen and Richie Sambora rolled into one. He hauled her roughly against him. Up close she could see a number of scars on his face that suggested he was either a fighter or he'd taken a number of spills from his bike. Oddly enough, they did not detract from his appearance. She thought she caught a flash of humor in his onyx eyes before he lowered his head and kissed her hard on the mouth.

The room had gone quiet. Summer was certain everyone could hear her heart drumming in her chest. Henrietta coughed politely. "Summer, dear? Aren't you going to introduce us to your friend?"

How she made it through the next few moments, Summer would never know. Although common sense told her to call the whole thing off immediately, she had no idea how to do it without causing her grandmother a great deal of embarrassment. She took a deep, shaky breath. "Grandmother, this is Cooper Garrett," she said. "Cooper, my grandmother, Mrs. Henrietta Pettigrew."

Henrietta offered her hand, and Cooper took it.

"So good to meet you, Mr. Garrett," she said graciously. "I'm glad you could make it."

"I'm sorry I held up your dinner party," he said regretfully. "My bike broke down on the way, and I had to make a few minor repairs."

Henrietta tilted her head to one side. "A motorcycle, eh? You must be a free spirit of sorts."

Cooper grinned, and the tight, almost menacing lines on either side of his eyes and mouth softened. "Believe me, ma'am," he said in a drawl that was thick as soft taffy, "I've been called a lot worse."

Someone chuckled. A collective sigh among the guests seemed to ease the tension that had followed Cooper Garrett into the room. For Summer, it wasn't that easy. She could feel the anxiety coiling in her stomach, the pressure building in her chest so that each breath was a struggle.

Henrietta turned to her granddaughter with a pleasant smile. "Summer, where are your manners? I'm sure Mr. Garrett would like to meet our guests."

Summer felt the color rush to her cheeks as she realized she was staring at the man. "Sorry, I wasn't thinking." She made the introductions, and the group nodded politely.

"Why don't we go into the dining room now," Henrietta suggested, and was immediately assisted by a man whose family had made their fortune in rare gems. "Mr. Garrett must be hungry after what he's been through."

"Please call me Cooper," he said, then glanced at Summer. "Hon, would you show me where I could wash up first?"

Hon? "Yes, of course," Summer sputtered, then forced herself to smile for the sake of Henrietta's guests. She could feel them watching her. Watching and wondering. "Come with me." She held her hand out, and he linked fingers with hers as though it were something they did often.

Summer led Cooper down the hall to the small bathroom tucked beneath the stairs. She followed him in and closed the door, realizing too late the room was barely able to accommodate them. "Who *are* you?" she asked tightly.

Turning on the elaborate brass faucets at the marble pedestal sink, Cooper gazed at her reflection in the mirror. "Warren's cousin," he said, noting the cut-glass soap dispenser with a frown. He squeezed a dollop of the gardenia-scented liquid into his palm and tried to work up a lather. "Didn't he tell you I was filling in for him?"

"Yes, but—"

"Yes, well, when you're desperate, you have to take what you can get." He squeezed more soap and worked at getting the worst of the grease off.

Summer took a long look at him, and her gaze came to rest on his dusty boots. "Couldn't you have cleaned up a bit?"

He rinsed his hands and jerked a guest towel from the rack. He turned, and Summer was reminded once more of their proximity. "You're lucky I showed up at all on such short notice," he said, scowling at her. "If you'd rather I leave—" He slung the towel over the rack, and it slid to the floor.

"No!" She stooped and groped for the towel which had fallen behind him. She tried to stand, lost her balance, and steadied herself by placing one hand flat against his chest. He was rock solid. She blushed and snatched her hand away. "I mean, you *have* to stay now that . . . that—"

"Lady, I don't have to do a *damn* thing. The only reason I'm here is because of Warren. He's got the hots for you and doesn't want to let you down. You ask me, I think this whole thing is ridiculous."

"It probably looks ridiculous to you, but it's for a good cause. My grandmother is—" She swallowed hard. "Very sick. She could die," she added, admitting it to herself for the first time. "She doesn't want to leave me all alone in the world. She's old-fashioned and doesn't think I can be happy without a man."

A smirk of sorts lifted one corner of his mouth, drawing attention to his full, almost sensual lips. "Maybe she's right," he said. "Could be a man is just what you need. I got the distinct impression Warren would be more than happy to fill that position."

"My personal life is not open for discussion," she said. "I just need this one favor. I'll even pay you for your trouble."

"And what would you say my time is worth under these circumstances?" he asked, his gaze dropping from her eyes to her slightly parted lips and finally to her breasts.

Summer could feel her body respond to his blatant perusal. Her cheeks warmed; a heaviness filled her breasts, and her pulse quickened. The small room was rife with sensual undercurrents. What annoyed her to no end was the fact that the man knew exactly what he was doing. He might be rude and crude, but those dark good looks and cocky attitude had obviously served him well in the past where the opposite sex was concerned. He probably thought she found him irresistible. She was determined to prove otherwise.

"I have no idea what your time is worth, Mr. Garrett. What exactly do bike mechanics make these days?" she asked, assuming that's what he did. It was a terrible thing to say, and she knew it, but the man seemed to have a knack for bringing out the worst in her.

"You'd be surprised," he said silkily. "But I wouldn't think of charging you. Besides," he added, "I'm not doing this for you. It's a favor to Warren, remember?"

"I don't want to be obligated—"

"You're under no obligation. But, if you want my help, I suggest you stop acting like some high-society snob and show a little appreciation." He propped one hand on the wall next to her head and leaned closer, so close, Summer caught a whiff of something tangy. "So what's the game plan?"

Summer could feel her shoulder blades pressing against the door as she tried to maintain a respectable distance from him. "Basically, we just have to act as if we're crazy about each other."

He seemed to ponder the thought longer than necessary, as though she were asking him to perform some monumental task like swim the Atlantic Ocean. Once again her irritation flared, and she added *insufferable* to his growing list of bad qualities.

"For how long?" he asked.

"Let's just concentrate on getting through tonight," she said. Oh, how she wished she'd never started this nonsense.

Cooper was about to respond, when someone knocked on the door. Summer opened it slightly and peered out. Mrs. Bradshaw gave her a huffy look. "Your grandmother requests your presence in the dining room immediately."

"Show time," Cooper whispered in Summer's ear. She shivered as his warm breath fanned her cheek. His soft chuckle assured her it had not gone unnoticed.

TWO

"I hope you don't mind," Henrietta said as Summer and Cooper entered the dining room, "but we decided to go ahead with our soup before it gets cold."

Summer felt embarrassed by the gentle reprimand, but she knew she and Cooper had held up the party long enough. "Oh, please do," she said, reaching for the chair next to her grandmother. To her surprise, Cooper nudged her hand aside and pulled it out for her. Then, shrugging out of his leather jacket, he draped it across the chair next to hers and sat down. She almost wished he hadn't come out of the jacket when she noted the rich lines of his body beneath the snug T-shirt. Summer realized she wasn't the only one who'd noticed. A couple of guests were sending covert looks his way.

Summer laid her napkin in her lap and picked up her soup spoon, watching Cooper from the corner of her eye as she did so. Her grandmother set a formal table; a man like Cooper probably wouldn't have the foggiest idea which utensils to use. But he surprised her once again by choosing the correct spoon without a moment's hesitation.

"I see Millie made my favorite baked potato soup," Summer said, offering her grandmother a stilted smile at her attempt to make polite conversation.

Henrietta nodded. "Yes. The weather is still cool enough to enjoy it."

Summer was thankful Henrietta had mentioned the weather, because suddenly everybody had something to say about it, no matter how mundane. At least it kept the conversation flowing.

"So tell me, Cooper," Henrietta said. "What do you do with your time when you're not riding motorcycles?"

He looked up from his soup. "Well, I like taking 'em apart and putting them back together again."

An investment banker by the name of Fred Sobol chuckled. "If I tried that, I'd probably have a few pieces left over when I was finished."

His wife, Anne, looked amused. "Darling, you've never quite mastered the hammer or the screwdriver. You'd best stick with banking."

The historian winked at her. "With Fred's head for figures, he doesn't *need* to know how to use tools. He can hire someone to make repairs for him."

Summer glanced up as a sudden uncomfortable hush fell over the group. The historian's face turned a bright red, as if he'd just realized he may have insulted Cooper by insinuating he was forced to perform actual labor because he wasn't smart enough to do anything else. Summer held her breath as Cooper regarded the man.

"Actually, I enjoy working with my hands," he said, "although I have a fairly good head for figures as well. I just can't imagine sitting behind a desk all day and letting my body go to flab."

More silence. Summer could almost imagine the other men sucking in their stomachs after the comment.

"Yes, well, you're certainly in good physical shape."

"My mother and I have a place way out in the

boonies. I plant a big vegetable garden each spring. Just staying on top of those weeds is all the exercise I need."

"You grow your own vegetables?" Henrietta said in delight.

"Yes, ma'am. I'd much rather eat home-grown vegetables than buy them from the grocery store."

"I know exactly what you mean," she replied. "I have my own little garden out back. I'm sure it's not as big as yours; in fact, I've had to cut back on what I grow because of my arthritis and the demand my charity work places on me. But you're right. Food does taste better when you grow it yourself."

Cooper smiled. "Tell you what. I usually end up giving away most of what I grow. I'll be sure to add your name to my list. You haven't tasted tomatoes until you've tasted mine."

Henrietta beamed at Summer. "I like him already," she said, then regarded Cooper once more. "You know, Summer never did tell me how the two of you met."

"She didn't?" Cooper glanced at Summer, but the look in her eyes told him she was not prepared for the question. He stifled a grin as he remembered the snide comment she'd made about mechanics' wages. Payback time. "Actually, we met at a biker's convention," he said easily.

Summer, in the process of swallowing a spoonful of soup, almost choked. "Cooper's right," she said. "I attended the convention on business. Worth Advertising was trying to land an account with one of the larger motorcycle dealers."

Henrietta nodded. "I see."

Once again a stillness fell over the group.

Cooper met Summer's gaze and nodded slightly, his way of telling her he was impressed with her quick thinking. "Bikers have a bad rep," he told the group, "because of gangs like the Hell's Angels and such. What most people don't realize is a motorcycle is much more economical than a car. We have a lot of family men coming into the shop these days for that very reason. We've also designed a smaller version of our most popular bike for women."

"Well, if I were thirty years younger, I might consider buying one," the banker said.

His wife eyed him speculatively. "You know, I think you'd look sexy on a bike."

He looked surprised. "Really?"

"We could get matching jackets and helmets." She nudged him, and her smile was seductive. "We could just take off on weekends and go wherever we liked."

"The two of us on a motorcycle?" he said, obviously shocked that she would suggest such a thing. "Our children would think we'd lost our marbles."

She shrugged. "Who cares what they think as long as we're having a good time."

The man glanced at Cooper. "Do women always react like this to bikes?"

Cooper nodded. "Chicks go wild over 'em. You shoulda seen Summer come after me."

Summer fixed him with a cool look. "You're getting carried away now, Cooper."

He slung his arm around her shoulder. "Go ahead and deny it, babe, but as I recall, I couldn't beat you off with a stick."

She blushed profusely at the chuckles he drew. "I think you have me confused with someone else."

"So you're saying it was love at first sight?" Henrietta asked.

Cooper grinned. "I think it was as far as Summer was concerned. I took more time coming around."

Summer gaped at him. She shot him a killing look. He'd obviously taken a bad fall on the way over and hit his head. Luckily, Millie chose that moment to serve the salads.

"You know," Henrietta began, her eyes growing soft, "it was love at first sight for my husband and me. I knew the minute I laid eyes on him that I wanted to marry him. My parents begged me to hold off, not rush into things, but now I'm glad we didn't wait. He was still a young man when he died. Had we followed their wishes and gone through a lengthy courtship, we would have had even fewer years together."

"I wish I'd had the chance to know Grandfather," Summer said, relieved that her budding relationship with Cooper was no longer the topic of conversation.

"You would have liked him, dear. He was a little unconventional at times, but that's one of the things I liked most about him." She smiled at Cooper as she said it, and it was obvious she equated the two. "When he was ready to propose, he enlisted a pilot to fly over my house with a banner asking me to marry him. People talked of it for weeks. He insisted on handling the wedding personally, hiring coaches with six white horses to drive the wedding party to the church. All the bridesmaids wore hoop skirts and straw hats. My gown came straight from Paris and cost more than most folks spent on a house in those days. I accused him of being extravagant; I'd never known anyone to fuss over me so. I felt . . . like Cinderella."

Henrietta's eyes misted as she remembered. "And when your mother was born, he took out a full-page ad in the newspaper announcing her birth and gave his employees the day off with pay." She shook her head. "He kept me on my toes, that man. I know most folks can't afford coaches with white horses or Paris originals, but they can still express their love in small ways." She waggled a finger at Summer and Cooper. "And they should never, ever take their love for granted. There are no guarantees in this life. Not all couples are lucky enough to grow old together."

Henrietta suddenly stopped talking and glanced around the table at the serious faces. "Oh, my, listen to me ramble on," she said as though embarrassed. "That's what happens when I allow myself more than one cocktail before dinner."

Cooper cleared his throat. "I believe that's one of the nicest stories I've ever heard, Henrietta."

Summer snapped her head around and looked at him. If Cooper was trying to be funny or make fun of her grandmother, she'd have his head the first chance she got. But the look on his face was sincere. She relaxed. "Yes, it was very nice," she agreed.

Once they had eaten dinner, Cooper asked if he could use the phone. A disgruntled Mrs. Bradshaw escorted him to the den. When he returned to the dining room with the housekeeper on his heels, he looked amused. "Let's take a ride," he told Summer, reaching for his coat.

She offered him a blank stare. "You mean on your motorcycle?"

He gave her a toe-curling smile. "You know how much you like riding at night, hon."

The look on his face was so intimate, so *knowing*, it was all Summer could do to maintain her composure with the wild currents racing through her body. The light in his eyes was blatantly sensuous, his tone suggestive. That, combined with his roguish image and maddening arrogance, added a deeper significance to his words. Summer felt as though he'd just announced to the group that he knew what she liked in bed.

Was she just imagining it, she wondered, or had the oxygen level suddenly dropped? The very air around her seemed to crackle. She could feel every eye watching her. But although she longed for escape, she knew it would be rude to leave her grandmother's dinner party so early, especially since it had been given in their honor. She tried to think of a diplomatic way to get her message across without causing further discomfort.

Henrietta never gave her a chance. "Oh, how romantic!" she exclaimed in such a way, one would have thought Cooper had just invited her granddaughter to take a gondola cruise along the canals in Venice. "Go ahead, dear," she told Summer. "The night is still young, no reason to hang around us old folks."

"Are you sure you don't mind?" she asked, wishing the woman would object instead of letting her ride off into the night with a perfect stranger and a man who obviously lived by his own rules. But then, Henrietta had no way of knowing these things.

"Why don't I get your coat," Cooper suggested, leaving no room for argument.

Summer tried to excuse herself as gracefully as she could. "We probably won't be gone long," she told her grandmother. She left the dining room and joined Cooper in the hall, where Mrs. Bradshaw was pulling her white swing coat from the closet, her face pinched with disapproval.

Summer didn't say anything until after Cooper had helped her into the coat and they'd stepped outside. "Why did you do that?" she demanded.

He didn't hesitate. "Because it was clear your grandmother was going to ask more questions, most of which neither of us could answer."

"Sort of like when you told her we'd met at a biker's convention?" she reminded tersely.

He grinned, and it took some of the severity from his face. "I just wanted to see how quick you were on your feet. I must say, I was impressed."

"Then my job here on earth is done," she said, sarcasm slipping into her voice.

He looked slightly amused. "Ah, the lady is not only smart and beautiful, she has a sharp tongue as well."

Beautiful? He was saying it only because he knew she was still sore at him for putting her on the spot. She followed him down the steps to his motorcycle, a massive-looking machine of black and chrome. Across the gas tank, scrawled in bold red letters, were the words NEW BREED. "I've never been on a bike before," she confessed, shivering, more out of nervousness than cold.

He tossed her a knowing look as he reached for his helmet and handed her a spare that had been strapped to the leather seat rest. "Why doesn't that surprise me?"

Summer ignored the hint of mockery in his voice as she slipped her helmet on, taking care with the hairdo she'd worked so hard to perfect. She fumbled with the heavy nylon strap under her jaw until Cooper brushed her hands away.

"Here, let me help you."

She gazed up at him as he slipped the strap between two metal rings and fastened it with deft fingers. His own helmet made him look different somehow. While it better defined the bone structure of his face, which was handsome despite being a little rough around the edges, it made him appear more perilous as well. Once again she was reminded that she knew absolutely nothing about the man.

"What's wrong?" he asked, noting the uncertainty in her eyes."

"I don't even know you."

He chuckled softly. "You're safe with me. I wouldn't think of letting anything happen to Warren's girl." He pulled his face shield down, swung his right leg over the bike, and straddled it, before starting the engine. The bike roared and vibrated like something alive. Summer took a small step back. Cooper tossed her a challenging look. "Well?"

She lowered her own shield and stepped closer to the bike, hesitating briefly before swinging her leg over as he'd done a moment before. Her stomach fluttered wildly as she suddenly found her breasts and stomach flush against his back and hips. She slipped her fingers between their bodies and located the leather strip on the seat, grasping it tightly. Her knuckles dug into the pockets of his jeans. Oh, well, it couldn't be helped.

An amused Cooper waited patiently as the woman behind him tried to situate herself on the bike without touching him. "Ready?" he called out.

"Yes," she said, trying to make herself heard over the noisy engine.

The bike suddenly lurched forward like a lion who'd spotted its prey, and Summer was flung back against the seat rest. She quickly let go of the leather strap on her seat and threw her arms around Cooper's waist, hanging on for dear life. She closed her eyes and leaned her head against his wide back, wishing, not for the first time in the past several hours, she'd never gotten herself into such a predicament to begin with. What had started out as a small white lie to protect her grandmother had backfired, leaving her in a vulnerable, not to mention potentially dangerous, situation.

At first it was horrifying, zigzagging through traffic, taking curves at a breakneck speed that forced the bike to lean dangerously to one side. Summer panicked and leaned to the other.

"Don't do that," Cooper shouted back. "You'll throw us off balance. Move *with* me, lean into the curve."

She was too terrified to argue. She edged closer to him and tried not to struggle against the next turn. Pressed tightly to him as she was, their bodies seemed to move as one. "Good girl," he said. "You'll get the hang of it."

After twenty minutes or so, Summer was able to lift

her head slightly and look around. They seemed to be flying along the interstate leading into downtown Atlanta. The skyscrapers loomed ahead; the cylindrical Peachtree Plaza Hotel gleamed like black ice against a perfect star-filled sky. Traffic became dense as they moved steadily toward the very heart of the city.

Cooper slowed the bike, and Summer breathed her first sigh of relief since climbing on behind him. They stopped at several red lights, and she couldn't help but notice the stares they received, mostly women who gazed at the biker with unabashed interest.

Cooper pulled into a parking space and shut the engine. Summer glanced around, finding they'd stopped at one of the parks in an undesirable location. "Let's walk for a while," he said.

Summer climbed off the bike first, noting how wobbly her knees had become. She could still feel the vibration in her thighs. She raised her face shield. "I don't like this," she said.

Cooper swung his leg over and joined her beside the bike. He pulled off his helmet and regarded her. "Which frightens you more, the thought of being mugged or of spending time alone with me?"

"I'm not afraid of you," she said stiffly. "I simply try to avoid this area of town. Especially at night."

"I grew up around here. People know me. You're safe." When she still hesitated, he helped her out of her helmet. The beehive that she had taken such pains with was pressed against her scalp. Pins stuck out in every direction. Cooper chuckled and stepped behind her. She tensed. "Chill, lady," he said, plucking several pins from her hair. "I think your hairdo is a lost cause."

Cooper found his eyes riveted to the blond tresses that fell in thick, generous waves down her back. Why she chose to wear it up was beyond him. His hands itched to touch it, let it slide through his fingers. He imagined her lying on his pillow, her hair fanning out all around her, of standing in a hot shower with it slicked straight back from her forehead. He had a vision of her straddling him, that gold mane falling against his chest like a silk curtain. Where had *that* come from?

Summer noted the strain around his eyes and mouth and wondered at it. She could sense his tension by the way his veins stood out on his forehead. Was he having second thoughts about bringing her there? She could only hope.

Cooper forced the sexy images aside. He had no business fantasizing about his cousin's girlfriend, especially when she'd made it plain from the beginning that she didn't particularly care for his type. They also didn't have the first thing in common other than the fact that they wanted to protect her grandmother. The decision to go along with it had been easy to make once he'd met Henrietta Pettigrew. He genuinely liked the woman; he only wished he could say the same for her granddaughter.

"Come on, prissy britches," he said, taking her hand. "You don't think I'd let anything happen to Warren's main squeeze, do you?"

She pulled away. It was the second time that evening he'd suggested she belonged to Warren, and she didn't like it. Nevertheless, it might serve her well if he continued to think along those lines, particularly if he felt any loyalty to his cousin. That way she could be assured of returning home in one piece.

"What?" he said when she continued to stare at him quietly.

"I'm not prissy," she said defensively. "I work in a male-dominated firm, and I manage to hold my own very well. Actually, I'm quite independent. If I want something, I go after it. I do not expect others to give me what I am perfectly capable of working for. Furthermore, choosing not to walk through a dark park in a bad section of town does not make me a priss. I'm merely using common sense."

"I'm impressed," he said, strolling toward a park bench and sitting. She hesitated a moment before following and taking a seat at the opposite end. "I just can't help but wonder what you see in my cousin."

"What's wrong with Warren?" she said defensively. "I happen to think he's a very nice man."

He shrugged and leaned against the bench, stretching his long legs and crossing them at the ankles. "*Nice* won't keep you warm on cold nights. You ask me, I think ol' Warren's neglecting you in the good-lovin' department. Otherwise, you wouldn't be so tense. You can tell him I said so."

Summer felt her irritation flare. She wasn't prudish by any means, but she also wasn't accustomed to a man speaking to her about such things, especially one she'd known only a couple of hours. He obviously had no manners, nor did he seem particularly concerned about his own cousin. "I can't believe you'd talk about Warren like that. For all we know, he could be seriously injured."

"He's fine. I called the emergency room from your grandmother's house. He has a broken leg, a sprained wrist, and a couple of cracked ribs. Nothing that won't heal. I'll visit him tomorrow."

"Well, I hope he won't take too long to recover," Summer said, knowing Warren could be quite a hypochondriac at times. It seemed as if he was always coming down with a cold or some other ailment, and he had more allergies than a classroom of kindergartners. Since they shared several key accounts, and her workload was already heavy, she knew she would be spending more evenings and weekends at the office. As usual, Henrietta would fuss.

Cooper noted the anxious look on her face and felt bad for poking fun at his cousin. Summer was obviously worried sick about the man. "Hey, I'm sure Warren's going to be good as new before you know it." She didn't seem to have heard him. He touched her shoulder gently, and she jumped as though a charge of dynamite had just gone off at her feet. "Good grief!" he said. "You're as tight as a rubber band." He immediately became wary. "Turn around."

She drew back, startled by his nearness. "I beg your pardon?"

Sighing his frustration, he took her by the shoulders and turned her so that her back was facing him. He slipped his hands beneath that mass of hair and began to knead her shoulders, but it wasn't easy with the bulky coat. "Take off your coat."

She tensed. "No." His hands remained firm on her shoulders. "It really isn't necessary," she said, and was met with more silence.

"Stop fussing," he said, sliding his hands beneath the hem and finding her deliciously warm inside. He skimmed her silk jump suit with an open palm and began kneading her shoulder muscles once more. She was tight. "Relax," he said.

His hands were big and warm, his fingers strong and sure as he massaged the band of muscles on either side of her neck. She felt her defenses weakening. Perhaps Cooper was right; she *had* let work and her grandmother's illness tie her in knots.

"Tilt your head as far left as you can," he said.

His breath fanned the back of her head, sending a tiny tremor up her spine. The back of her neck tingled. She closed her eyes and leaned her head so that her ear brushed the top of her shoulder. By the time she had stretched her neck from side to side and front and back, Cooper had worked his way just below her shoulder blades. Summer felt herself being lulled into a sense of well-being that simply didn't jibe when you took a close look at the situation. Here she was, sitting on a park bench in a seedy section of town with a man she barely knew, who happened to have his hands all over her. And she was enjoying every minute of it. Had she been a cat she would have curled into his lap and started to purr. It suddenly struck her that he might be hoping for just such a reaction.

Cooper felt the sudden tensing of her body, the ramrod stiffening of her spine. "What's wrong?" he asked, his hands becoming still.

Summer felt immobilized. She was out of her element here. Although she was accustomed to dealing with men on a daily basis, it had been a long time since she'd sat in the moonlight with one and enjoyed being caressed. "Are you"—she paused—"trying to seduce me?"

Cooper chuckled softly, sending another ripple of awareness through her. "It wouldn't be the first time I've engaged in sex in a public place, but you look like a woman who prefers privacy. If I'd wanted to seduce you, I would have taken you to my place."

"Assuming I would go," she replied with cold sarcasm.

"Assuming I would ask," he drawled with distinct mockery.

Summer felt her face grow warm at the gentle rebuke. She tossed her head in defiance, shrugged off his hands, and stood. "You are incredibly rude," she said.

"I'm truthful," he said. "I don't try to sugar-coat everything I say. Perhaps that's what you're used to." He studied her in the light of a lamppost. She was undoubtedly the loveliest creature he'd ever seen. And he wanted her despite the fact she belonged to Warren, despite everything. "I would think a woman of your intelligence would appreciate a man who tells it like it is."

She faced him. His steady gaze made her pulse

quicken; he looked dark and sinister bathed in shadows as he was. "What's that supposed to mean?"

He stood and closed the distance between them. "When I look into your eyes, I see a woman who's desperate to prove herself worthy. Of what, I don't know."

Her bottom lip trembled; she averted her gaze. Words tumbled from her. "You think you've got me figured out after knowing me all of three hours. You're very perceptive. What else have you gleaned from our brief encounter?"

He looked as though he were weighing the question. "The truth?"

"Why not? You're a man who tells it like it is."

His look was bold and assessed her frankly. "I think you need to get laid."

At first she thought she'd misunderstood. When the full impact of his words hit her, she simply stood there, blank, amazed, and very shaken. Then, suspecting that was his intent, she quickly regained her composure.

"If you're trying to shock me, you're wasting your time," she said icily. "I've wheeled and dealed with the best of them. The language isn't always pretty, and you're not the first man to make lewd suggestions."

"I'll bet you cut them off at the knees every time," he said, giving her a charming half-smile.

"Something like that." Even as she said it, Summer realized she was more intrigued than repelled by his distasteful remark. It was completely irrational the way her body was responding to his nearness—she felt as giddy and breathless as an eighteen-year-old. She could feel the sexual magnetism that made him so confident. She felt a lurch of excitement within; all her senses flared to life. For one maddening heartbeat she dreamed of being crushed within his embrace, and while the thought filled her with a sense of deep longing, she knew any involvement would be perilous. She was a woman who not only craved security but felt as though she should be in control, both physically and emotionally, at all times. Cooper Garrett made her feel as though she were standing on a patch of thin ice. No doubt he would rescue her if it gave beneath her, but at what price to her heart?

Cooper brushed his hand against her cheek, and it reminded him of the petal softness of a magnolia bloom. Her facial bones were delicately carved, but she had a chin of stubborn determination. He knew they shared an intense physical awareness of each other, he felt it heighten with every beat of his heart, with each breath he took. But he seriously doubted that she would admit such a thing, even to herself.

"What are you thinking?" he asked in a voice that echoed her own longings.

Summer brushed his hand aside. His mere touch had upset her balance, filling her with a strange inner excitement. She tried to remember the last time her body had responded to a man in such a way. Cooper's black eyes were so galvanizing that she couldn't look away, couldn't break the fierce hold they had on her.

"I should be getting back," she said, feeling the need to escape his probing looks and return to her normal surroundings, where she could relax, let her guard down.

A lazy smile played at the corners of his mouth. "You're a big girl. Besides, it's Friday night. Don't you old debutantes *ever* cut loose?"

Much to her annoyance, Summer blushed, then became irritated at the heavy dose of censure in his voice. And just when she was beginning to think he might have a few redeemable qualities about him. "What makes you think I was a debutante?"

He shot her a disarming grin. "Baby, it's written all over your pretty little face. You even kiss like one," he added, remembering how stiff and unyielding her lips had been when he'd touched them earlier. "Or maybe you were feeling shy with all those people watching. Could be I made a simple error in judgment. Maybe I should give you a second chance."

He was making fun of her. Again. He had an uncanny knack for discovering things about her on his own, then tossing them back in her face as though she owed him an explanation. Her irritation veered sharply to anger. "You are, without a doubt, the most egotistical man I've ever met!" she said, throwing the words at him like a fistful of rocks. What made her even more furious was the fact that she'd allowed him to reduce her to such a state. "Has it occurred to you that I'm not *asking* for a second chance, that maybe I don't give a damn *what* you think of me?" The smug look he offered told her he didn't believe it for a minute, and his eyes seemed to take much delight in her heaving breasts.

Summer felt exposed as he boldly appraised her.

"I've had enough for one evening," she said tightly. "I'll grab a cab home." She turned.

Cooper reached out and closed his hand around her wrist, bringing her to a dead halt. "I don't think so." He pulled her around, and in one fluid motion she was in his arms, her breasts flattened against his broad chest. She tried to resist, twisting in his arms and pressing her open palms against his chest, but she was powerless. He locked his hands against her spine. "Don't fight me," he said, his voice husky with need. "You've been sending me mixed messages all evening. I think it's time I find out what you *really* want."

Summer opened her mouth to object, and his own came down on hers hungrily. He crushed her to him, shattering her last coherent thought.

His lips were hard and searching, almost brutal as he forced his tongue inside, devouring the satin lining of her mouth. It was urgent and hot, and Summer felt as though her lips had been singed when he raised his head.

Cooper saw that her eyes were unnaturally bright. Was she crying? "I hurt you." It was not a question but a statement.

She hitched her chin upward. "Yes, you did."

His eyes took on a glazed look of anguish. He raised his big hands to her face, cupping her cheeks. "I'm sorry," he said. "I don't know what happened. This whole evening has been so strange." He stroked her bottom lip with his thumb as he spoke.

Summer noted the trembling hand and forgave him. "Next time try to be more gentle," she whispered.

The tense lines along his forehead relaxed. He leaned forward and replaced his thumb with his tongue. He traced her full lips, his touch no more than a whisper. When he captured her mouth once more, the kiss was slow and surprisingly tender. He dropped his hands to her waist. Parting her lips slightly, Summer slipped her arms around his neck. She could feel his steady heartbeat against her breast, smell his manly scent.

Cooper pulled away, and his lips reappeared at her closed eyelids. He kissed the tip of her nose, the length of her jaw, and nibbled an earlobe. It wasn't enough. As he pressed his lips against the hollow of her throat, he imagined her warm and naked in his bed. Touching her. Tasting her.

Cooper decided the bulky coat Summer wore simply wouldn't do. Without breaking the kiss, he slipped his hands inside. It was like stepping in from the cold. He slid his palms downward, followed the swell of her hips, then grasped them tightly, pulling her body against his. His need was great, and he nudged her to let her know he was hard. But as his passion grew to new heights, he could feel her withdrawing. She was no longer responding. He raised his head slightly, and they both sucked in air as if they had been deprived of oxygen for a long time. "Kiss me back," he demanded.

Summer met his dark gaze, and the look in his eyes almost took her breath away. Although her body yearned for him, she knew the risks involved in having sex these days. She couldn't afford to lose her head over a man like Cooper, who probably took as many chances in the bedroom as he did on the road. She pulled back. "I can't," she managed to say, biting her bottom lip to keep it from trembling.

Cooper saw the resolution in her eyes and cursed himself for getting carried away.

His black eyes hardened, and he released Summer with such force, she almost stumbled. "I don't know what kind of game you're playing, but I don't like it worth a damn."

"Oh, really?" Summer said, her voice dripping with sarcasm.

"Really. Come on, I'll take you home." He suspected he'd hurt her feelings, and her sarcasm had been a cover-up, but, dammit, what'd she expect? One minute she was all soft and kissing him, and the next thing he knew, she didn't want anything to do with him. How much could a man take? He was almost to the point of believing she and Warren deserved each other. He stalked toward his bike.

Summer was left standing there, feeling foolish. He didn't even know her, yet he'd already made up his mind what kind of woman she was. She felt her defenses rising. How many times had she been judged unfairly? Even when it came to her job she found herself working harder than everyone else to prove herself.

"Wait!" she said as Cooper reached for his helmet and climbed onto the bike.

He glanced at her, irritation marring his handsome face. She looked like a lost child in her pristine coat with her blond hair hanging loose and gleaming beneath the lamppost. "I'm going to give you about five seconds to get your skinny butt on this bike, then I'm leaving without you."

"You wouldn't."

"One . . ."

She sighed. Of course he'd leave her. He had nothing to lose. "Cooper—" She stepped closer.

"Two . . ."

"What if I told you you were wrong about me?" she said quickly.

He studied her in silence. He could see a battle raging inside her—her green eyes were troubled—but he had no idea what it was about. He wasn't even sure he *wanted* to know. He should never have agreed to Warren's crazy idea; all it had gotten him was a headache and a hard-on. But he was intrigued by her, and although he would probably regret it later, he had no desire to say good night to her. Not yet. "Prove it," he said.

"Okay." Summer hitched her chin high as she closed the distance between them and joined him on the bike. As the engine roared to life, she slipped her arms around his waist and wondered if she'd just made a date with the devil himself.

THREE

Dirty Harry's Bar and Grill was located only a few blocks from the park. As Cooper pulled behind the building, the roar of his engine startled a stray tabby and sent him scurrying into the night. He parked and killed the engine, and the noise from the bike was replaced by loud country-western music.

Cooper helped Summer with her helmet before removing his own. Lugging both helmets, he led her through the back door into a smoke-filled room that smelled of sweat and cheap cologne. The band was playing an old Garth Brooks song, "Friends in Low Places."

Cooper took Summer's hand and put his mouth to her ear so she could hear. "Stick close," he said, his breath fanning her earlobe and sending an involuntary shiver down her spine that made her think of the kisses they'd shared only moments before. "These cowboys will take one look at you and pull out their lassos." He led her toward the bar. The bartender, a balding, middle-aged man with wire-rimmed glasses, smiled the minute he saw Cooper. "Hey, buddy. How's it hanging?" He noted Summer.

"Have a seat." He indicated two empty stools.

Cooper waited for Summer to sit before taking a seat next to her and setting the helmets on the bar. "Summer, meet Harry," he said, nodding to the man. "We go way back."

Summer offered her hand, and Harry made a production of raising it to his lips for a kiss. She chuckled. "Oh, my, a *real* gentleman." She shot Cooper a thoroughly enchanting smile. "Which makes me wonder what the two of you could possibly have in common."

Cooper pretended to look offended. "Don't let him fool you," he said. "Harry gave me the beating of my life when I was only fifteen years old."

"You had it coming, kid, and you know it." Harry turned to Summer. "If I hadn't taken a firm hand with this guy years ago, he'd probably be sitting in a jail cell. Now, what can I get you to drink, sweetheart?"

Summer shrugged. "Well, I suppose a glass of white wine would be nice."

Cooper chuckled. "Harry doesn't carry wine. Let me order for you." He looked at the bartender and winked. "Make her a Lace Panty, and I'll take a draft."

"A Lace Panty?" Summer said, arching one blond brow. "I don't think I've ever heard of that one."

"Trust me, you'll love it."

"You want me to hang that up for you?" the bartender asked, nodding toward her coat. "It looks like it's worth some bucks. I'd hate to see it get ripped off."

Cooper handed it to him, and the man disappeared behind a curtain.

When her drink was served Summer took a sip. It had a caramel flavor. "That's delicious. What's in it?"

"Oh, a little of this, a little of that. Harry and I came up with it some years back. It's our secret recipe. I could tell you, but then I'd have to kill you."

She took another sip and licked her lips. Cooper

watched her pink tongue dart along her bottom lip, and something inside him quickened. He took a long drink of his beer.

One of the band members started playing a fiddle, and the place went wild. Cooper suddenly had an urge to get as far away from the noise as he could. "You ready to go?" he asked Summer.

Summer, trying to see over the crowded dance floor, looked surprised. "We just got here."

Harry slid another draft in front of Cooper. "What's your hurry, man? The lady's having a good time. You ready for another one?" he asked Summer, motioning to her empty glass. She nodded.

"You drank the first one already?" Cooper asked as Harry hurried away to fix another.

She shrugged as she tapped her fingers against the bar, keeping in time with the music. "It was good. Tasted like a liquid candy bar."

"Well, they're not as innocent as you think," Cooper said as Harry set another drink in front of her. "Go easy on her, Harry. I don't think she's used to the stuff."

"Would you chill out, for Pete's sake!" the other man said, sticking a straw in her glass.

Summer smiled at the bartender, who seemed to be going out of his way to be nice to her. Cooper, on the other hand, acted as if she were cramping his style. "Would you like to dance?" she asked him.

"We couldn't get on the dance floor if we tried," he said, noting her eyes were unnaturally bright. She put her lips on the straw and sucked greedily. "Hey, slow down." Cooper took the drink from her and asked Harry for a glass of water.

"Why are you acting so paranoid?" Summer demanded. "You all but accused me of being a stick-in-the-mud earlier. I'm just trying to have a good time, and you're doing everything in your power to prevent it."

Cooper glared back at her. "Fine. Don't let me stop you." He slid her glass in front of her and got up from the stool. "I'm going to the bathroom." He walked away without another word.

"So how long have you and Cooper been seeing each other?" Harry asked.

Summer blinked at him. His face look slightly fuzzy and off balance. "We just met tonight," she said, picking up her drink. "I doubt we'll see each other again."

"How come?"

"Oh, he thinks I'm dull as dishwater." She shrugged. "Maybe he's right. Even my grandmother accuses me of taking life too seriously, and she's seventy years old. Do you know, I haven't been out on a real date since—" She paused and tried to count the months on her fingers, then got confused and had to start over again.

"Excuse me, miss?"

Summer stopped counting and glanced over one shoulder, where a man stood wearing a cowboy hat. "Yes?"

"Would you like to dance?"

"Dance?" She looked across the dance floor, where couples were gathering for a slow number. "Gee, I don't know."

"Go ahead," Harry urged. "I'll keep Cooper company while you're gone."

"May I take my drink with me?"

"Sure, whatever you like." He chuckled as she followed the man to the dance floor.

Cooper returned from the rest room and frowned when he noted Summer's empty stool. "Where'd she go?" he asked the bartender.

"She's dancing."

"*Dancing?*" Cooper turned around and found Summer in the arms of a cowboy. "I told you to keep an eye on her," he blurted out to Harry.

"Hey, she's over twenty-one. She can dance if she feels like it. What's wrong with you, buddy?"

Cooper sat down on his stool but didn't take his eyes off Summer. He felt his anger flare at the way the cowboy held her, the way he whispered in her ear. Summer laughed, and the sound reached Cooper's ears. She was obviously having the time of her life. Well, to hell with her, he thought. Warren had asked him to fill in for a couple of hours, not play baby-sitter. He gritted his teeth and turned to Harry, who seemed to be enjoying the whole thing. "Let me pay up."

The other man looked surprised and a little startled. "You're not leaving?"

"She can find her own way home. From the looks of it, she shouldn't have any problem." Cooper pulled several bills from his wallet, tossed the money on the bar, and made his way out the back door. The cool night air was like balm on his face after sitting in the stuffy club. He unlocked the chain securing his bike, taking his time in case Summer decided to stop playing belle of the ball and come looking for him.

Once it was obvious Summer had no intention of looking for him, Cooper pulled on his helmet, climbed onto his bike, and roared out of the alley. Like Harry'd said, she was over twenty-one and could do as she damn well pleased.

Cooper had gone only a couple of miles before he pulled off on the side of the road and killed the engine. "Dammit to hell!" He sat there for fifteen minutes, wondering what he should do. He couldn't just leave her back there to fend for herself in a room filled with horny men wearing ten-gallon hats and pointy-toed boots. The last thing she needed was a bunch of losers pawing on her. Not that Harry wouldn't look after her, but he had no business dumping her in his friend's lap when he was the one who'd brought her there in the first place.

As Cooper started his engine once more, he realized he was more angry with himself than with anyone else. He should never have taken her into such a dive. What could he have been thinking? It just proved that he had no idea how to treat a real lady. He turned the motorcycle around and headed back to the bar.

When Cooper walked in the back door, he muttered a sound of disgust. Summer was literally surrounded by men. As he stalked toward her, he noted there were several drinks in front of her as well as two or three empty glasses. Harry spotted him right away and grinned.

"We haven't had this much action since Tanya Tucker came in and agreed to sing us a song."

"I hope you're proud of yourself," Cooper shot back angrily.

"Hey, you brought her here, pal."

"Get me her coat and call a cab."

"What about your bike?"

"How far do you think we'd get before she fell off?" he snapped, then realized he had no business being angry with his friend for the predicament he was in. "I'm leaving it out back," he said a bit more gently. "Everything's locked up."

"Nobody's going to lay a finger on it once they know who it belongs to," Harry said confidently.

"And I'm supposed to feel proud of that fact?" Cooper replied, giving Harry a hostile look before moving in on Summer's groupies. He and Harry had an unspoken agreement not to talk about the past or even make references to it. He had to assume it was a slip on his friend's part.

Cooper nudged one of the men ogling Summer. "Get lost." The man stepped aside without another word.

Summer smiled lopsidedly the minute she spotted Cooper. "Hi, I was beginning to think you'd left me."

Cooper glared at the men circling her like wolves hunkering over prey. "Party's over, guys," he said, and was met with a great deal of grumbling. "The lady is going home now to her husband and six kids." Harry passed him the coat over the bar, and Cooper held it in one hand as he helped her from the barstool. She stumbled and he caught up with her. "Come on, now," he said. "You know how Junior frets when you're not there to rock him to sleep." Several of the men stared at her.

Summer gazed back at Cooper dumbly, unable to make sense of what he was saying. "But I'm not finished with my drink," she said, slurring her words. "And I told that nice man with the rhinestone vest I'd dance with him."

"Well, you'll just have to come back another night. Besides, you're scheduled to take that blood test first thing in the morning."

"Blood test?"

"So we can find out how you got that rash *you know where*." Some of the men moved away.

Rash? Summer was still trying to figure out what was going on as he helped her toward the front door. She was unsteady on her feet, but he managed to lead her across the room without mishap. "Hurry up," he said, shoving her through the front door without benefit of her coat. The cab was nowhere in sight.

"It's cold out here," she protested, a shiver snaking up her body. Her teeth chattered.

"Here's your coat," he said. "Put your arm in this sleeve." He held it out, and she aimed at the opening several times without hitting it. Finally, Cooper muttered an obscenity and worked at getting her arms in the sleeves. It was like trying to force a cooked fettuccine noodle through a straw. He glanced over his shoulder several times to make sure the rednecks hadn't followed them out. Where was that damn cab? He buttoned Summer's coat and noted she was swaying. "How many drinks did you have?" he demanded.

She offered him a blank look. "I don't know. Three or four. Maybe more."

"Damn, Summer! Do you realize there are two shots of booze in each drink?" She looked shocked. "Just because you can't taste it doesn't mean it's not there." He let out a sigh of frustration. "I can't take you back to your grandmother's house in this condition. She'll have me locked up." His eyes clouded with uneasiness.

Summer stood there quietly, noting his worry and indecision. "I'm sorry," she said as a sense of inadequacy swept over her. "I acted like a fool back there. I embarrassed you in front of your friends."

Cooper, still in a dilemma as to where he was going to take her, responded impatiently. "What?"

She colored fiercely. "I humiliated you in front of your friend Harry." She was so ashamed of how she'd acted that she buried her burning face against his shoulder and burst into tears.

Cooper suddenly felt a strange surge of affection toward her. "I shouldn't have taken you into that place to begin with." Why had he? What had he hoped to prove? That they had nothing in common? That perhaps she was, as he'd suspected from the beginning, too good for him?

He saw the cab a distance away. "Hush your crying," he said gently, and tipped her head back. Her eyes were wet, her cheeks tear-stained. "It's okay," he tried to assure her. "We need to get you home and into bed. You'll feel better in the morning." Even as he said the words, he doubted it was the truth. She was going to feel like hell when she woke up.

Once the cab had pulled to a stop, Cooper helped Summer inside and closed the door. He got in on the other side. She automatically leaned against him. He put his arm around her, feeling very protective toward her at the moment.

"Where to?" the driver asked.

"Summer?" Cooper shook her slightly. "Where do you live, honey?" She mumbled something incoherently, and he had to repeat the question twice before he understood. He repeated it to the cabdriver.

Five minutes into the ride, Summer was sleeping soundly. Cooper could hear her even breathing, smell her perfume, and the fresh, clean scent of her hair. As before, his body stirred in response to her nearness; his whole being was filled with a sense of longing, a feeling of urgency that tied his gut in knots. And to think, only moments before he'd felt quite chivalrous toward her. Perhaps it had something to do with the fact that one of her hands was curled in his lap, so close to the part of his anatomy that was giving him the most trouble at the moment. He wished she would accidentally brush her fingers against him, wished he could take her hand in his and press her palm against the aching muscle. The mere thought made him break into a sweat.

He didn't need this, didn't want it. He was suddenly eager to escape the confines of the cab and get as far away from the woman as he could. He could feel himself holding his breath until Summer's ritzy condo came into sight. When a security guard stepped out of a small booth nearby, Cooper informed the man Summer was ill and he was seeing that she arrived home safely.

The guard took a closer look at Cooper, stepped forward, and peered into the window. "Miss Pettigrew, are you okay?" he asked. "Miss Pettigrew?"

Cooper shook her once more. "Summer, wake up."

She opened her eyes and tried to focus. "What s'matter?"

"Tell this man you're okay," Cooper said, motioning to the guard, "and that I'm not trying to kidnap you."

Summer looked at the uniformed man. There seemed to be two of them. She blinked several times, and the two bodies seemed to merge into one that she suddenly recognized. "Oh, hi, Jack," she said, finding it difficult to pronounce her words. "Everything's 'kay. My, uh, frien' is just trying to get me home safely. I had too many Lace Panties tonight."

Jack frowned. "Would you like me to call your grandmother?" he asked.

"Oh, no, thas not n'sary. Mr. Garrett here is my very bes' friend. He can come and go anytime he likes, 'kay?"

The guard looked doubtful. "Mr. Garrett, may I see your driver's license?"

Cooper sighed and reached into his pocket for his wallet. He pulled out his license and handed it to the man. "Is this how you welcome all your visitors?" he asked.

"I'd like to make a copy of this if you don't mind."

"Suit yourself."

The guard was gone several minutes. When he returned, he handed Cooper his license. "Just so you'll know, I plan to run a check on you, Mr. Garrett. We're real careful about who we let in. Especially when it comes to our single ladies."

"May I deliver Miss Pettigrew to her door now?" Cooper asked. "Or do you plan to frisk me as well?"

The guard waved them through without another word, but he didn't look happy about it. "Man, oh, man," the cabdriver said as he checked the numbers on the doors. "You'd think we had Princess Di in the backseat." He pulled into a slot and put the car in park while Cooper tried to nudge Summer awake.

"You're home," he told the limp woman. "Do you think you can walk?"

Summer suddenly felt dizzy. Her stomach churned. "I don't feel so well."

The cabbie mumbled something under his breath and looked the other way. Cooper all but pulled Summer across the seat and out the door, then managed to get her into a standing position long enough to pay the driver. He closed the door and the cab pulled away, squealing its tires. It occurred to him he didn't have a ride home, but he didn't have time to worry about it at the moment. "Come on, Summer," he said sternly.

"I'm going to be sick."

"Yes, you probably will be," he agreed, "but try to wait until we get inside. Take a deep breath."

Summer did as she was told, but it didn't seem to help the feeling of nausea. Cooper led her to a corner unit of two-story town homes that had been built of antique brick in a graceful Queen Anne–style architecture. Each unit had its own miniature yard and petunia-filled flower bed. The circular drive had been paved with cobblestone; the grounds resembled an English garden, complete with wrought-iron benches and lampposts. Definitely a high-rent district, but classy in a subtle, unassuming way.

Once they reached her door, Cooper leaned Summer against one wall, took her purse, and checked inside for her keys. He pulled them out and chuckled when he noted each key had been neatly labeled. He unlocked her door and helped her inside.

As Cooper unbuttoned Summer's coat, he took in his surroundings with a great deal of curiosity. Standing in the small foyer, he noted the butler table and brass scrolled mirror and a tall vase of fresh flowers that sweetened the air and made him think of being on a country road in spring. From where he stood, he could see the living room that had been decorated in various shades of white, cream, and beige, accented with a splash of color here and there that added eye appeal. White saloon-style doors led into another room, which he suspected was the kitchen. A flight of stairs stood to his left. "Where's your bedroom?" he asked.

Eyes half closed, Summer pointed to the steps. Cooper shook his head sadly. As he figured, he was going far beyond the call of duty. He draped her coat over a highly polished mahogany coat rack, shrugged off his jacket, and lifted her high in his arms. She opened her eyes and shot him a frantic look. "I have to throw up."

"Two seconds," he said irritably.

He took the stairs as quickly as he could and entered the first bedroom he came to. He was only vaguely aware of the soft mint paint on the walls that added a soothing touch to the room. He found the bathroom easily enough and set her down in front of the toilet. He lifted the lid. "Go for it."

Summer wasted no time. As she leaned over the mint-green toilet bowl and emptied her stomach, Cooper held her hair back, then tucked it in the back of her jump suit. He opened the linen closet and grabbed a washcloth trimmed in delicate lace. He was almost afraid to use it, then noted the others were just like it.

Cooper wet the washcloth and waited patiently while Summer finished being sick. He simply stood there, wishing he could help and feeling inadequate because he couldn't. Finally, Summer moaned aloud and sank to the floor like a drooping daisy. Cooper flushed the toilet and closed the lid, then reached beneath her arms and pulled her up. Once again it was like working with a limp noodle, but he added a little soap and scrubbed from forehead to chin. Finally, he rinsed the cloth and patted her dry with a clean towel. She was lovely without makeup, her skin healthy and unblemished and glowing with pale peach undertones. "You want to brush your teeth?"

Stupid question, he thought. She could barely hold her head up.

"Sit tight for a minute," he said, almost afraid to let

her go for fear she'd fall. He grabbed her toothbrush from a dainty porcelain holder and squirted a generous amount of toothpaste on it. "Open your mouth, Summer."

She did as she was told. Cooper brushed her teeth as best he could, then helped her over to the sink to rinse. "Now, doesn't that taste better?"

She mumbled incoherently.

"Come on, you need to go to bed." He led her back into the bedroom and set her on a satin comforter of cream and mint green with splashes of peach. She leaned back and tried to curl into a ball. "Oh, no, you don't," he said, noting her badly stained jump suit. He couldn't let her climb beneath the sheets wearing it. Not when it was so obvious how particular she was. He pulled off her black heels and reached for the zipper at her throat. It whispered as he slid it all the way down past her navel.

Peeling the jump suit from her shoulders, Cooper tried not to stare at the lacy black bra she wore that made her skin appear translucent. He eased her back on the bed and wrestled the jump suit past her waist and hips, where he was greeted once more with black lace in the form of bikini underwear. He moaned. The woman might appear conservative on the outside, but underneath it all she was tempting as hell.

He could feel the perspiration beading his brow. Damn Warren's soul for getting him involved in this! He tried to remember what, if anything, his cousin had ever done for him to garner such loyalty.

He sighed heavily. "Sit up, Summer," he ordered in a voice that sounded like a cross between a snarl and a growl. He'd heard vicious Doberman pinschers make nicer noises. "We have to get you under the covers." If she heard him, she didn't give any indication. He pulled her up and, encircling her waist with one arm, yanked the bedcovers down. Her scent lingered on the pastel sheets. Her skin felt like rose petals, and he reminded himself that he was the cause of all this. If he hadn't taken her to Dirty Harry's in the first place, she would not be in such bad shape. With that in mind, he lay her back gently and tucked her long, shapely legs beneath the covers.

He dragged in a shaky breath and wiped his brow. There now. He'd done his duty. He was exonerated.

Cooper's broad shoulders heaved as he sucked in another deep breath and turned to go. He was almost out the door when he heard the rustle of covers.

"Cooper?"

He snapped his head around so fast, it made him dizzy. Was she going to be sick again? He didn't think he could stand by and watch her go through it a second time. Especially since it was his fault. "Yeah?"

Summer was gazing at him sleepily. "Please don't leave."

"Oh, damn," he muttered.

Summer awoke the next morning to a full bladder, but as she raised herself up from the bed, the room seemed to tilt dangerously to one side. She almost groaned aloud at the dull throbbing at the back of her head, then realized her stomach didn't feel so good either. Was she coming down with something? She stood woozily and made her way into the bathroom. Once she'd relieved herself, she made a beeline for the sink and her toothbrush. Her mouth felt and tasted as though a herd of gazelles had grazed on her tongue during the night. She brushed her teeth twice, dried her mouth, and looked into the mirror.

Her bloodshot eyes and wild hair startled her. She was a mess! But the real scare came when she realized she was still wearing her bra and panties from the night before. Why hadn't she slipped into a gown before going to bed?

Her mind searched for answers. The last thing she remembered was going into a cowboy bar with Cooper Garrett. At one point he'd seemed to disappear, at which time she'd met a man named Tex or Rex or something like that. She'd even agreed to go to breakfast with him. After that, everything sort of blurred. Definitely not a good sign!

She walked into her bedroom and froze when her gaze fell on a pair of scuffed boots. Shock rendered her motionless for a moment; her mouth formed a perfect O. Finally, her gaze crept upward. The man had his back to her, but she would have recognized the scoundrel no matter what. Who else had hair the color of black shoe polish and shoulders wide enough to pull a covered wagon? And . . . and he was wearing her bathrobe of all things!

"Excuse me," she called out in a voice shrill enough to break glass and send little arrows of pain darting through the back of her skull.

Cooper turned over in the bed and smiled at the disheveled, half-naked vision before him. "Good morning, sweetheart."

FOUR

Sweetheart? Panic seized her. Summer backed away, horror-stricken as she struggled once more to remember what had happened after she'd left Dirty Harry's. The details were sketchy at best.

Summer suddenly noted the look in Cooper's eyes, bold and assessing, and her heart gave a wild lurch as she realized she was still in her underwear. She yelped and turned a vivid scarlet, then ducked into the bathroom. Her embarrassment and humiliation was heightened by the sound of male laughter coming from the next room.

Blast the man! Who did he think he was? Here she was, feeling next to death, and he seemed to be enjoying every minute of it. Summer snatched an oversized bath towel from a rack and wrapped it around her sarong-style. It smelled of rose-scented soap and male flesh. Cooper had taken a shower. Since the towel was completely dry, he must have done so the night before. But why?

She sat on the edge of the bathtub and covered her face with her hands. Lord, what had possessed her to act so irresponsibly? Here she was, basically a teetotaler, and she'd tossed back those drinks like a real pro. And that wasn't the worst of it! Oh, no, that didn't even come close to the shame of waking up next to a man she'd known less than twelve hours or prancing about in black bikini underwear as though she were part of a burlesque show.

She had to get rid of him. Her grandmother would ask questions, naturally, but she would think of something. With the decision made, she squared her shoulders and marched into the bedroom. She found him lying on his back with his hands stacked beneath his head as though he had every right to be there.

He gave her a toe-curling grin. "I sure could use a cup of coffee."

"Why are you here?" she demanded.

"You asked me to stay," he replied matter-of-factly. "Don't you remember?"

She tossed him an accusing look. "No, I *don't* remember."

"Yes, well, I'm not surprised. You were pretty far gone at the time. I took the liberty of anticipating how you'd feel this morning," he added, "by placing a bottle of aspirin and a glass of water on your night table."

Still trembling, Summer reached for the bottle, opened it, and popped two tablets into her mouth before draining the glass of water.

The pounding in her head seemed to get worse. She met his gaze but found her eyes straying to his wide chest and the thick mat of hair that covered it. Her robe did very little to hide that part of his anatomy. "You slept in my bed?" she asked at last.

He nodded. His poker-face expression told her nothing.

She dreaded hearing the answer to her next question. "Did I undress myself?"

"You were in no condition." He saw the uncertainty

in her eyes, and he knew he was a real heel for letting her believe the worst, but he was having too much fun to stop. Besides, she had it coming after all she'd put him through.

"I want you out of here," she said, her voice as cold and bitter as a December wind. "Now!"

He arched one dark brow, swung his legs over the side of the bed, and stood. "You're not even going to fix me breakfast?"

The killing glare she shot him was all the answer he needed. Cooper planted his hands on his hips and pretended outrage. Not an easy task considering how he was dressed. "Well, that's a fine how-do-you-do," he said. "I can't believe you'd just kick me out after . . . after all the nice things I did for you last night. The least you could do is thank me."

Summer colored fiercely. "*Thank you?*" she sputtered in disbelief. Surely there wasn't a man alive who could match his arrogance. "I'm supposed to *thank you* for what you did? I should cut your liver out and feed it to my neighbor's cat. But you're not worth dulling a perfectly good blade."

He shrugged. "Fine. Be that way. But if you think I enjoyed doing what I did for one minute, you're wrong. I went through with it only because I knew no other man would." He shuddered. "Talk about nasty. Why do you think I showered immediately afterward?"

She felt as though he'd slapped her. "You rodent!" she cried in utter contempt. "You are the most boorish, uncouth man I've ever met. You are vile and despicable, lower than the lowest life-form. You are vermin!" she added shrilly. "A maggot!"

Cooper cocked his head to one side. "Could you please be more specific?"

The humorous light in his eyes only incensed her

more. She whirled around and stormed from the room as ferociously as a tornado.

Cooper realized he'd pushed her too far. He hurried after her. "Summer, wait—"

She was already halfway down the stairs. "Go to hell!" she spat out over her shoulder. She cleared the steps and marched into her kitchen, where she found the door to the laundry room ajar. She pointed. "Put on your clothes and leave this instant!"

"I can't."

"What do you mean, you *can't?*" she said between gritted teeth.

"They're still wet. I never got around to putting them in the dryer last night."

"I don't care if they're on fire. I don't care if your underwear is crawling with red ants. I want you out of my house *now!*"

He'd never seen a female look so angry. The woman had a temper that would stop a charging bull. "Wait," he said, holding both hands up as though he were the victim of a stickup. "Before you kick me out, I have something to tell you."

She covered her ears with her hands. "I refuse to listen to any more of your trash."

He grabbed her wrists and pulled them toward him. "Tough. 'Cause you're going to listen anyway. Nothing happened between us last night, okay? I was just trying to have a little fun with you."

Her eyes became daggers. "Liar! And I thought you couldn't get any lower."

"I can get plenty lower, believe me, but I try to draw the line at having sex with an unconscious woman. The only thing that happened is you got sick, and I had to clean it up. That's the reason I took a shower and washed my clothes."

She studied him closely. "So we didn't—"

"No. You did such a good job of passing out that they'd have covered you with a sheet if you'd been in a hospital. You woke up only long enough to ask me to stay. I figured I'd better hang around in case you got sick again."

Her anger flared to new heights. "And you let me believe we were intimate!" she sputtered, backing away from him. "Do you have any idea how frightened I was not knowing if I'd contracted a disease or gotten pregnant? And you think that's funny?"

Cooper opened his mouth to defend himself just as she reached for a decorative teakettle and threw it at him. He ducked in the nick of time, and the kettle slammed into the wall behind him, sending a small picture askew. "Dammit to hell!" he shouted. "Are you crazy? You could have hit me with that!"

Summer gasped aloud once she realized what she'd done. "Oh, my heavens!" she cried, covering her mouth with one hand. "I—I didn't mean to—" She reached out for him and he backed away, eyeing her skeptically. "I've never done anything like that in my life," she confessed. "You had me so upset. I wasn't thinking."

"Give me my clothes."

"But they're still wet."

"Two minutes ago you were willing to let red ants gnaw on my privates."

Summer hurried into the laundry room and pulled his clothes from the washer. She tossed his clothes into the dryer and turned it on. "They'll be dry before you know it," she said. "In the meantime, I'll make coffee and fix your breakfast."

His eyes were guarded. "Why are you suddenly being nice to me?" he demanded. "Afraid I'll swear out a complaint?"

"Don't be ridiculous," she said as though it were no big deal when, in fact, her insides were still quaking.

"Besides, you'd be too embarrassed to go to the police. How would it look, me getting the upper hand on a big, tough biker like yourself?"

She was starting to piss him off. "*Excuse me*, but I wouldn't actually say you got the upper hand," he said, beginning to pace. He had to work off his anger, the restless energy that made him want to shake her silly one minute and kiss her senseless the next. "I just wasn't expecting you to start throwing things. Someone with your fine *breeding*," he added with a sneer.

Summer tried her best to look remorseful. She chanced a look in his direction. Just knowing he had nothing on underneath the robe made her a little breathless. As he continued to pace, she studied him. His legs and feet were strong and sturdy-looking, slightly muscular, and covered with dark hair. The robe flapped open at the bottom each time he turned, giving her a brief glimpse of his thighs. He paused when he caught her staring.

"What are you looking at?"

"You have nice legs."

He crossed his arms over his chest and regarded her. "Don't try to suck up to me, Summer, because it won't work."

She smiled in spite of herself. Lord, what had possessed her to throw that kettle at him? She stepped closer, ready to apologize again.

He backed off. "Keep your hands off me."

"Don't be silly," she said. "I'm not going to hurt you."

He gaped at her. "You think I'm *afraid* of you?"

"Well, you certainly act like you are."

"I'm not afraid. It's just that I can't defend myself against a damn *woman*. If you were a man, I'd have already decked you, but—" He paused and looked thoughtful. His eyes narrowed into black slits. "Maybe I *can* teach you a lesson after all."

Summer saw the menacing look and retreated a step. "I don't think I like whatever it is you're planning," she said.

He pulled a chair from the square pine table, grabbed her wrist, and dragged her to it. She struggled, and the towel came loose and clumped around her feet. She squealed and reached for it, but Cooper yanked her closer. He sat down in the chair and pulled her across his lap.

"What are you doing!" she cried.

Cooper's voice sounded more like a snarl when he spoke. "I'm doing what your grandmother should have done long before now." He brought his hand down on her fanny in a solid whack.

"Ouch!" She kicked. "Let me go!" she ordered, her pretty features contorted with shock and anger.

"That's for offering me mechanics' wages when I tried to do you a favor last night out of the kindness of my heart."

"You have no heart!" she replied, and was rewarded with another slap that hurt her pride more than her behind.

"And that one was for teasing a bunch of horny men in a cowboy bar," he said. "You put both of us in a dangerous situation."

"You're an animal!" she sputtered. "Not even fit to be let in the house."

The doorbell rang. Obviously the neighbors had heard the ruckus and decided to investigate. Good! Maybe they'd call the police. The idea of watching them lead Cooper away in handcuffs would be worth any scandal that might ensue. "Let me go," she said between clenched teeth, "or I swear I'll—"

"You'll what? Throw something else at me? Punch

me in the face? And you call yourself a lady?" Even as he spouted off at her, he realized he no longer had the urge to smack her again. He glanced down at her bikini-clad bottom, and his gut tightened at the sight of the tempting swell. He couldn't resist touching her any more than he could resist taking his next breath. But the minute his hand made contact, he knew he was lost. She was firm but womanly. *Exquisite* was the word that came to mind. He could no longer deny the strong attraction he felt for her.

Summer's heart slammed to her throat as Cooper's hand came down on her once more, this time in a caress. She could feel the heat of his open palm burning through her satin-and-lace panties. She glanced over her shoulder, and their gazes met and locked. His eyes smoldered like black coals. She thought she felt heat on her skin, but told herself it was just her imagination. The fire in her belly was real. She suddenly couldn't get enough oxygen into her lungs. "Cooper?" His name came out sounding like a croak.

"Summer, I—" He shook himself. He hadn't meant this to happen. The tables had turned on him, and he was in no way prepared. Her dreamy-eyed look and the slightly parted lips told him she was at her most vulnerable, and he didn't have the first clue what to do about it.

Neither of them heard the key turning in the lock at the front door, or the approaching footsteps.

"Oh, my word!" Henrietta Pettigrew came to a dead halt in the doorway, her chauffeur on her heels. He looked away respectfully. The color drained from Henrietta's face, and the genteel lady who never became rattled, even under the most harrowing circumstances, looked as though she might shatter into a million pieces.

She clutched her chest. "Please wait for me in the car, Axel." He nodded quickly, as though eager to escape.

Henrietta took a deep breath. "What in heaven's name is going on here?" she demanded.

Without warning, Cooper released Summer, and she slid to the floor, bumping her knee in the process. She winced and reached for the towel, wrapping it about her haphazardly. "I know it looks bad, Grandmother," she said, "but it's not what you think."

Cooper stood and nodded lamely. "Good morning, Mrs. Pettigrew, it's good to see you again."

Henrietta looked at him. "Why are you dressed in my granddaughter's bathrobe, young man?"

He looked embarrassed. "It was all I could find to put on once I took my shower."

Summer cringed inwardly, knowing he was making matters worse. "What Cooper is trying to say—"

Henrietta hushed her by putting one hand up. "On second thought, I'd just as soon not hear your explanation," she said coolly. "You're both consenting adults. What you do in private is your business. Besides, I wasn't spying on you," she told Summer. "When you didn't return for your car last night, I became worried. I called several times after my guests left, and I've been trying to reach you all morning."

"That's my fault," Cooper said. "I took the phone off the hook so Summer could sleep in this morning. She wasn't feeling well last night."

"Oh?" Henrietta regarded her granddaughter. "Are you ill?"

"Yes, but I'm better now. It must've been something I ate."

Henrietta looked from one to the other. "I'm glad to hear it. I'll expect you to come for your car around lunchtime. *Both* of you," she added, eyeing Cooper. "We didn't get a chance to talk much last night. Since this . . . uh . . . romance seems to have progressed further than I suspected, I'll look forward to seeing more of you. Hopefully, you'll be dressed in men's clothing next time." Without another word, she turned and made her way to the foyer and out the front door.

Summer and Cooper stared at each other again. "Do you think she's upset?" he asked.

"I'd venture a wild guess in that direction, yes."

"Will she do something like cut you off?"

"Cut me off?"

"Your inheritance. Like write you out of her will or something?"

Summer was insulted, and it showed. "Do you think I care one way or the other what she does with her money?"

He glanced around the spotless kitchen with all its conveniences. "Well, you obviously live very well."

"That's right. And I happen to pay my own way."

He crossed his arms and held them over his face as though fending off another possible blow. "Okay, let's not fight again. I was just wondering what you had to lose if she stayed mad at you."

Summer crossed her arms. "Her respect maybe?" she said, sarcasm slipping into her voice. "I mean, it isn't often she drops by and finds me in my underwear getting spanked by a man she barely knows wearing my bathrobe."

"You had it coming, and you know it."

"Don't start with me, Cooper." She turned for the coffeepot. The aspirin hadn't helped her headache. Neither had the events of the morning.

"So what are we going to do?" Cooper asked, sitting down in the chair once more.

Summer plugged in the coffeemaker. "*We* aren't going to do anything," she replied. "I'm going to tell her the truth."

He laughed. "Oh, that ought to go over well."

"What's *that* supposed to mean?"

"She probably thinks we're serious about each other; otherwise you'd never have let me spend the night. The fact that she found you across my lap can be explained away easily enough. We were just two people in love having a little fun."

"You call that *fun?* I shudder to think what you do for an encore."

"Hey, I'm kidding, okay?" Cooper stood and crossed the room. He reached out and tucked a stray lock of blond hair behind one ear.

"I thought it was every woman's fantasy to be dominated in bed."

"I'm not into pain, if that's what you're asking. I have no desire to be brutalized."

Cooper reached for another strand of gold hair and toyed with it. "I'm not talking about cruel and inhumane treatment, babe," he said, his voice so smooth, it lulled her into a sense of well-being when she knew she needed to shield her emotions and remain alert. "I'm talking about releasing one's darkest secrets and inhibitions in the bedroom. Where it's safe. I'm talking about using all five senses and whatever else it takes to give our bodies the pleasures they were designed for. Imagine two people so enmeshed, it's impossible to tell where one leaves off and the other begins. No holding back."

Summer was held rapt by the erotic images he'd planted in her brain. Her body felt heavy and warm, her insides had become soft and liquid. She reeled her thoughts in and steeled herself. "What new game is this?"

He twirled her hair around his index finger. They locked gazes. "No game," he said softly. "But a man must make love to a woman's mind before he can hope to have her body."

An unwelcome blush crept up her neck and spread across her cheeks. She pulled her hair free and stepped back. "That's *exactly* why I want out of this situation," she said. "Instead of helping me, you're making things worse."

"Worse? How?"

"You make me . . . uncomfortable."

"Uncomfortable in a good way or a bad way?"

"I don't like it."

His eyes met hers disparagingly. "Then I suggest you follow your instincts and tell your grandmother the truth. You got commode-hugging drunk and woke up next to a man you'd known less than twelve hours. What she walked in on this morning will appear tame after that." He shrugged. "I gotta go."

Summer nibbled her bottom lip as she remembered how her grandmother had reacted when she'd walked through the door earlier.

How could she confess the truth to her grandmother when there was a chance she could make the woman's condition worse? How would she live with herself?"

"Cooper, wait," she said. "I can't tell her. As much as I hate lying to her, I can't risk telling the truth."

"Just how sick *is* she?" he asked.

The play of emotions on his face made Summer wonder if he was having second thoughts. "I haven't been able to reach her doctor. I'm afraid he's avoiding me because it's bad news."

"Or maybe he's following the old doctor/patient confidentiality rule."

"Avery's an old friend. He knows how close my grandmother and I are. I can't imagine him keeping anything from me unless my grandmother specifically asked him to. And I can't see her hiding information from me unless it's serious, and she can't bring herself to tell me." She felt the first pangs of guilt. "I hope what she saw a few minutes ago doesn't affect her condition."

Cooper saw the deep concern in her eyes. He wanted

to put a hand on her shoulder, comfort her, but he was afraid she'd pull away. "Look, I'll go another round with you if that's what you want. We'll meet your grandmother for lunch and pretend we're crazy mad in love with each other. In the meantime, you try to talk to her doctor. Maybe it's not as bad as you think. If that's the case, we'll pretend to have a serious fight and break up. I doubt Henrietta will mourn for long once Warren takes over. I'm sure Golden Boy will meet all the qualifications."

The dryer buzzed in the next room, and he hurried inside for his clothes. His jeans were still damp, but he didn't care. He stepped into them and zipped them up. He shrugged out of the bathrobe and tossed it to Summer, who was doing her level best not to stare. But what woman wouldn't find her gaze riveted to that powerful, well-muscled chest and flat stomach or the coarse blue-black hair?

She noted the scar right away, a jagged four- or five-inch welt that marred the flesh near his navel where the hair whirled captivatingly. There was also scarring at the top of one shoulder, where it looked as though someone had bitten him, and a perfectly round indentation not far from that spot that made her wonder if someone had burned him with a cigar.

"Summer?"

She snatched her head up. He'd caught her staring. Gawking, actually. "Yes?"

His voice was slightly husky when he spoke. "I'm not going to leave if you keep looking at me that way."

Her face flamed. She crossed her arms and glanced the other way. Darn her roving eyes! No wonder the man was so full of himself.

He pulled the T-shirt over his head and tucked it in. He couldn't hide his amusement. She was doing her level best not to look at him, but it was too late. She'd caught an eyeful, and it did his heart good to know she liked what she'd seen. "Mind if I use your phone?" he asked, giving no indication of the direction his thoughts were going.

She glanced in his direction and was relieved to see he was clothed. "Help yourself."

He shot her a sheepish grin. "I guess I ought to put the one in the living room back on the hook." She waited until he left the room before slipping on the bathrobe and pulling off the towel. She tied the robe securely about her waist. His scent still clung to the fabric. She had the crazy notion to bury her face in the material. What was wrong with her?

Cooper returned. "It definitely looks better on you," he said, motioning to the robe. He made his way to the wall phone, grabbed the phone book from a shelf beneath it, and flipped through the pages until he found what he was looking for. The silence hung heavily in the air as he dialed and waited for an answer. "Yeah, I need a cab," he said when a voice came on the line. He rattled off the address. "That long, huh? Okay." He hung up. "It's going to be an hour or so before they can get to me."

She opened her mouth to respond, but he hurried from the room. She heard him on the stairs and wondered what he was up to. He returned a moment later, carrying his boots.

"At least have a cup of coffee before you go," she said, deciding she could prove she indeed had good breeding.

"I take mine black."

She filled a cup and set it before him, then prepared one for herself.

Sitting in the chair once more, Cooper pulled on his socks and boots, and reached for the dainty white coffee cup edged in gold.

Summer joined him at the table. "Cooper, I know this whole thing has been quite an ordeal for you."

He liked the way she said his name, liked the sound of her voice in general. In fact, he was finding it awfully damn hard to find something he *didn't* like about her. He imagined her whispering his name in his ear as they made love, or crying out as she reached orgasm. It didn't matter how blue her blood was; if he ever got her in the sack, she'd forget all about being a lady.

"I can't imagine *what* possessed Warren to do something so irrational," Summer went on.

Cooper realized he'd drifted away from the conversation. "Maybe he hit his head in the accident," he replied. "Don't worry about it." He stood. He needed to put some space between them. He couldn't wait to get back on his bike. Maybe a ride in the cool air would clear his head. "So what time's lunch?"

"Noon. That gives us a couple of hours."

"I'll pick you up at eleven-thirty."

She nodded. "Maybe afterward we can visit Warren."

He shrugged. "Whatever," he said tersely. "We certainly don't want the poor guy to think we've forgotten about him." He went into the foyer for his jacket. "I'll wait for my cab outside."

"You don't have to do that," she called out, following him into the next room, where he was already slipping into his leather jacket. His shoulders seemed to double in size. "Cooper, is something wrong?"

He glanced over his shoulder. She stood there in her bathrobe with her hair tumbling about her shoulders, looking sexier than any woman had a right to. Apprehension coursed through him. How had she managed to get under his skin so quickly?

"Everything's fine," he muttered, and reached for the door handle.

Summer covered his big hand with hers. "No, it isn't," she said. "You're angry with me. Why?"

The pleasure of her touch was as pure as sunshine, but he snatched his hand away as though she'd put a hot brand to his flesh. He averted his gaze, knowing if she looked into his eyes, she'd see more than he was ready to share. How would she react if he told her he had strong feelings for her despite the fact they were little more than strangers?

He'd never met a woman quite like her, one that drove him mad with desire one minute and made him want to protect her the next. What would she have thought of him if he'd fallen back on his old ways and taken on half the guys in the bar the night before? Lord knew it wouldn't be the first time. He had enough scars on his face and body to prove it.

No, he couldn't tell her. She'd think he was a nut case. Maybe he was. Maybe she was making him nuts.

"I need to get going," he told her. "I've got a lot to do before I come back for you."

Summer would have had to be blind not to notice his response to her touch. Disappointment settled like an iron weight in her chest. "Sure, I understand," she said, clasping her hands together in front of her. He let himself out and closed the door behind him, leaving her feeling troubled and confused.

Summer found herself still wondering about Cooper's sudden change in mood as she looked up the number for the hospital where Warren had been taken. After being passed around from one crisp voice to the next, her coworker finally answered. She could hear the grogginess in his voice.

"How are you?" she asked brightly.

He sighed. "Well, considering the fact I have a broken leg, a sprained wrist, and several cracked ribs—"

"Are you in a lot of pain?"

"They've been pretty good about giving me something," he told her. "But the medication must be wearing off, because I'm starting to feel every bump and bruise. Speaking of bruisers, how'd it go last night with my cousin?"

"I don't like to kick a man when he's down," Summer said, "but I can't believe you sent someone like Cooper. Why didn't you just call the city jail and ask them to release one of their prisoners?"

Warren chuckled, then groaned from the pain in his side. "I couldn't find anybody else," he said. "Besides, Cooper's not such a bad guy once you get to know him. Most folks don't even bother because of his reputation as a badass." Warren paused, mumbled something to somebody on his end, then spoke. "A friend of mine just walked in. Can I call you back?"

"Don't bother," she said quickly. "I'll be by later to visit."

"You're awfully quiet back there, Mrs. Pettigrew," her chauffeur said, eyeing his employer in the rearview mirror. "Are you feeling okay?"

Henrietta realized they were almost home. She had been so lost in her thoughts, she'd missed the passing scenery. "What did you think of that little display back there, Axel?" she said.

"Aw, they're just a couple of kids having fun. You'll have to admit your granddaughter tends to take life too seriously sometimes."

"You've always had a soft spot for Summer," Henrietta said with a slight smile.

He nodded. "Yes, ma'am."

"And it's a good thing, considering how hard Mrs. Bradshaw was on her at times."

"She certainly made the girl toe the line," he said.

"Which is precisely why I kept the woman on for so many years. I would have spoiled the girl rotten. Just like I did her mother. And then, who knows? She might have taken off. Just like her mother," she repeated, almost in a whisper.

"Don't be so hard on yourself, Mrs. Pettigrew. With the world like it is today, one should not apologize for having a generous heart."

Henrietta remained thoughtful for the rest of the ride. She waited until they had pulled through the gate and parked in the circular drive in front of the house before she spoke.

"Axel, would you please be kind enough to contact that nice investigator who's done work for me in the past? I think I'm going to require his services."

Once more the driver's eyes sought hers in the mirror. "Of course, ma'am."

"And you saw nothing this morning, correct?" It was a rhetorical question. After thirty years of acting as driver, butler, and handyman, he was her most trusted employee and confidant. Not to mention her closest friend.

"How could I when I never even got out of the car."

They exchanged smiles in the mirror.

Cooper was back at eleven-fifteen and found Summer dressed in jeans, a simple chambray work shirt, and a sweater vest in an old quilt pattern. She wore Doc Martens on her slender feet, and her hair hung in a neat braid down her back.

"Well, this is a nice change," he said, deciding as pretty as she'd looked the night before, he preferred this casual side of her.

She was happy to note he'd dressed up a bit. His jeans looked new, and his navy polo shirt unwrinkled. Of course, he still hadn't gone anywhere near a barber or a razor, and he wore the same leather bomber jacket that only emphasized his biker image.

"How are you feeling?" he asked, noting she still looked a bit pale.

"Better. I took a brisk walk, then spent twenty minutes in a hot shower. I think from now on I'll stick to my occasional glass of champagne at weddings and forgo the Lace Panties." She paused and realized they were still standing in the foyer. "You're early," she said, checking her wristwatch. "Would you like a soft drink?"

He checked his own watch as though surprised to find he'd arrived back sooner than he was supposed to. "It must be running fast," he said, pretending to make adjustments. He wasn't about to confess he'd done all he had to do at breakneck speed so he could get back as soon as possible. "Sure, I'll take something to drink if it's not too much trouble."

Summer was taken aback by his polite tone. "I hope diet is okay," she said, going to the refrigerator.

He shrugged. He cared more about her company than the drink. "That's fine."

He took a seat at the table and watched as she grabbed an ice tray from the freezer and dumped several cubes into a glass. He found his eyes riveted to her jean-clad bottom and remembered how she'd looked that morning in skimpy black panties. Her hips were full and round, filling out the seat of her jeans in a way that made his palms itch to touch her again.

He remembered how lush her breasts had appeared as he'd undressed her the night before, satiny globes that almost spilled from the cups of her lacy black bra. His body stirred as he envisioned himself taking her nipples between his teeth and nipping them lightly, of rubbing baby oil into the soft mounds until they glistened. He would massage her entire body with the oil, concentrating his efforts on her thighs, where she would be most sensitive. He imagined how she would look against the sheets. Shiny. Slick. And then he would dip his fingers inside her, and she'd be just as wet, just as slippery.

Summer turned and caught him staring at her as though entranced. His gaze seemed to burn right through her clothes, and tiny pinpricks shimmied up her spine. It was a purely sensual experience, amazing because he hadn't even touched her.

Summer had never felt so self-conscious in her life. She tried to hide it as she carried the glass to the table and set it down, taking great care not to touch him.

"You're uncomfortable with me," he said, stating the obvious.

She rocked back and forth on the heels of her shoes, feeling almost girlish under his bold gaze. Nobody would ever have suspected she was a bigshot ad executive who earned close to a six-figure income. But she'd had better luck in advertising than in romance. "A little, I suppose." She met his gaze. "I still don't know you all that well."

He felt as though he knew her very well after the previous night, but then, he hadn't been unconscious part of the time. He decided not to bring it up and make her feel worse than she already did. "Aren't you going to join me?"

Summer prepared herself a glass of ice water and took a chair next to him. They were quiet for a minute. "So your bike was okay when you went back for it?" she asked.

He nodded as he sipped his drink.

"Most people would be afraid to leave an expensive motorcycle parked in that area of town," she said. "You're lucky it was still in one piece."

"I suppose."

"Warren said—" She paused at the dark look he shot her.

"When did you talk to Warren?" he asked, his tone coolly disapproving.

"I called him earlier," she replied, feeling defensive once more. "To let him know we'd be by to visit him later."

Cooper's gaze locked with hers. "And what did good ol' Warren have to say?"

Summer noted the sudden edge to his voice. She didn't like the way it made her feel. Nor did she care for the cold look in his eyes. "I don't think I care to carry on this discussion." She stood and started for the sink. He grabbed her wrist and pulled her to a halt.

She shook off his hand. She refused to let him stir her to anger. "Let's get something straight, Cooper," she said, her voice deceptively calm. "You don't use that tone with me, and you *certainly* don't put your hands on me unless I want you to."

He stood, and Summer was reminded once more of his size. Nevertheless, she refused to be intimidated by the man.

"I asked you a simple question," he said. "What did Warren say?"

She sighed. "He said people considered you a badass, okay? Is that what you are, Cooper? Or is it just an act you put on to keep people from getting close to you?"

He was so confused by her words that he merely stared at her for a moment. "What are you talking about?"

She hitched her chin high. "I don't think you're so bad. If you were, you'd have left me in that bar to fend for myself. But you didn't. You came back for me, saw that I got home safely, and took care of me while I was sick. You even stayed in case I got sick again during the night." She smiled knowingly. "You're not going to convince *me* you're so bad."

It ticked him off that she thought she knew him so

well. She didn't know a damn thing. If she did, she never would have invited him in for a soft drink, and she never *ever* would have asked him to spend the night no matter how much she'd had to drink. "You women always have to read something into every little thing, don't you?" he replied, his voice ringing with sarcasm. "Maybe I stayed 'cause I was hoping to get laid. Did you ever think of *that*, Einstein?"

She was still smiling that aggravating smile. "Right."

"Oh, for Pete's sake! You have to be the most exasperating woman I've ever met."

"Maybe I'm the first woman ever to stand up to you, *tough guy*," she said, stabbing her finger against his chest with each word.

A shadow of annoyance darkened his face. "You're a real hellcat, aren't you? No wonder you go for wimps like Warren."

"Have you always been jealous of your cousin?" she countered icily.

"Jealous?" he said incredulously. "Of *Warren?*"

"It makes sense to me. He's handsome and personable," she said, knowing most of the secretaries at work had had crushes on him at one time or another. "He's got a lot on the ball careerwise."

"And you think I lack those qualities?"

"I didn't say that. You and your cousin are special in your own way."

"So you're telling me Warren is special to you?"

She didn't hesitate. "Yes, he is," she said, remembering how kind Warren had been when she'd first joined Worth Advertising as their token female. Some of the older men had resented her, and she'd been assigned the smaller, less important accounts. It wasn't until Warren had gone to Mr. Worth on her behalf and asked that she be allowed to assist him with a major project that she'd won a grudging respect from the others.

Cooper watched the thoughtful expression on her face. It didn't take a mind reader to know she was thinking of Warren. She was right. He *was* jealous, but it had nothing to do with his cousin's looks or career advancement. He envied the man for having won Summer's affection. Not only that, it peeved him that Warren was better suited for her. He'd grown up in a loving home with all the advantages and had graduated from an Ivy League college. Cooper's mother had quit high school to marry his father, who had deserted the family when Cooper was just a toddler and his mother pregnant with his little sister. With little education, his mother cleaned houses for the rich and took in ironing. Still, it was only barely enough to keep them going, but she refused to let Cooper quit school and work full-time.

He'd picked up whatever work he could before an older kid had taught him how to pick pockets and scam people. Then came gambling. He'd already earned a reputation as a fighter; guys weren't afraid to put their money on him no matter how big his opponent. He got a cut of the profits, of course, and decided it was an easy way to make good bucks. But his career came to a screeching halt the minute his mother saw his battered face. He would never forget her anguish.

"You have shamed your family!" she'd cried. "Do you think I'm working this hard to raise a brute? What kind of example do you think you're setting for your sister?"

That had been his turning point. How could he expect his little sister to respect him when he'd lost respect for himself? He'd decided to make some changes to his life, and he'd done well. Even so, he realized Summer was still too good for him. She was out of his league.

That made him want her all the more.

The phone rang, and Summer snatched it up. "Hello, Grandmother," she said. "No, we didn't forget about lunch. As a matter of fact, we were just about to walk out the door."

Summer hung up the telephone and leaned her head against the wall, feeling very frustrated. "I don't know how we're going to pull this off," she said. "You and I can't be in a room five minutes without arguing."

Cooper surprised her by chuckling softly. When he spoke, she realized he was right behind her. She hadn't even heard his footsteps. She turned and found him only inches away.

"You still don't get it, do you?" he said softly.

She shifted her gaze. "Get what?"

"I've wanted you since the moment I laid eyes on you." He hooked his finger beneath her chin and raised her head so that she was looking directly into his eyes. "And, much as you'd like to deny it, I think you feel the same. Instead of admitting it, we've been walking around testy and irritable with each other." He smiled, almost gently. "If we keep it up, somebody's liable to get hurt."

She suspected he was right. She'd been tense and on edge since meeting him, except for that period of semi-consciousness. It was physical attraction in its purest form. Lust, plain and simple. Not the sort of stuff that made deep, lasting relationships. "Cooper, this is all wrong," she said. "I'm simply not ready—"

He silenced her with a kiss. He moved his mouth over hers slowly, tantalizingly, sending her thoughts into a wild spin. Her body began to respond in ways that alternately frightened and delighted her, upsetting her balance while sending currents of desire through her.

The kiss deepened as Cooper's tongue explored the insides of her mouth with demanding mastery. Summer curled her arms around his neck, suddenly unable to get close enough to him and the musky scent of his cologne. He pulled away for a split second, and she moaned a protest. His lips reappeared at the base of her throat, moved upward to the line of her jaw before toying with an earlobe. Finally, because he could no longer resist, he reached out and cupped her buttocks in his palms.

He squeezed her hips gently and pulled her closer, rubbing his aching member against her so there was no doubt what he wanted. He heard her small gasp of pleasure, felt her respond. She cried out softly, a pleading, desperate sound that told him she was as eager as he was to finish what they'd started.

If she had been anyone else, he would have taken her there. He suspected their first coupling might not be all hearts and flowers or whatever she was used to. His need for her had become too great. All he wanted at this point was to have her wet and wanting, to know the pleasure of her sheathing him tightly, arching against him so he could fill her completely.

Cooper lifted his head and looked into her eyes. He knew desire when he saw it, and it did him proud to know he wasn't the only one getting hot and bothered over a simple kiss. It was clear she wanted more.

No, he was not going to take her like some rutting animal who could not control his instincts. When the time came, she had to be ready and willing. Besides, they had someplace to be.

Cooper pulled away and tossed her a cocky smile. "We'd best get going," he said. "Your grandmother will be worried. Anyway, I think that's enough kissing for one afternoon, seeing as how you're not completely ready."

Summer was tempted to throw the teakettle at him again.

FIVE

Summer climbed on the back of Cooper's motorcycle a few minutes later after donning a pricey suede jacket and matching gloves her grandmother had given her for Christmas the previous year. She wasn't as hesitant to slip her arms around his waist as she'd been the night before; it was either hang on tight or fall off. Those choices made it simple.

Cooper changed gears with his right toe and eased the throttle, and the bike rolled forward at a respectful pace. He crossed the parking lot, started to pull out onto the main road, then braked quickly as a car changed lanes and moved into his path. The bike came to a slightly jolting halt, and Summer was thrust forward on the seat. Her face warmed at the intimate contact, and at the way the two of them fit together so perfectly, her soft curves molding against his masculine contours.

Once Summer adjusted herself on the bike so that she wasn't flattened against Cooper, she began to relax. The ride wasn't as frightening as before, and she felt more comfortable on the turns, leaning into each one with him instead of fighting them.

They arrived at the Pettigrew estate twenty minutes later. Once Cooper had parked and helped her with her helmet, Summer led the way up the steps and to the front door. She rang the bell, and it was answered immediately by Mrs. Bradshaw.

"Good afternoon, miss," the housekeeper replied formally, stepping aside so they could enter.

"Hello, Mrs. Bradshaw," Summer replied. "You remember Mr. Cooper." She shrugged out of her jacket and pulled her gloves off and handed them to the woman. Cooper did the same. The housekeeper hesitated before taking his leather jacket as though she feared it might be flea-ridden.

"Mrs. Pettigrew is in the den," she said. "Lunch will be ready shortly."

Once again Summer led the way through the elaborate foyer and down the wide hall, where their footsteps were muffled by expensive wool rugs. She paused at the doorway leading into her grandmother's informal den and knocked even though the door was open. Henrietta rose from her desk and offered them a somewhat stilted smile. Summer suspected she was still worried about the scene she'd witnessed that morning.

"Come in," she said, greeting her granddaughter with a kiss to the cheek. She shook hands with Cooper. "So nice to see you again, young man. And I must say I prefer that outfit to the one you had on earlier."

"Thank you, Mrs. Pettigrew."

"Please, I asked you to call me Henrietta. Why don't we sit down?" she suggested, making her way toward a plump floral sofa and matching club chairs. She took a chair and waited for them to sit before continuing the conversation. "I'm afraid we didn't get a chance to chat much last night, and I'm always interested in learning about my granddaughter's, uh, friends."

Cooper joined Summer on the sofa and took her

hand in his. "I'd like to think your granddaughter and I are more than friends," he said, giving Summer an intimate smile.

Henrietta nodded slowly, then looked at Summer. "How long have you been seeing each other?"

They answered simultaneously.

"Six months."

"Six or eight weeks."

Summer shot Cooper a frantic look before returning her attention to her grandmother, who looked confused. "Actually, Cooper and I have known each other longer, but we didn't start dating until a couple of months ago."

"And you've waited until now to tell me?" Henrietta asked.

Summer shifted uncomfortably on the sofa. "I knew if I told you, you'd insist on meeting Cooper right away. I thought he and I should take some time to get to know each other better first."

"Part of it was my fault," Cooper said. "I was afraid you wouldn't approve of me."

"Oh? Is there any reason I shouldn't?" Henrietta asked. "Other than the fact you have a penchant for my granddaughter's clothes?"

He chuckled. "I can assure you I'll stay out of Summer's closet in the future. The reason I put off meeting you was that I knew I was so different from the sort of man you were accustomed to seeing your granddaughter with."

"Different doesn't necessarily mean bad," Henrietta replied. "I shudder to think what this world would be like if everyone were exactly the same. What a person looks like on the outside matters little to me. I'm more interested in the stuff that's *inside*." She paused and eyed him thoughtfully. "I wonder what I'd see if I were able to look past that rugged exterior of yours."

Now it was Cooper's turn to look uncomfortable. He

was not used to answering personal questions; in fact, he'd spent much of his life protecting his secrets. But he genuinely liked Henrietta, and he realized, under the circumstances, she had a right to ask questions. He would have to be blind not to see how deeply she loved her granddaughter. He envied Summer that.

"I made a few mistakes in my younger days," he said at last, being deliberately vague. "I like to think I learned from them." He glanced at Summer, then focused once more on her grandmother. "I grew up poor," he said with an easy smile, "so that taught me to appreciate even the simplest things in life." Henrietta nodded but said nothing. She didn't have to. He could see the understanding in her eyes. He suspected she'd seen a lot of poverty in her charity work. Not to mention pain and emotional suffering. "I don't have a college degree, but I read a lot. I try to treat people fairly and honestly, and I've found in most cases they respond likewise." He shrugged. "That about sums it up."

"And what are your intentions regarding my granddaughter?" Henrietta asked.

Cooper could see that Summer was uneasy as well, and he tried to reassure her with a smile before responding to the other woman's question. "Contrary to what you walked in on this morning, I have no desire to compromise Summer in any way. You've raised her to be a lady, and I have tried to treat her like one. As for what the future holds—" He paused. "I'm hopeful, but I won't rush your granddaughter into anything."

Finally, after what seemed an eternity, Henrietta smiled. "You put that very nicely, Cooper."

Mrs. Bradshaw interrupted from the doorway. "Excuse me, Mrs. Pettigrew. Lunch is served."

"Oh, good," Henrietta said, starting to get up. Cooper hurried over to assist. "You're very kind," she said, accepting his help, "but I won't have you and Summer treating me like an invalid."

"That was not my intent," he said. "I simply believe a man should act a certain way while in the presence of a lady."

Henrietta chuckled. "My, but I believe you could charm the skin off a snake if you put your mind to it."

Following closely behind, Summer suspected her grandmother was probably right.

Once they were seated at one end of the long mahogany dining table, Millie carried in three plates containing prime rib sandwiches, a small scoop of cole slaw, and another of potato salad. A sour-looking Mrs. Bradshaw filled their glasses with tea. Summer noted the look of contempt on her face as she served Cooper, and her ire rose.

"Is something wrong, Mrs. Bradshaw?" Summer asked politely.

The woman froze as Henrietta and Cooper glanced up at her. "No, miss," she said stiffly. "Why do you ask?"

"You don't look as though you feel well. I hope you haven't let the strain of grandmother's illness wear you down."

"I'm quite well, thank you."

"I keep telling Grandmother she needs to hire more help. This big old house is too much for one person to handle."

Mrs. Bradshaw drew herself up in such a way, one would have thought Summer had just accused her of pilfering the silver. "I appreciate your concern, miss," she said sharply, "but the day I can't take care of this house will be the day they put me in my grave." She walked out of the room without another word.

Henrietta gazed at Summer in surprise. "What was *that* all about?"

"She's never approved of me," Summer said.

"Nonsense. Mrs. Bradshaw is very fond of you. She just has a different way of showing it."

"You can say that again," Summer mumbled as she picked up her napkin.

Cooper, who'd already started on his sandwich, noted the sudden tension in the air. "This is quite a spread," he said. "The meat is so tender, it melts in my mouth."

Henrietta beamed over the compliment. "Once I told Millie you were coming for lunch, she decided to whip up something extra nice. I think you've already earned a soft place in her heart."

He grinned. "And I thought it was Mrs. Bradshaw I'd won over," he said, drawing chuckles from both women.

Henrietta glanced at her granddaughter. "Why are you staring at your plate, dear? Is something wrong?"

Summer looked up. "Didn't the doctor put you on a special diet?"

"Oh, that." Henrietta waved the statement aside. "You know I don't have time to worry about every little thing I put in my mouth."

"You're going to have to *take* the time," Summer replied sternly. "For your own good."

"You know what your problem is, Henrietta?" Cooper said. "You spend so much time taking care of others that you ignore your own needs."

Summer looked pleased. "Thank you, Cooper. That's *exactly* what I've been telling her for years now."

"Are you two trying to gang up on me?" the older woman asked, looking from one to the other.

"If that's what it takes," Summer replied. "You should be eating more fish and chicken. I'll move back home for a while if that's what it takes," Summer threatened.

"Oh, heavens!" Henrietta cried. "Anything but that." She glanced at Cooper. "I wouldn't have a moment's peace if she moved back. She'd be on my back from morning till night. I don't want to think what it would be like having her and Mrs. Bradshaw under one roof again." She appealed to her granddaughter. "I promise I'll try to follow Dr. Cook's instructions."

Summer smiled. "See? I knew we could work this out."

They chatted easily among themselves as they ate. Fortunately, Henrietta seemed to be in a talkative mood, which meant Summer and Cooper weren't forced to answer a lot of questions. "By the way," the older woman said, glancing at Summer. "You haven't forgotten about Wednesday night?"

Summer scanned her brain, but nothing came to mind. "What about it?"

"It's the annual AIDS benefit, dear. We never miss it."

Summer didn't have to be reminded how important AIDS research was to Henrietta. She, too, had become more involved in her grandmother's causes over the years, and as heartbreaking as some of the causes were, she'd derived a great deal of satisfaction in the simple act of helping others. "I'm sure I just overlooked it," she said. "Of course I'll be there."

Henrietta looked at Cooper. "I'd be honored if you would join our little fund-raiser this year," she said. "Helen Reddy will be entertaining us. It's about time my granddaughter attended one of these benefits with a handsome man on her arm instead of tagging along behind her granny."

"I'd love to come," Cooper said.

Summer could feel a blush creeping up her neck. She gave an embarrassed cough. "Uh, *sweetheart*," she said, giving Cooper a tense look. "You told me you were going to have to start working more hours because of increased bike sales." She looked at Henrietta. "Cooper sells twice as many motorcycles this time of year," she said.

"I'm sure I can spare *one* evening for a good cause," he said smoothly. "Besides, it's about time I became more involved with the community."

Summer's eyes clouded with anxiety, but she forced herself to smile. "But, *dear*, the dinner is one thousand dollars per plate."

Henrietta looked offended. "Now, Summer, you *know* I always take care of the costs, and since Cooper is my guest, I will cover his meal as well."

"I'm afraid I can't let you do that," he said.

Both women looked at him. "Oh, but I insist," Henrietta replied.

"Then, I'll have to take a rain check. I don't allow ladies to pay my way."

Summer could see that her grandmother was as stunned as she was. She merely gazed at him for a moment, blank and amazed. Was he crazy? The cost of the dinner itself would take quite a chunk of his salary. "You'd have to wear a tux," she said in a small, tight voice.

He shrugged. "I'm sure I can scrounge one up somewhere." A faint light burned in the depths of his dark eyes. For some reason he found her discomfort amusing. "Something with a little style and pizzazz," he added with a hearty wink.

Summer suddenly had a quick and disturbing vision of him appearing at the plush Peachtree Plaza Hotel in a lavender tux with sequins.

"What time shall I plan on picking you up?" Cooper asked, interrupting her train of thought.

"Huh?" She blinked several times. "Perhaps it would be best if we took my car," she said. "I'm afraid my hair won't survive a helmet. I could pick you up at your place . . . say around seven."

"I'll just borrow a friend's car," he told her. "I'll come by early so we can swing by and pick up Henrietta as well."

"That's awfully kind of you," the woman said. "I'm sure my driver would enjoy having a night off."

"Then, it's settled."

He took a bite of his sandwich, but one corner of his mouth quirked at the corners as Summer fixed him with an icy look. It was obvious she didn't want him to go, and she most certainly didn't want him to provide transportation. She was probably afraid he was going to pick her up in some rusted-out pickup truck. For a brief second he entertained the thought of arriving at her doorstep on a donkey, and he almost smiled.

With lunch behind them, Henrietta invited Cooper out back to look at her gardens. Summer excused herself on the pretense of having to make a phone call, and promised to join them shortly. She waited in the den as Cooper helped Henrietta into a light jacket and led her out the French doors, then crossed the hall and headed for the kitchen. She found Millie stacking the lunch dishes into the dishwasher and Mrs. Bradshaw writing out a grocery list at a large oak table. They looked surprised to see her.

Millie smiled. "Did you need something, Miss Pettigrew?"

As often as she'd tried to convince the women to be less formal, neither of them were inclined to do so. "I want to discuss my grandmother's diet," Summer replied.

Millie looked confused. "Oh? I didn't even know she was on one."

"That's the point, she *isn't*. But she's supposed to be."

"That's pretty much up to her, isn't it?" Mrs. Bradshaw said. "She's a grown woman, not a child."

Summer regarded the housekeeper, trying to remind herself she wasn't ten years old anymore. She was an independent, well-educated woman. "No, it's *not* up to her. Not as long as I have anything to say about it, and I plan to see that she adopts a healthier lifestyle no matter what. Even if it means hiring additional staff."

She reached into her purse and pulled out several leaflets of paper. "I tried to locate my grandmother's doctor at his office the other day, but he wasn't in. However, his nurse was quite helpful. She gave me a copy of the diet Dr. Cook prescribed." She handed the pages to Millie.

"My grandmother has devoted half a century to caring for others. I think it's only fitting we take good care of her now." Summer started for the door, then turned, her gaze seeking out the housekeeper once more. "Also, my grandmother is to take light exercise. I think a twenty-minute stroll on the property would be sufficient to start with. If anybody can convince her to do it, Mrs. Bradshaw, it will be you. She loves you like family. I assume you feel the same." She had the pleasure of seeing the woman blush before she pushed through the swinging door leading into the dining room.

Summer almost slammed into Henrietta, who was about to enter the kitchen from the other side. "I knew it!" the older woman said. "You were in there telling them to starve me. They'll probably be boiling weeds from my garden for breakfast."

"Nobody's going to starve you," Summer replied. "Where's Cooper?"

"Oh, he had to leave," she said. "He had an appointment and asked me to tell you he'd catch up with you later."

Summer gritted her teeth. The skunk! He knew she wouldn't be happy with him for agreeing to escort them to the benefit, so he'd decided to slip out without saying good-bye. "That's fine," she said, going to the hall closet for her jacket. "I've got to visit a friend in the hospital."

Henrietta didn't seem to be listening. "Cooper's bringing his rake and hoe next time so he can work in my garden. I don't believe I've ever had a guest do that sort of thing. Your taste in men has certainly changed. But I rather like him, despite my earlier reservations. And I can tell he's absolutely smitten by you."

Summer slipped into her coat. "You can?"

"Oh, yes." Henrietta glanced over her shoulder to make sure they were alone. "I'll have to admit I had a few doubts about him this morning, but I feel better about it now. And the two of you make such a nice couple," she added dreamily. "Him so dark, you so fair. You'd have beautiful children."

Summer, in the process of stuffing her gloves into her shoulder bag, snapped her head up. "*Children!*" She shook her head. "Stop right there, Henrietta Pettigrew. Nobody said anything about marriage and children. You're doing it again. The minute I look at a man twice, you're ready to hire a minister and catering service."

Henrietta looked surprised. "Well, you talked like . . . I mean, the two of you *acted* like you really cared about each other. I just thought—" She pressed one hand against her breast.

Summer didn't miss it. She watched all the light go out of her grandmother's eyes. In fact, she suddenly looked quite pale. "We *do* care for each other," she amended quickly. "I just don't want to rush into anything. As he said earlier, he's very different from the sort of men I've dated in the past. I need time to get used to him." She started for the door. She needed to escape the conversation.

Henrietta followed. "He may not be suave and debonair like some of the gentlemen you've dated, but you'll have to admit he's good-looking in a rugged sort of way. He seems honest and hardworking."

Summer was quickly growing weary with the subject. "Must we discuss this now?"

"I'm just trying to tell you that money and position aren't everything. I would have married your grandfather if he'd sold dirt for a living. His being rich was just an added bonus, but in the end all that money couldn't save his life when it was discovered he had a rare blood disease. Nor could it bring back my only child when she decided to run off with some hippie and live like a vagabond."

Summer opened the door and hurried out onto the wide veranda. She was in no mood to discuss her parents and the mistakes they'd made. "Cooper and I need more time before we start thinking about something as important as marriage," she said. "I don't want any lingering doubts."

"Be careful that you don't take too much time," Henrietta said. "At your age you should have already married and started your family. You'll be thirty before you know it. That biological clock of yours doesn't stop ticking just because you're afraid to make a commitment."

"I don't believe I'm hearing this."

"Look what happened to Mary Ann Drummond. She was as bad as you where her career was concerned. By the time she was ready to start having babies, her ovaries had dried up like raisins. She's raising poodles instead. And don't you think her poor mother's heart is broken?"

"Please go inside, Grandmother. You'll catch a chill. I have to go," Summer said, giving her grandmother a peck on the cheek.

"You haven't heard one word I've said."

"The entire neighborhood heard you." Summer opened the door to her car.

"So I'll see you Wednesday?" Henrietta called out. "For the benefit?"

"Yes, Wednesday," she replied. But even as she closed her door and strapped on her seat belt, her mind was already searching for an excuse not to go.

Summer drove to the same hospital where Henrietta had been rushed during her heart attack. She paused at the information desk to get Warren's room number, then squeezed into an elevator of other well-wishers. She found Warren's room easily enough and waltzed through the door with a bright smile on her face.

"Hi, handsome," she called out the minute she spotted her friend and coworker. He brightened at the sight of her. "I see the accident didn't mess up that good-looking puss of yours," she said. She ruffled his hair and gave him a playful kiss. She noted the cast on his leg and wrist. "Now, don't worry about a thing. Auntie Summer is here to take good care of you. Just tell me where it hurts."

He grinned. "If I told you, you'd probably break my other leg."

"Maybe you *should* tell her, Warren," a male voice said. "She seems eager enough."

Summer whirled around at the sound of Cooper's voice. He was leaning against the sink near the bathroom door. She'd waltzed right past without seeing him. "Oh, my," she said breathlessly. "I didn't know Warren had company."

"Obviously," he said, his black eyes boring into hers.

"Am I interrupting anything?" she asked.

"Of course not," Warren told her. "I've been counting the hours until your visit. What took so long?"

Still embarrassed that Cooper had witnessed her giddiness upon seeing her friend in one piece, Summer took a seat in the chair next to Warren's bed and folded her hands in her lap. "My grandmother insisted I have lunch with her," she said, deliberately avoiding mentioning the fact that Cooper had been with her as well. She had no desire to rehash the previous night's events with Warren, and from the looks of him, he probably didn't feel like listening. She noted the bulk under his hospital gown and figured they'd taped his ribs as well. "So, you're feeling kinda crummy, huh?"

"Like I was in a car wreck. But I'm better now that you're here."

"When do you think they'll release you?" she asked.

"I was hoping to get out tomorrow, but my doctor insists on keeping me until Monday, because he wants to see all my test results."

"And when are your parents coming?"

"They're leaving Florida on Monday. They plan to drive halfway, spend the night in a hotel, and get here on Tuesday. Mr. Worth has already been by. He said to take as long as I needed. I just hate leaving you in a bind at the office."

Summer knew it wouldn't be easy balancing both workloads, but it couldn't be helped. She would manage somehow. She forced a bright smile and tried to sound optimistic. "I'll be fine. Right now you just concentrate on getting better. Is there anything you need?"

"Other than a little TLC, I'd like to have a pair of pants and a clean shirt in case I'm discharged tomorrow. You haven't lost your key to my place, have you?"

Summer felt the heat rise from her neck, knowing how it must sound to Cooper, then wondered why she cared one way or the other. Warren had given her a key the previous summer before leaving on vacation because he hadn't trusted anyone else to take care of his ficus trees and see to his mail.

"I'll run by this afternoon," she told him.

Someone tapped on the door and Summer turned as a middle-aged man in a white jacket stepped into the room, holding a clipboard. Warren looked pleased to see him.

Summer decided to make herself scarce while Warren's doctor examined him. "I'm going to grab a cup of coffee in the cafeteria," she told him. "You want me to bring you anything?"

Warren nodded eagerly. "How about a slice of pecan pie?"

"You got it."

"I'll go with you," Cooper said, following her out.

Summer punched the button for the basement, where the vending machines and cafeteria were located. The metal doors whisked open, and she stepped in with Cooper right behind. A shadow of annoyance crossed her face.

He saw the look and realized he was the one who had a right to be mad at the moment. How could she let him kiss her senseless one minute and simper over his cousin the next?

"What's bugging you?" he muttered as if he had no idea.

Summer shot him a killing glare. "Don't play dumb with me, Cooper Garrett," she snapped. "We agreed to try to bail you out of further social obligations, and you did just the opposite. Now I'm back to square one. Not only am I forced to continue lying to my grandmother, I have the added pressure of trying to pretend we're a couple when we're not. You could easily have gotten out of going to that benefit." The elevator came to a stop, but Cooper reached passed her and pressed a button that kept the doors from opening. She opened her mouth to protest, but he interrupted.

"Maybe I didn't want to get out of it."

Summer eyed him as he stepped closer, forcing her

into a corner. The elevator seemed to shrink in size as his thighs grazed hers. His finger remained on the button. She drew back, but there was no escape. She suddenly felt claustrophobic, depleted of oxygen. "What possible reason could you have for wanting to carry on this ridiculous charade?" she demanded with what little breath she possessed.

He tilted his head forward, and his eyes flashed a brilliant onyx. His lips hovered over hers enticingly. She felt ready to snap. Part of her *wanted* to be kissed, that side of her that dealt with feelings and emotions and gave no heed to logic and common sense. "I've already told you," he said, his voice so low and husky, she felt the hair on her arms rise. "I wanted you from the minute I saw you. I've decided I'm going to have you no matter what."

"You can't make a decision like that without my consent," she said. "And I've already told you—"

His lips descended, cutting off the rest of her statement. The kiss was hungry and devouring, hot, setting her mouth aflame and making her forget all the reasons she should be protesting. Summer clutched the front of his jacket, half afraid her knees wouldn't hold her. When he finally raised his head, she felt weak and confused.

"I'm willing to play this your way," he whispered against her slightly parted lips. "I'll court you like a gentleman if that's what it takes. But don't make me wait too long, Summer, because I'm not a patient man when it comes to getting what I want." As his lips captured hers once more, he told himself she was as good as his. He *would* have her. Even if it meant stealing her away from his cousin.

SIX

Summer was late for work on Monday due to an accident that tied traffic up on the interstate for forty-five minutes. She closed her eyes and took a deep breath. This was not the time to get rattled, she reminded herself, knowing she had an important meeting in less than an hour.

Summer picked up her car phone and dialed her secretary, Joyce, and discovered she had a number of messages. She used the time to return calls and discuss various ideas with clients. By the time she pulled into Executive Park Plaza, where Worth Advertising leased the entire top floor of offices in a modern glass and steel-framed building, she had managed to take care of her most pressing business.

With minutes to spare, Summer climbed from her car and hurried inside the building, making her way through the lobby to the elevators, which tended to be tied up this time of day. Luck was with her. One of the doors was standing open. She stepped in and punched the button to the tenth floor, then smoothed the wrinkles from her navy jacket and winter-white pleated skirt. By the time she entered the conference room where Edwin Worth met with his advertising people each Monday, she felt less frantic. Joyce was waiting inside with a cup of coffee and a number of files containing key accounts.

"Thanks, Joyce," Summer whispered, taking a seat at the long mahogany table with her male coworkers. The Monday-morning meetings, or grill sessions, as some of the employees referred to them, had terrified Summer in the beginning. Straight out of college, she was certain her ideas sounded corny and naive, but Warren had assured her she'd brought a freshness that was long overdue to the firm. She never knew if he was being honest or if it was just another ploy to get her in the sack.

Joyce made her way out of the room as Edwin Worth stepped inside with his young male secretary, Max, a man in his twenties who was as fastidious in his appearance as he was in his job. The CEO sat at the head of the table; Max took the chair to his right, pen and pad poised and ready.

"Before we get started," Worth began. "I want to let all of you know Warren Spencer was involved in a car accident Friday night." He gave them a rundown of his injuries. "He should be released today, but he's going to be out of commission for a while. I had Max send flowers on behalf of the company," he added. "Now, then. I've got a busy day ahead of me, so let's try not to drag this out."

For the next hour they went around the table discussing current projects while Max scribbled furiously. Leaning forward, hands clasped together, Worth listened carefully and asked questions. His eyes, a startling blue, were alert and intelligent. Max had told Summer that Worth achieved the look with contact lenses. His eyes were really a dull, washed-out hazel.

When it was her turn, Summer updated Worth on her accounts, including the one she'd recently been assigned, a string of weight-loss centers for women called The Body Works, which had the potential of becoming a multimillion-dollar account. The owner eventually wanted to go nationwide with his centers, and he was willing to spend any amount of money to achieve that goal and see they were successful.

"I've spoken to Mr. Flynn only a couple of times by phone, and he had a few ideas as to the image he wanted to create. I'm going to try to convince him otherwise when we meet for lunch this afternoon."

"What if Mr. Flynn doesn't like your ideas?" Worth said. "What will you do if he insists on going with his original plan?"

"I'll simply do my best to point out why my ideas are better."

"And if he's adamant?"

"Mr. Flynn is prepared to invest a lot of money in our services because we're experts in the field; we know how to attract consumers. I don't think it would be fair to Mr. Flynn to use his suggestions merely to placate him, when I know they're not going to draw as many customers." She paused. "I realize the final decision is his, of course."

"Just make the client happy," Worth said. "This is an important account."

Summer nodded. She knew Worth would never have agreed to give her the account in the first place if Sam Flynn hadn't requested working with a female. Since his diet centers were being designed specifically for women, he'd wanted someone who knew exactly what today's modern woman was looking for.

"By the way," Worth said. "What have you heard from Gridlock Tires?"

Summer shifted in her chair. "I've tried to contact them several times, but they haven't returned my calls. I can only assume they're checking with our competitors, but I got the impression they were pleased with our ideas."

Worth didn't respond. Once he'd been updated, he offered various suggestions concerning the larger accounts. Although he'd announced his retirement several years back, he still spent a couple of hours a day at the office and insisted on knowing what was going on in his company at all times.

"Before I forget," he said, "I was contacted over the weekend by a nonprofit organization called The Good Shepherd. This group tries to find adoptive parents for handicapped children. Unfortunately, most couples are looking for healthy male babies and don't want to take on the financial and emotional strain of raising a child with health problems. Since The Good Shepherd is operating on a shoestring, they can't afford to hire a firm like ours. I gave them the names of a couple of agencies I thought might be able to assist them. If any of you knows of a good freelance person who might give them a cut rate, I'd appreciate your passing their names on to Max." He checked his diamond-studded Rolex. "If there's nothing else, I have work to do." He nodded toward the group and left the table with his secretary close behind.

Summer spent the rest of the morning working on preliminary sketches for The Body Works.

Joyce tapped on the door and peeked in. "Mr. Worth wants to see you in his office," she said. "What'd you do this time?"

Summer glanced up from her sketches. "No telling," she said. "You know what a loose cannon I am."

"Well, I'd tread gently if I were you. Max said he and his wife just had a raging battle on the phone over what she charged on a recent shopping spree in New York. That woman spends more money on clothes than Ivana Trump."

"Just what I need," Summer muttered. She checked

her reflection in a small mirror and started out of her office as Joyce ran an index finger across her throat in a slashing motion. "Very funny," she replied. "Just remember. If I go down, I'm taking you with me." She made her way toward the suite of offices on the other side of the building, which was referred to as the Worth Penthouse.

Max greeted her warmly and told her to go right in. His real name was Maximilian; Summer often wondered what kind of woman would stick her son with a name like that. Although he was the only male secretary employed at Worth, he seemed to fit right in with the girls. All the men claimed he was gay, of course, but Summer had once remarked that it was nobody's business as long as Max did his job. That hadn't earned her any popularity votes with her male counterparts, but Max had been deeply touched when he'd learned through one of the secretaries that she'd taken up for him. As a result, he kept Summer abreast of what was going on in the company, giving her information the others weren't privy to.

"Just don't ask him how his wife is," he whispered.

Summer winked. "Thanks for the tip." She knocked on one of the double doors leading into Worth's inner sanctum, then opened it and walked in. He was in the middle of a phone call. He motioned Summer to have a seat, and she sank into one of the comfortable leather chairs facing his desk.

Worth hung up and smiled at Summer. If he was in a hostile mood at the moment, he hid it well. "Thank you for coming right over," he said. "I've got a tennis date at noon, but I wanted to touch base with you before I leave." He glanced down at a leather notebook in front of him. "I'm aware that you and Warren share several key accounts," he said. "Is that going to present a problem for you while he's away?"

Summer had learned long ago that Edwin Worth

didn't like hearing about problems. He called it whining, and his company was no place for crybabies. No matter how bad the pressure, you stayed cool and pretended you were on top of things. "Nothing I can't handle, Mr. Worth," she said confidently. Secretly, she suspected she would be pulling sixty-hour work weeks *plus*, to keep up.

"Good girl," he said, his tone telling her she had given him the correct answer. "Warren should be gone only a couple of weeks. I know your girl will help you as much as she can," he said. "I wish I could spare Max, but he's up to his eyebrows in work." He closed the notebook and stood.

Summer stood as well, knowing she'd been dismissed.

"One last thing, Mr. Worth," she began. "About that organization you mentioned. The Good Shepherd?"

"Yes. I wish we could help them, but if word got out we were cutting deals for nonprofit organizations—" He paused and winked.

"I would be willing to do the work on my own time free of charge," she said.

"That's very generous of you, Summer," he said, giving her a fatherly pat on the shoulder, "and as much as I appreciate your generous heart, I can't possibly allow you to take on more than you already have. You simply can't afford to waste your time on nonpaying clients when you're juggling million-dollar accounts." He brushed a tiny fleck of something white off his jacket sleeve. "Besides, you're going to be under enormous pressure while Warren's gone. I don't know why you'd *want* to become involved in something that has the potential of being . . . well, depressing."

"It doesn't have to be," Summer replied. "Not if it's presented in a positive way. I would try to show that each child, no matter how handicapped, has something special to offer."

Worth cupped her elbow in his palm and led her

toward the door. "Just concentrate on doing the very best job you can on your present accounts. Try to touch base with Gridlock Tires if you can, see if they're still interested in doing business with us."

Summer watched him hurry toward the elevator and press the button leading to the lobby, and she knew the matter was closed as far as Edwin Worth was concerned.

Giving a dejected sigh, she made her way toward her office, where Joyce was in the process of taking a telephone message on a pink slip. "Hold on," she told the caller. "Ms. Pettigrew just stepped in." She pressed a button on the phone and looked up. "There's a Cooper Garrett on line one. I asked the name of his company, but he said it's a personal call. I don't know what he looks like, but he's got one heck of a sexy voice."

Summer's body reacted swiftly to the news. Her stomach fluttered as though a battery of moths had just taken flight. "Tell him I'm not in."

Joyce looked surprised. "But I just told him you were."

"Tell him—" She paused and sighed her frustration. "Oh, never mind, I'll tell him myself," she said.

Summer stepped inside her office and closed the door, then stared at the blinking button on her phone for a full minute before reaching for it. "Hello, Cooper," she said, feeling at once breathless and light-headed as she remembered his promise in the elevator. "I'm sort of busy right now—"

"I wanted to see if you were free for lunch."

"Sorry, but I have a previous engagement."

"Okay, how 'bout dinner?"

"I've, uh, already made plans."

He was silent for a moment. "Is this for real, or are you trying to brush me off?"

"It's for real. I have to meet a client for lunch, and I'm picking Warren up from the hospital after work."

"I could pick up Warren."

"I told him I'd be there." She remembered how pathetic he'd sounded on the phone. "I'd hate to disappoint him."

Cooper frowned on the other end of the line. "Okay, what about tomorrow? I think it'd be a good idea if we got together before the benefit. To sort of get our stories straight."

She sighed. "Cooper, I'm not going to be able to go to the benefit," she said. "With Warren out, I simply have too much work to do. Besides—" She paused. She'd already told so many lies lately that one more wouldn't hurt. "I'm not feeling well," she said, affecting a weary tone that she hoped was convincing. "I think I'm getting some kind of bug. It's been going around the office for weeks now."

"I'm sorry to hear it," he said. "Are you taking something for it? Is there anything I can get you?"

His concern was so genuine that she was instantly consumed with guilt. "I'll be fine," she said quickly. "I just need to get to bed early and take care of myself for a few days. I'm sure it'll blow over."

"So you're going to call Henrietta and cancel?"

"Yes. I know she'll be disappointed, but once I explain things, she'll be okay."

"My phone number's unlisted," he said. "Let me give it to you in case you need something."

"That's not necessary," she said, not wanting him to think she was one of those helpless, clinging women who couldn't survive without a man. "I'm a big girl, perfectly capable of taking care of myself." She suddenly realized she'd come off sounding harsh. "I have to go now, okay?" she said, softening her tone. She hung up and went back to sketching, but her mind wasn't on her work. She found herself pausing every so often and staring into space. Finally, she shook herself. She had a pre-

sentation in a few short hours. She had absolutely no
business daydreaming about Cooper Garrett!

Cooper heard the click in his ear telling him she'd
hung up. So this is how she planned to play it. He hung
up the phone and leaned back in his chair, propping his
feet on his desk as he considered his next move. He'd be
lying to himself if he didn't admit he was somewhat confused. He liked knowing where he stood with a woman,
but with Summer he didn't have a clue. One minute she
was responding to his kisses as though she couldn't get
enough; the next thing he knew she was trying to run as
fast as she could in the opposite direction.

He chuckled softly. He'd never met a woman who
seemed so determined to prove to herself and the world
that she didn't need anybody. It was up to him to show
her that needing other people in your life didn't make
you a weak person.

Summer Pettigrew didn't know the kind of man she
was dealing with. Once he made up his mind to have
something, he let nothing and no one stand in his way.

He would have her. Simple as that.

Joyce knocked on Summer's door at noon and announced her appointment had arrived. Lunch had already been delivered from a nearby deli. Knowing how
hectic her client's schedule was, Summer planned to give
her pitch while the owner of The Body Works ate his
lunch.

Sam Flynn, a striking, well-built man in his late for-
ties, stepped through the door wearing an expensive
dove-gray double-breasted suit and Hermès tie. With his
deep tan and aviator sunglasses, he looked like someone
who'd just spent two weeks in the Virgin Islands. He
removed his glasses and tucked them into the pocket of
his jacket as Summer greeted him with a handshake and

motioned him toward the sofa. "I took the liberty of ordering lunch," she said as Joyce carried in a tray of food. The food had been removed from the sack and placed on china that Worth Advertising kept in a kitchen for just such purposes, and two crystal goblets were filled with ice for the bottled water. "I hope you don't mind."

"As long as it's healthful," Flynn said. "I abhor junk food."

"As do I," she replied, hoping he never learned of the Godiva chocolates and honey-roasted peanuts she kept hidden at the back of her desk drawer.

"Why don't you go ahead and get started on your lunch while I show you what I have in mind for your weight-loss centers," Summer suggested. "I think you'll find the whole concept exciting." She thanked Joyce and waited until the woman let herself out before beginning her presentation.

"Now, then. Are you comfortable, Mr. Flynn? Do you have everything you need?"

He took a bite of his sandwich. His pale eyes took her in as though seeing her for the first time. He shot her a smile that had a come-hither look written all over it. "Call me Sam."

Summer took a deep breath. "Okay. When you first contacted me, you wanted Worth to hire an assortment of models to pose for the ads regarding your weight-loss center."

He nodded and chewed.

"After giving it some thought and checking the demographics of your future locations, I would like to offer another suggestion."

Flynn stopped chewing. "What was wrong with my idea?"

"Let me explain," Summer said. She stepped away from the sketchpad where she'd drawn several thin women in bodysuits wearing ankle and wrist weights.

"You're trying to hook women by making them think this is how they'll look once they sign a contract with your weight-loss centers."

"That is how they *can* look if they commit themselves to my program," Flynn replied, pointing to the sign.

Summer offered him a slight smile. "Not all women are going to be able to achieve this look no matter how hard they work at it, Sam."

Summer paused to let him digest the information. "Sam, I don't think it's fair to add more pressure to what women already have on them. Believe me, if you start putting up billboards with skinny, drop-dead-gorgeous models on them, you're going to make women feel intimidated, guilty, and resentful. Not only that, how do you think the average woman is going to feel when, after six months of hard work, she hasn't achieved that look? She's going to want to get out of her contract."

Flynn put his sandwich down and wiped his hands. It was obvious he wasn't happy. "What do you suggest? You want me to put a bunch of ugly women in my ads so I can make everybody feel good about being overweight?"

"You told me from the beginning you didn't want to open just another string of weight-loss centers. I believe your exact words were, 'They're a dime a dozen.' You want your centers to be different, and since you're in the early stages of planning, we'll have time to make necessary adjustments."

He nodded. "I definitely want something different."

"And I think we can accomplish that in a big way. But I think it's important we agree on the fundamentals, and that's why I called this meeting." His gaze dropped to her legs, and she feared she'd lost his attention. "Mr. Flynn?"

"Sam," he reminded her, meeting her gaze once more. "Okay, let's hear your ideas."

"I think your ad should portray women from all walks of life who simply want to get healthy and feel better about themselves, period." Summer turned the page. The sketch showed a group of women dressed in everything from business suits to blue jeans.

"These are the women you're trying to reach out to," Summer said. "The *average* female. Not all of them are going to look great in bodysuits; in fact, some might have to come in wearing their old sweats. But at the bottom of the ad, I think you should ask women an important question. 'When's the last time you did something nice for yourself?' Then, in bold letters, simply add, 'The Body Works.' "

Flynn took another bite of his sandwich. He seemed to be playing with the idea. It hadn't clicked yet, but Summer had given enough presentations to recognize he was trying to keep an open mind.

"This ad is honest, and that's what women want. You're not promising to make them look like Heather Locklear. What you *are* promising is that they'll feel better *about* themselves once they start doing something *for* themselves. No matter what size they are."

"I'll have to think about it."

Summer shrugged. "Take all the time you like."

He looked surprised. "You mean I'm not going to get a hard pressure sale?"

"That's not the way we do things here, Mr. Flynn." She sat down and reached for her own sandwich. "You're welcome to check with our competitors. When you're ready to do business, we'll still be here."

He studied her closely, as though photographing her with his eyes. Once again his gaze fell to her long legs. "You've never been in one of my weight-loss centers, have you?"

"No, I haven't had the pleasure."

"Perhaps it's time you had a look. I have one that just

opened in Jacksonville, Florida, and I'm looking at locations in West Palm Beach. We could fly down in my private jet for the weekend. Soak up a little sun while we're there."

"It sounds wonderful," she said. "That way I'll have a chance to meet *Mrs.* Flynn."

He gave an indiscreet cough. "I'm afraid that's not possible. My wife is terrified of flying."

"I'm sorry to hear that," she said. "Perhaps I can meet her another time. In the meantime, why don't you make the necessary arrangements, and Joyce and I will arrange our schedules accordingly."

"Joyce? Your secretary?"

"Also my assistant. I never go anywhere without her."

He laughed softly. "You're either very coy or very dimwitted," he said. "Which is it?"

"Well, I've never been accused of being dimwitted," she said with a polite smile.

He put his hand on her knee. She didn't so much as flinch. "This account could mean a lot to your career," he said.

Summer met his gaze. It was not the first time a client had made a pass at her. Fortunately, most men were professional in their business dealings. "Yes, it does mean a lot to me. But at the risk of repeating myself, I must remind you this is simply not the way we do things here at Worth." She pushed a button next to her, and Joyce's voice came on the intercom. "Joyce, would you please show Mr. Flynn his way out." Her tone was cool but professional.

Joyce appeared at her door in a matter of seconds. The friendly, personable woman who'd greeted Flynn when he'd first arrived now looked like a female pit bull who'd just had her tail yanked. Joyce had been with Summer long enough to know that a client was not asked to leave unless there was a real problem, and the fact that Flynn still had his hand on Summer's knee was a clear indication of the direction things had been going.

"Mr. Flynn?" the secretary said tersely. "Please allow me the extreme pleasure of escorting you to the elevators."

Sam Flynn shrugged and removed his hand from Summer's knee. He stood, then straightened his jacket so casually that one would never have guessed something was amiss. "Worth Advertising isn't the only game in town, you know," he told Summer. "If you change your mind, you know where to reach me." He walked to the door and gave Joyce a killing glare. "I know my way out."

Summer buried her face in her hands. "Dammit!"

Joyce sat down beside her and put her arm around her shoulder. "Are you okay?"

"No, I'm furious. I can't believe I wasted all that time for nothing. I'll be okay as soon as I count to ten."

There was a knock at the door. Both women looked up. Cooper Garrett stood in the doorway holding a paper sack. He noted the expression on Summer's face and hurried over to her. "What's wrong?" he said quickly. "Are you feeling worse?"

Summer shook her head, hoping to clear it. Of all times for Cooper to show up! She'd completely forgotten about telling him she wasn't feeling well. "I just had a little trouble with a client, that's all." She glanced at Joyce. "Joyce, meet Cooper Garrett. Cooper, this is Joyce Cox, my assistant."

Cooper could tell she was upset. "What kind of trouble?" he asked after nodding a quick greeting at the woman.

"Oh, the slimeball made a pass at her," Joyce said angrily. "You probably passed him in the hall. Tall, athletic guy with aviator sunglasses?"

Cooper's look turned dangerous. "Did he lay a hand on you?"

"He practically had his hand up her skirt when I walked in," Joyce replied in a high-pitched voice.

Summer shook her head. "You're exaggerating—"

"We'll just see about that." Cooper spun around on his heel and exited the office without another word.

Summer shot to her feet. "Why did you tell him?" she asked Joyce.

Her assistant looked surprised. "I thought he was a personal friend of yours."

Summer hurried out of her office, where she found Cooper stabbing buttons on the panel next to the elevator. Luckily, Sam Flynn wasn't in sight. The man had obviously left the building. Not only that, the hallway was clear of other personnel. She sighed her relief. "Cooper, wait—" She spotted Flynn coming out of the men's room at the same time Cooper did. He barreled past her and caught Flynn by the arm.

"What do you think you're doing?" the man demanded.

Cooper spoke through gritted teeth. "Keep your voice low, or you're going to be ordering dentures by the time I get finished with you."

"Cooper, stop!" Summer cried.

"Who the hell are *you?*" Flynn asked, eyes wide as saucers.

"I'm the guy who's going to rearrange your face for taking indecent liberties with a lady."

Summer touched Cooper's shoulder gently. "Let him go," she said, holding her breath for some sort of response. His face remained a glowering mask. "Please," she added.

Cooper hesitated a full minute. Something in his expression changed, a momentary softening that was barely discernible even to her. He shook the man hard before releasing him. "Don't you *ever* touch her again, you got that?" Flynn nodded quickly. "Now, get out of my sight before I change my mind and bust you up anyway."

Sam Flynn didn't have to be told twice. He disappeared through the door leading to the stairs. When Cooper turned, he found Summer staring at him, her face shadowed with alarm. "Is that how you handle your differences?" she asked, her voice so quiet, he had to strain to hear.

"He had no right to put his hands on you."

"And who decides that? You?"

He looked away, unable to meet that frightened-doe look she gave him. He felt awkward now that he'd had a chance to cool down, embarrassed that she'd seen him at his worst. "I couldn't let him think he could just treat you any old way he liked."

She took a step closer. "So you decided to chase after him like a raging bull and create a scene at my place of employment. Were you hoping to get me fired, or just make me a laughingstock?"

"You looked upset when I got here."

"I *was* upset. But I would have handled it." She took a deep breath and realized she was trembling. "Please leave while I still have a job."

He held up both hands. "Fine, I'm outta here." He followed the same path out that Flynn had taken a few minutes before.

Summer tried to get herself under control. If Worth ever found out one of his clients had been threatened, he would have her head. She could only hope none of her coworkers had overheard.

"Is everything okay?" Joyce asked.

"They're gone."

Her assistant joined her. "Did Cooper beat him up?"

"Came close to it," Summer said.

"Oh, my," the woman said. "How romantic."

Summer gaped at her. *"Romantic?"*

"When's the last time a man was willing to fight for you?"

"Now that you mention it, never." She followed Joyce inside, noting there was a new bounce to her step.

Summer arrived at the hospital shortly before six and parked as close to the entrance as she could. She rode the elevator to Warren's floor and checked with the head nurse, an older woman who wore a perpetual scowl, to make sure his doctor had released him.

"Yes, he's all set to go," she said, her voice as crisp as the stark white uniform she wore. "And not a moment too soon," she added. "He's driving the younger nurses crazy with all that flirting."

"Sounds like he's on the mend."

"Well, you'd best get him out of here before I break his other leg," the woman mumbled, then called out to an orderly. "Please wheel Mr. Spencer to the lobby," she said. "And blindfold him so he can't find his way back."

Summer chuckled and started down the hall toward Warren's room, where she found him watching a soap opera. "Hey, stud. I hope you're all packed and ready to go. I have a feeling you've worn out your welcome."

He looked happy to see her as he reached for his crutches. "You must've talked to Nurse Attila the Hun."

"Oh, so you're on a first-name basis."

Warren stood on his good leg and tucked the crutches beneath each arm. "She's just jealous 'cause she's not getting any. I was tempted to tell her she'd have better luck if she put a bag over her head, but she's already threatened to give me an enema, so I decided to serve the rest of my sentence in silence." He pulled open the drawer of his night table. "Looks like I got everything."

Summer picked up the small overnight bag she'd packed for him. The orderly arrived with his wheelchair. "Your limo's here," she announced.

Warren frowned. "I don't want to make my exit in one of those," he said, nodding toward the chair. "I'm afraid it will emasculate me in front of the nurses."

"Hospital policy," the orderly said.

"Get in the chair and let's go," Summer said, "before the head nurse emasculates you. She's probably out there sharpening her ax as we speak."

"You talked me into it," he said, hobbling toward the chair. The orderly showed him how to position his crutches so that he didn't injure anyone in the elevator. "It feels good to be going home," Warren told Summer. "The food here stinks. What d'you say we stop by the store on the way home and grab a couple of thick, juicy steaks? You can cook while I lie on the couch and tell you all the awful things they did to my poor body while I was here."

"Why don't we see how you feel once I take you home?" she suggested. "I can always run out later."

"I feel great. They gave me a pain pill twenty minutes ago."

The orderly smiled at Summer and winked. "I'll be surprised if he can stay awake until he gets home."

Sure enough, Warren conked out about ten minutes into the ride. By the time Summer parked in front of his apartment, he was snoring loudly. "Wake up, Warren," she said, touching his arm lightly so she wouldn't risk hurting him. "You're home."

Warren opened his eyes and blinked at her several times, as if he weren't sure where he was. "Home?"

"That's right. That all-adult community where the babes lie around the pool in next to nothing. The one that frowns on children, pets, Mom, and apple pie. I'll come around and help you." Summer let herself out and hurried to the other side. She opened the door, and Warren, who'd drifted off again, almost fell onto the pavement. She squealed and caught him just in the nick of time. "Wake up, Warren," she snapped. "Before you end up hurting one of us."

"Okay, okay," he mumbled, trying to peer out from beneath heavy eyelids.

Summer managed to get his crutches in place, pull him into a standing position, and together they moved toward the door at the speed of a crawl. Reaching his front door, Summer unlocked it and steered him in the direction of his bedroom. His attempts were clumsy at best. "You're going to have to practice walking with these things," she said, suspecting he would be wearing a cast for some weeks.

"You're not going to make me practice today, are you?" he said groggily.

She chuckled. Men turned into such wimps when they were sick. "I'll give you the evening off if you're a good boy."

"Will you make me a pot of homemade vegetable soup like Mom always did when I was sick?"

"I don't do homemade. But if I can find something in a can, you got it, buddy."

"You're too good to me. I should have hog-tied you and forced you to marry me a long time ago."

They'd made it as far as the bedroom door. Summer stepped through first and waited for Warren. "Okay, try to balance yourself on one leg while I take your crutches," she said. She took them from him and leaned them against the wall, then slipped his arm around her shoulder. "We need to turn around," she said, trying to position them so the backs of their knees were against the mattress. "Okay, on the count of three, we're going to sit down. Keep your leg with the cast straight out and—"

"Just count, okay?" he said impatiently. It was obvious he was struggling to keep his eyes open.

"One, two, three."

They started to sit, but Warren lost his balance due to the heavy cast, not to mention his drugged state. His weight landed on his fractured wrist and he howled. He immediately flipped to the other side and fell on Summer.

She felt as though a boulder had toppled onto her. "What happened?" she cried.

"I think I broke my damn wrist. Again."

Summer tried to push him up, but it was impossible. "Can you sit?"

"I'll have to try and push myself up with my good arm. Damn," he muttered.

"Now what?"

"All this time I've been trying to get you in my bed, and now that you're here, I'm too banged up to do anything about it."

She tried to laugh, but he was cutting off her oxygen supply. "You're squishing my guts out," she managed to say.

"Go ahead and take me, Summer," he said, sounding groggy once more. "Just be gentle."

Laughter bubbled up inside of her. Truly, she had never been in a more ridiculous situation. "They must've fed you well in that hospital," she said. "You weigh a ton."

He yawned and lay his head on her shoulder. "All muscle, baby. All muscle."

"Don't you dare fall asleep on me!"

"Am I interrupting anything?"

Summer looked up to find Cooper leaning in the doorway. His jaw was set in a hard line. What was *his* problem? She was the one who was supposed to be mad for the ruckus he'd caused at her office. Although she had decided to forgive him, she expected a little humbleness on his part beforehand. "Would you mind pulling your cousin off me?" she said.

Cooper noted the man had fallen asleep with a smile on his face. "It doesn't look as though he *wants* to be pulled off. If it's all the same to you, I think I'll just mosey on and leave the two of you alone."

"Don't you *dare* walk out of here, Cooper Garrett!" she said. "Not until you get me out from under this . . . this slab of flesh."

Cooper crossed his arms and leaned against the door frame. "What's it worth to you?"

She glared at him, finding it more difficult to breathe. "Very . . . funny. I can always count on you to . . . to do and say the right thing in an . . . uncomfortable situation." She pounded Warren's back with both hands. "Wake up, Warren," she said loudly, startling him.

"What's wrong?" he said, eyes flying wide open.

Cooper made his way to the bed, slipped his arms around his cousin's chest, and pulled him up so that Summer could roll out from beneath him. She gasped for air.

"Hey, Cooper," Warren said, giving the other man a silly, lopsided smile. "You want to sign my cast?"

"Let me get a razor blade first," Summer said sweetly, "so he can do it in his own blood."

"You're still sore about this afternoon, aren't you?"

"I don't want to talk about it. If you can just help me get his bathrobe off and get him settled on the bed, you can leave."

"The guy had it coming, and you know it."

She glanced up. "Okay, so maybe he did. But that gave you no right to barge in and act like some kind of . . . of barbarian. What if my boss had been there? I could have been fired on the spot."

"You know what your problem is?" he said. "You're

so determined to prove you don't need anybody that you can't appreciate the simple fact that someone cares enough to stand up for you. Well, I don't need your thanks or appreciation, I would have done the same for any woman."

She blushed, feeling foolish now. "Thank you, Cooper," she said somewhat grudgingly.

He blinked, certain he'd misunderstood. "What?"

She raised her eyes to his. "Thank you. For coming to my defense." She gave him a tight smile. "Nobody's ever done that sort of thing for me before. I guess it took me by surprise."

His shoulders relaxed. "Oh, well." He finally shrugged. "You're welcome." He glanced down at his cousin. "I guess we need to do something about him."

Together they wrestled the sleepy man out of his bathrobe. Cooper dragged the bedcovers down while Summer pulled Warren's slippers off his feet. She covered him. "Warren? I'll make you that soup now if you like," she said, hoping he had a can in his cabinet.

He opened his eyes. "You're not going to leave after that?" he asked anxiously.

Summer blinked several times. He expected her to spend the night? She looked to Cooper for help. Surely he'd hang around in case Warren started hurting in the middle of the night or had to go to the bathroom. She tried not to get irritated when Cooper didn't offer; after all, she'd insisted on picking up Warren at the hospital when he'd offered to do it. Perhaps Cooper had made other plans. "Sure, I'll stay," she said, forcing a smile.

Warren looked content as he drifted off to sleep.

Summer made her way into the kitchen and checked several cabinets before she found a can of tomato soup. A wide opening in one wall looked out into the combination living room and dining room. She was aware that Cooper watched her every move from the other side. "I have to run home for fresh clothes," she said. "Would you mind staying with Warren until I get back?"

"I thought you were sick."

"What?"

"You told me on the phone this morning you weren't feeling well."

She blushed. "I'm . . . uh . . . better now."

"Obviously." It irked him that she'd miraculously recovered from what ailed her so she could play nursemaid to his cousin. "That's great," he said. "Now you won't have to back out on our date for Wednesday night."

"Sorry, but I've already canceled with my grandmother." She was surprised the lie slipped so easily from her tongue. Practice made perfect, she supposed.

"Oh? She didn't mention it when I stopped by earlier."

Summer snapped her head up. "You went by Grandmother's house?"

"I had some free time on my hands, so I weeded her garden. Actually, I just left her place, and she was still looking forward to the benefit."

"You're not making this any easier on me," she said, knowing she had no choice but to attend the event.

"Nor do I plan to."

She shot him a quick glance and grabbed her purse. Once again he was letting her know he had no intention of backing off. She hurried for the door, desperate to put some space between them before he realized he was getting to her. Again. She could feel his eyes boring into her back. He knew exactly what he was doing. She could run, but she could not hide because he'd already figured her out. He knew which buttons to push, and she suspected he would keep on pushing till he got it right.

"Try not to burn Warren's soup," she called over her shoulder.

SEVEN

By the time Summer arrived back at Warren's place, she was nursing a headache that had Cooper's name all over it. The more she tried to avoid spending time with him, the more she found herself thrown into one situation after another with him. It couldn't be healthy, all this emotional turmoil. Every time she thought she had her feelings under control, Cooper had only to look at her that certain way to send her pulse racing. One touch, one kiss, and she was a goner.

She parked in front of the apartment complex and switched off the ignition, then sat there for a full ten minutes, reminding herself *why* she had no right to get involved with the man.

He was reckless and insensitive and downright crude at times. He could be charming one moment, brutal the next. How was she to know which was the real Cooper? He was not the sort of man who would be willing to stay with one woman for long; he would upset the even balance of her life, break her heart, and never think twice about it. They were from different worlds; what did they really have in common when it came right down to it?

She would have to be tough as nails. She couldn't, she *wouldn't* allow herself to think of what it was like being kissed by him. She refused to be drawn in by those dark eyes and blatant sensuality.

Squaring her shoulders as though preparing for battle, Summer reached for her overnight bag and the hunter-green suit she planned to wear to work the next day. She'd changed into her grungiest jeans and sweatshirt. She didn't want Cooper to think she was dressing up for him; in fact, she planned to do everything in her power to appear unappealing.

Perhaps *then* he'd give up this crazy idea to possess her, when all he really wanted was to play house with her for a while.

Warren's door was unlocked. She let herself in and stepped into the living room, where she found Cooper watching basketball on a large-screen TV. He gave her a grin that immediately set her on edge. "You didn't have to go to so much trouble on my account."

He couldn't even smile at her without making her think of sex. Well, she wasn't about to be taken in by that look, that smile. "Did Warren eat his soup?" she said evenly.

"Yeah. I had to slap him around a few times to keep him awake, but I got it down him."

She pursed her lips. That was the other thing about him, he couldn't be serious for one minute. What made her think he could have serious feelings about her? She hung her dress in the front closet and returned to the car for her briefcase and laptop computer. She set both on the table, opened the briefcase, and glanced through it to make sure she had all her files. The doorbell rang. She glanced up. "Are you expecting someone?"

"I ordered us a pizza," he said, rising from the sofa. "I hope you like yours with everything on it."

"Thanks, but I'm not hungry."

He shrugged, wondering at her sour mood. "That just leaves more for me." He opened the front door, paid the delivery boy, and carried a large pizza box into the dining area, where Summer had already set up her work center. "You want something to drink?" he asked, going into the kitchen.

"No."

He returned with two root beers and a roll of paper towels. "Well, just in case you change your mind," he said, setting a can before her. He tore a couple of paper towels off the roll, opened the pizza box, and placed a slice on each towel. Summer tried to ignore the enticing aroma, but her stomach growled loudly.

"See? You're hungrier than you think."

"I try to stay away from fattening foods during the week," she said. "It helps me keep my weight down."

He seemed to consider it. "I'm not sure it's going to look as appetizing by the weekend," he replied. When she didn't respond, he simply watched her. "Do you always bring work home with you?"

She pulled out a chair and sat down. "Usually."

"Could be you're working this hard because you're the only woman at Worth Advertising?"

Summer looked at him. His full bottom lip was greasy from the pizza. She imagined herself kissing him, tasting what he'd just put into his mouth, and she almost shivered at the thought. She pried her gaze from his lips. "Why are you asking me these questions?"

"I just want to know why you're pushing yourself. I don't want your job interfering with our relationship," he said, and had the pleasure of watching her mouth fall open.

"What relationship?" she sputtered, glancing up sharply.

"Now, Summer," he said in that cajoling voice that made her feel five years old again, "don't start playing hard to get. We both know what we want. The sooner you admit it, the better."

"I already *know* what you want, and it doesn't have anything to do with undying devotion and commitment." She took a bite of her pizza.

He reached for another slice. "Ouch! You cut me to the bone that time, Summer. Why do you think I rushed to your defense this afternoon? I couldn't stand the thought of some twerp manhandling my woman."

She almost choked on her pizza. "*Your* woman? Are you crazy?"

"When it comes to you, I am," he said silkily.

"Oh, you're too slick for me, Cooper Garrett," she said, chuckling because he made no secret of the fact he was trying to woo her. "Of course, it's okay if *you're* the one doing the manhandling, right?"

He arched one dark brow. "I don't recall ever forcing myself on you. In fact, if I remember correctly, I'm the one who called a halt to our last encounter."

Summer felt her cheeks grow hot as she remembered how she'd almost lost control while he'd been kissing her in her kitchen. Just how far would she have gone if he hadn't brought it to an end? She was afraid even to think about it. She had been so cautious in the past where the opposite sex was concerned.

And here she was about to lose her head over some biker whose idea of a long-term relationship was a couple of drinks at a cowboy bar and a tumble in somebody's king-sized bed.

Summer sighed heavily and raised her gaze to his. "I really should try to get some work done."

"What are you working on?"

The man was determined to distract her. "A number of things."

"Anything interesting?"

She shrugged. "The big Ford dealership is moving to

a new location, and they want something new and different. I've got a couple of fast-food restaurants eager to change their image and—" She stopped as her enthusiasm fizzled out. "I thought I had an ace in the hole with a large tire manufacturer, but they haven't bothered to call me back, so I don't know what's going on. I'm not involved in anything terribly engrossing, if that's what you're asking."

"What do you consider engrossing?"

She looked at him, then back at her files. "There's an account I really wanted to work on," she said. "I even offered to do it free of cost in my spare time." She told him about the Good Shepherd program and her ideas.

"So what's the problem?"

"My boss thought I'd be taking on more than I could handle."

"But if you're doing it on your own time—"

"He thinks my other accounts will suffer," she interrupted. "But I wouldn't let that happen. I have a very capable assistant who's dying to take on more responsibility."

"So do it. The secret about liking your job is doing something that doesn't feel like work."

"And if my boss finds out?"

"What's the worst that can happen?"

"I could find myself standing in the unemployment line."

Cooper laughed. "Henrietta Pettigrew's granddaughter in the unemployment line? I doubt it."

"I've already told you, I make my own way in this world."

"Oh, right. I keep forgetting how proud you are of that fact."

"Darn right," she said.

"You're one tough lady," he said.

She shot him a dark look. "I really do have a lot of work to do."

"Okay, I'll be quiet."

They polished off the pizza, and Summer continued working while Cooper cleaned up and found other things that needed doing. He busied himself with nonessential tasks and kept the coffee flowing. When Warren called out, he was only too happy to give him another pain pill, hoping it would knock him out for the rest of the night.

By three A.M. he found himself nodding in front of an infomercial about aluminum siding. He glanced at Summer, who was still bent over her sketchpad. Although he'd caught a glimpse of her work and saw that she was damn good at what she did, she'd made it plain she didn't approve of him watching over her shoulder. "Are you going to work all night?" he asked, wondering if he should put on another pot of coffee. He didn't see how she could drink that much caffeine without going through the ceiling.

Summer glanced up as though she'd been in a trance. She checked her wristwatch. "I didn't realize it was so late."

"It's not late, it's early."

"I guess I'd better hit the sack."

"I really don't mind staying in your place," Cooper said.

Summer stood and stretched, and his eyes narrowed as her breasts rose high with the movement. Noting it, she quickly dropped her arms to her sides. "That's okay. I told my assistant I'd be working here in the morning if she needed me. I have only two appointments scheduled, and the first one isn't until three. I figured I'd get Warren packed and wait for his parents." She suddenly yawned. "Now, where do you suppose Warren keeps his extra linens?" she asked, going to the hall closet.

"Extra linens?"

"Ah, here they are." Summer pulled out a set of sheets and a blanket.

"What's that for?"

"I need to make up the sofa," she said. "You don't expect me to sleep in the bathtub, do you?"

He followed her into the living room, then stood there blank and amazed. "But I thought—"

She pulled the cushions off the sofa and tugged at the mattress inside. It unfolded before her. "What did you think?"

He shrugged. "I just figured you'd sleep in Warren's bed."

"What!" She gaped at him. "Why on earth would I do that?"

"Well, because the two of you are . . . you're—"

"We're what?"

"Lovers?"

She stared at him wordlessly, first bewildered, then indignant. "Did Warren tell you that?" she demanded, planting her hands on her hips.

"Not in so many words, but he led me to believe there was something going on between the two of you. I just assumed—"

"You assumed wrong," she snapped. "We're good friends and coworkers and nothing more."

"Does *he* know that?"

"I've told him a number of times. If I haven't gotten through to him by now, then he's deaf, dumb, blind, *and* stupid."

Cooper laughed. He felt as though a big weight had been lifted off his shoulders. "So you're basically unattached."

"And I have every intention of staying that way, thank you very much."

He tweaked her nose. "That's to be seen, sweetheart." He reached for his jacket and slipped it on. "What time's breakfast?" he asked.

She couldn't hide her astonishment. He actually expected her to prepare his breakfast? "You're incredible," she said, shaking her head. "I don't do breakfast."

He slipped his arms around her waist and pulled her close. "Incredible, huh? And you haven't even been to bed with me yet. Just wait, babe, I'll show you incredible. But only when I think you can handle it." He kissed her hard on the mouth. When he raised his head he was smiling. "Forget breakfast. I'll drop by with coffee and doughnuts. Walk me to the door?"

As Cooper took Summer's hands in his, she realized he wasn't giving her much of a choice. He literally dragged her to the front door, then gazed down at her in a way that sent the tingling from her toes to her calf muscles. She knew she had no business standing there wearing a dumb, expectant look on her face. She was giving the man mixed messages. While her brain told her to back off, her body refused to respond.

The amused glint in his eye told her he knew she was struggling with indecision. "Now, be a good little girl and kiss papa good night."

"Forget it." She turned.

He chuckled, snaked an arm around her waist, and pulled her against him. Her bottom made contact with his crotch, and he groaned inwardly. Summer heard his quick intake of breath, felt his erection. "Cooper—"

Bracing her against his body with one hand, he lifted her hair away from her neck and nuzzled the downy softness. She shivered. He moved his mouth upward, then to one side, where he nibbled the back of her ear. "I love it when you turn that pert little nose up at me like you wouldn't give me the time of day. God, you smell good," he said. "I want to taste you, Summer."

"You shouldn't be saying these things to me."

"Who told you that? Your grandmother? Or did you read it out of some book on dating etiquette?"

His voice was so husky that her insides took on the consistency of buttermilk. Her knees trembled. Once again he'd managed to find all the right buttons. She could feel herself weakening despite the promises she'd made to herself earlier. "I hardly know you."

"I know all I need to know about you," he said, turning her around in his arms. He looked into her green eyes. "Why don't we share that mattress tonight? Warren won't interrupt us. He's zonked for the next eight to ten hours." When she glanced away, he put a finger under her chin and forced her to look at him. "You already know how much I want you," he said gently. "Don't you want me back just a little?"

She was so close to complying. She could feel every nerve in her body crying out for him. "Yes, but—" She tried to think, but she was so tired. "This just isn't the time or place, Cooper. It doesn't feel right."

He saw the exhaustion in her face and knew that was part of it. He wouldn't press. "How will you know when the time is right?"

Her answer was a long time coming. "I'll know."

Cooper arrived back at Warren's apartment shortly before nine the following morning. He rang the doorbell several times before he heard footsteps from the other side, followed by the sound of the chain sliding free and the dead bolts snapping open. Summer squinted at him. Her hair fell in disarray, wild and untamed-looking, and the strap holding her gown had slid down one arm.

"I woke you."

"You're a genius," she mumbled, still half asleep. Leaving the door open, she dragged herself back to the sofa bed.

"I knew you'd be thrilled to see me again," Cooper said, following her in. He set a box of fresh doughnuts on the table and watched her fall in an unladylike heap onto the mattress. "Is the coffee ready yet?" When she merely grunted, he walked into the kitchen and saw that it was not. He dumped the old filter, put a fresh one in, and spooned coffee into it before pouring a pot of water into the top.

He left the kitchen and made his way toward the living room, where she was lying on her stomach, hair fanned across her shoulders. The gown was of thin white cotton. He could see her panties. Hot pink. He swallowed. "Did Warren wake up during the night?"

"If he did, I didn't hear him," she said, her words muffled by the pillow.

"Fine nurse you are," he said, grinning. "I'd better check on him." Cooper hurried toward the bedroom. His cousin was already awake. "How're you feeling?"

"I hurt like a son of a gun, and I need to use the little boys' room."

"Good thing I stopped by," Cooper said, reaching for the crutches.

"Is Summer here?"

"Yes, Nurse Nightingale is passed out on your sofa right now. She and her laptop partied till the wee hours. Do you think you can sit up?"

Warren tried to rise, then moaned. "It feels like every one of my ribs are cracked."

"Well, you haven't had a pain pill since about three A.M. You're probably suffering withdrawal." Slowly, they managed to get inside the bathroom. Hands gripping his crutches, Warren stared at the john.

Summer knocked on the door. "Is everything okay in here?"

Warren looked confused. "How am I supposed to—" He glanced at Cooper. "You know."

"Hey, don't look at me, pal," Cooper said, backing away.

Summer frowned, knowing there was no way Warren could hold himself up and do all that was necessary to urinate. "Oh, for Pete's sake, Cooper, you have to help him."

Cooper shot her a dark look. "Why don't *you* help him?"

"*Somebody* needs to help me," Warren said anxiously. "I haven't gone since I left the hospital."

"Okay, I'll help him," Summer said, stepping closer.

"No!" Cooper held his hand up to stop her. The thought of her touching another man's genitals was more than he could stand. "I'll do it. Close the door," he ordered.

Summer stepped into the hall and closed the door so hard, it almost knocked a picture off the wall. What burr had gotten into his underwear? First he comes in and wakes her from the best sleep she's had in months, now he was ordering her around like a drill seargeant. She pressed her ear against the door and tried to hear what was happening on the other side.

"Okay, Warren, I'm going to help you sit on the john," Cooper said. "I'll hold your crutches once you're in place. The rest is up to you."

Summer realized what was going on and burst into laughter.

"I heard that!" Cooper shouted angrily.

She tried to stifle her giggles as she hurried into the kitchen in search of fresh coffee.

Once Cooper had helped his cousin back to bed, he came into the kitchen wearing a dark scowl. Sitting on a stool beside the counter, Summer tried to keep a straight face. She failed miserably.

"It's not a damn bit funny," Cooper muttered.

"You'd think a grown man could do one or two things for himself."

"I don't know why you're making such a big deal out of it," she said innocently. "I offered to take your place."

"Let's just drop it, okay? Warren needs a pain pill." He reached for the bottle next to the sink, opened it, and dumped one into his palm.

"It hasn't been eight hours yet."

"Well, I'm giving him one anyway so he'll stop whining." He took a glass from the cabinet and filled it with water. "Why don't you grab a couple of doughnuts and pour him a cup of coffee while you're standing there doing nothing. I'm having a real problem watching you prance around in that skimpy gown."

He carried the pill and water into the bedroom. When he came out, he had Warren's robe slung over one shoulder. He tossed it at her. "Now you have no excuse to strut around like some lingerie model."

"It's what I live for," she replied haughtily. She slipped into the robe and tied the belt, then leaned against the cabinet and sipped her coffee in angry silence. The man was very definitely getting on her last nerve, but she was determined not to get into a verbal battle with him.

He stepped closer, planting his hands on either side of the counter. "Is that what you're trying to do?" he asked, his voice husky. "Make me want you so bad, I can't think about anything else? If so, it's working." He pressed closer. Summer gasped aloud as his rigid sex made contact with her belly. She tried to back away, but was trapped between him and the cabinet. "Feel that?" he said. "It kept me up most of the night."

She could feel the heat searing her cheeks. "You're embarrassing me."

"*You're* embarrassed? Did you see the look on Warren's face when you waltzed into the bathroom in that . . . that excuse for a gown?"

"He wasn't embarrassed, he had to pee, for heaven's sake!" Summer could only gaze back at him in utter bewilderment. Why was he making such a big deal out of a simple cotton nightgown? One would have thought she was wearing tassels and a G-string. "Why are you acting like this?"

"Maybe I just don't like watching you flaunt yourself."

"*Flaunt* myself? Have you lost your mind?" She pressed one hand against his chest, and he took a step back. "Besides, who are you to tell me how I can or cannot dress? I'll walk down Main Street buck naked if I feel like it."

He continued to stare at her for a moment, then looked away. He raked his hands through his hair. She was right, he was beginning to sound like he'd lost all his marbles. "I have to go to work." He turned and reached for a pencil, then scribbled a number on a sheet of paper next to the phone. "Warren says his parents should arrive around lunchtime. Call me if something comes up."

He turned and started out of the room, and Summer gave a sigh of relief. It was short-lived. He retraced his steps and stood there for a moment, his gaze flitting about the kitchen as though trying to avoid looking at her. "Listen, I don't know why I act like such a jerk when I'm with you." He looked confused, utterly baffled. He took a step closer, and this time he met her gaze. They stood there looking at each other for a breathless moment. Summer was certain he was going to kiss her, and she knew she would welcome it. Instead, he raised a hand to her cheek and touched it lightly. "I'll see you later."

She watched him walk away. The sound of the front door closing left her feeling empty and frustrated. She longed to kick something.

Warren was dozing when Summer stepped into his bedroom a few minutes later carrying a small plate of doughnuts and a cup of coffee. "Do you feel like eating?" she asked, setting them on his night table.

He took his time rising, grimacing with every move. "Mmm. I'll bet you whipped those up from scratch."

"Get smart with me, and I'll crack another rib," she threatened, sitting on the edge of the bed. She offered him the cup of coffee. "Be careful, it's hot."

Warren watched her as he took a sip. "Oh, man, I must be dreaming. Here you are, wearing my bathrobe, bringing me breakfast. I must've done something right in my life. Did anything happen between us last night?"

"In your dreams, pal."

"Speaking of dreams. Did I hear you and Cooper arguing earlier, or was I having a nightmare?"

"You probably heard us fussing," she said wearily. "Your cousin is a jackass."

Warren reached for a doughnut and took a hearty bite. "Yes, well, Cooper certainly has a way with the ladies."

"He's probably the reason female tarantulas kill their partners after mating," she said dully.

He gazed at her steadily. "You got it bad for him, huh?"

"Yeah." Summer sighed heavily. "How can I be falling for him so fast and so hard when the man irritates me the way he does?"

"Maybe you're not as irritated as you think. Could be a case of raging hormones making you jittery." Warren looked thoughtful. "Has Cooper told you anything about himself?"

She gave a snort. "Oh, yes, he's a wealth of information about himself." She paused and shot him a sidelong glance. "Is there something I should know?"

"I'd feel better if he told you."

"Don't start holding back on me now, Warren. If he's done something . . ." Her words trailed off as she waited.

"Cooper didn't have it so easy growing up," he finally said. "His mother married someone her family didn't approve of, and there was a bitter fight. Then Cooper's father abandoned the family, leaving behind a pregnant wife and a young son. My parents offered to help, but Cooper's mother was too proud to accept handouts from anybody, especially the family who'd turned their back on her. It was downright silly if you ask me. You have this family living in the same town, and they don't even speak to one another for years. I met Cooper for the first time by accident when we bumped into each other at a club one night. We sort of became friends, although we didn't have much in common except for being cousins.

"Anyway, from what I gather, he grew up dirt poor, and the kids teased him something awful. He learned to fight at an early age."

"Which explains that massive chip on his shoulder," she said, feeling sorry for the man who'd had to depend on his fists all his life. She, too, knew how it felt to be teased and ridiculed, and just like Cooper, she'd built up defenses. Perhaps they had more in common than she'd realized.

Warren yawned before going on. "The only people he was close to were his mother and his younger sister, Angie. His mother's a devout Catholic. She worked two and three jobs to support them. Cooper got a job cleaning up some bike shop before he was old enough to get a work permit. Anyway, he came home one day and found some guy trying to have his way with Angie. An old boyfriend who was tired of hearing the word no. Angie was almost raped."

Summer was almost afraid to hear the rest of the story. "What happened?"

"Cooper beat the guy within an inch of his life. Just about broke every bone in his body. There was a hearing. Some folks felt Cooper went overboard.

"But fighting had always come natural to Cooper, and he earned himself quite a reputation. Some rich guy had a large barn on his property up past Marietta, where he held cockfights. He heard about Cooper and decided it would be more interesting to watch a couple of men go at it, so he set it up. The way I heard it, Cooper was getting the best of his opponent, so the guy pulled a knife from his boot and tried to cut out Cooper's belly button."

Summer shivered as she remembered the jagged scar. "It's a wonder he lived through it."

"He almost didn't. He lost a lot of blood and spent some time in the hospital. As soon as his mother knew he was out of the woods, she tore into him like a rabid pit bull. In the end Cooper promised he wouldn't fight again."

"Has he kept his promise?"

"As far as I know. When you have a reputation like Cooper, you don't have to fight. He was promoted from janitor to salesman at the bike shop, and motorcycles became the love of his life. Anyway, here he is, a guy who graduates high school by the skin of his teeth, and he goes and designs a bike that has the big boys at Harley-Davidson begging for the patent."

Summer wanted to question him further, but was interrupted by the ringing of the doorbell. She glanced at the clock on Warren's night table. "I wonder who that could be." She got up and started for the door.

"Summer?"

She glanced back. "Yes?"

"What I just told you about Cooper? I'd rather you not say anything. If he wants to tell you, fine, but he's kind of private. I just thought you should know."

"Thanks, Warren." She made her way out of the bedroom, crossed the living room, and hurried toward the door. When she opened it she found herself looking into the faces of Warren's parents, Natalie and Ben Spencer.

"Summer, how nice to see you again," his mother said, stepping inside. "How's our boy?"

Summer had met the Spencers on several occasions when they'd visited Atlanta. "He's hanging in there, Mrs. Spencer. I know he'll be glad to see you."

Natalie and Ben nodded soberly and made their way to their son's bedroom.

When Summer stepped out of the bathroom half an hour later, she was dressed in the hunter-green suit with matching heels. She'd made up her face and tucked her long hair into a bun. "My, don't you look nice," Natalie said, holding a plastic garbage bag.

"She sure does," Ben agreed. "I keep saying what a good-looking couple she and Warren would make."

Summer blushed. Although she'd convinced Natalie she and Warren were merely friends, Ben had never made a secret of wanting to see the two get together.

They were in the process of discussing the best way of getting Warren into the car, when the front door opened and Cooper stepped into the room. Ben and Natalie stopped what they were doing and stared at him, then sputtered a hello. He nodded politely, crossed the room, and kissed Summer on the mouth. "Hi, sweetheart. I was in the neighborhood and thought ya'll might need help getting Warren to the car."

EIGHT

For a moment Ben and Natalie simply stood there, looking dazed. "You two know each other?" Natalie asked.

"Certainly looks that way," Ben said. "He just kissed her and called her sweetheart."

Natalie looked slightly embarrassed. "You're looking well, Cooper. The motorcycle business must agree with you."

"I have no complaints," he replied coolly.

"We called your mother on the car phone," Ben said. "She invited us to lunch and gave us directions to the house. We can't wait to see the farm."

"I can't believe how little I get to see my own sister," Natalie said.

Cooper's expression was cool. "Neither can I."

There was a brief, uncomfortable silence. "How's Angie? We heard she married. Was he a boy from the neighborhood?"

Cooper shook his head. "Actually, she married a pediatrician."

Natalie looked impressed. "A doctor. Oh, my!"

"I thought maybe you could use my help getting

Warren to the car," Cooper said, obviously wanting to get on with the business at hand and leave. "He's not real handy with his crutches yet."

"I would appreciate it," Ben said.

Things moved quickly after that, and Summer suspected Ben and Natalie felt ill at ease with their nephew. Warren seemed oblivious of the tension as he made his way to the car, struggling with his crutches but determined to do it on his own. Once he was in the backseat, Natalie fussed over him, propping a pillow beneath his broken leg and another behind his back. Cooper shook his hand and Summer leaned forward, giving him a chaste kiss on the cheek. "Take care of yourself," she said.

"Just don't let my ficus trees die," he replied, grinning. "And call me if you need help on those accounts. I have copies of everything in my briefcase."

"I'll lock up," Summer told Ben as he climbed into the driver's side of the car. Natalie was already in, her seat belt strapped in place. They said their good-byes and the car disappeared through the security gate a minute later. Summer went inside the apartment for her things. Cooper followed.

"Can I help you with anything?" he asked.

She gave him a tight smile. "Don't you think you've done enough?"

He closed the door behind him and leaned against it. "Yeah. I'm sorry if I embarrassed you. Ben and Natalie rub me the wrong way. They think they're too damn good for everybody. My grandparents were the same way."

"Has it ever occurred to you that maybe you rub *them* the wrong way?"

"I've known that for years. The only reason I tolerate them is because of my mother. Natalie's the only relative she has left."

"People change, Cooper. Maybe your aunt and uncle aren't the same persons they once were."

He stepped closer. "I like you in that color."

"You're changing the subject."

"You're much more interesting as far as subjects go. In fact, I find you intriguing as hell."

She could feel the heat of his body, feel herself being drawn by his sensuality. "I have to go to work."

"Your first appointment isn't until three. It's not even noon yet."

She took a step back. "But surely you have to get back."

He shrugged. "I sort of manage the place. I come and go as I please."

"Yes, well, I don't have that luxury." She started to turn.

He grasped her upper arms, bringing her to a complete halt. "Stop running from me," he said.

"I'm not run—"

He cut off her words with a kiss. Giving a deep moan of pleasure, he slipped his arms around her waist and pulled her closer as his tongue pushed past her lips and made a clean sweep of her mouth. Summer felt her body go weak. When he pulled away, his black eyes searched hers. "Let's make love, Summer."

Her eyes suddenly became round as saucers. "What, *here? Now?*"

"What's wrong with here and now? We're not likely to be disturbed. Unless your grandmother has a key to the place."

There was a tingling in the pit of her stomach as Summer considered it. She turned slowly and made her way toward the dining area, pressing her palms against her cheeks, trying to weed through her emotions. "I'm not . . . uh . . . prepared for intimacy," she said at last.

"I am." He reached into the front pocket of his jeans and tossed several foil packs onto the table.

Summer tried to still the currents racing through her body. She felt him move closer, felt the energy that flowed from his body to hers like a magnet. Her heart beat out a frantic message; her insides were as erratic as a summer storm. She ached for his touch; she dreamed of being crushed within his embrace. The thought of their bare flesh touching made her breathless and dizzy. But what about the emotional risks?

"I want you, Summer," he said softly, his warm breath brushing the back of her neck like dandelion fluff. "I need you."

Summer shivered. All her self-control seemed to fizzle out at the confession. Cooper *needed* her? She turned around and looked into his eyes. They blazed and glowed with desire, yet there was a softness, a vulnerability that she hadn't noticed before. Was this man going to break her heart before it was over? "I want you, too, Cooper," she said on a whisper.

His look became even more intense as he studied her, searching for signs of doubt. He saw his own desire mirrored in her green eyes. He reclaimed the square foil packs and stuffed them in his pocket once more. Taking a deep, unsteady breath, he leaned forward slightly and lifted her in his arms.

"What's this?" she said, surprised by his unpredictability.

His laugh was low and throaty. "You didn't think I'd just drag you into the bedroom by your hair, did you? On second thought, don't answer that."

Summer lay her head against his shoulder as he carried her into Warren's bedroom. She suddenly felt shy and self-conscious. He set her on the bed gently. "Would you close the blinds and draw the drapes?" she asked.

Cooper could see that she was anxious, and he tried

to lighten the moment. "Afraid I'll see some cellulite?" he said, moving toward the windows, where he did as she'd asked. The room dimmed, but not so much that he wouldn't be able to make out every delicious detail of her body. He walked toward the bed, offered his hands, and she took them. Once he'd pulled her to a standing position, he slid his hands inside her jacket and helped her out of it, then draped it across the back of a chair. Turning her around, he unzipped her dress and peeled it from her shoulders, planting soft kisses on her bare skin. It whispered down her body and pooled at her feet. She stepped out of it, and he laid it across her jacket.

The sight of her standing in her slip made his mouth go dry. He couldn't resist touching the gossamer fabric, and he knew enough about women's lingerie to know hers hadn't come from a department store. His hands were unsteady as he raised them to the neat bun she'd fashioned at the nape of her neck. He pulled the pins free, and her thick hair tumbled past her shoulders to the small of her back. Then, very slowly, he turned her around so that she was facing him once more. "You're beautiful."

The look on his face made her feel beautiful. "Thank you."

Cooper knelt before her and removed her heels, then skimmed his hands up her thighs to her waist, where he tugged off her panty hose.

Cooper stood and kissed her lightly before he peeled the straps of her slip off her shoulders and pushed it down, past the swell of her hips and long legs. He'd meant to put it on the chair with the rest of her things, but the sight of her in skimpy bikini underwear and a lace bra sent his thoughts into a tailspin. He drank in the sight of her. He reached between the cups of her bra and unfastened the hooks. Summer shrugged out of it and let it slide down her arms. She stared at her feet, unable to meet his gaze; but she could feel his eyes on her, making her body flush.

His black eyes glowed with passion. "Take off your panties," he ordered softly.

Summer took a deep, shaky breath, slid her fingers inside the waistband, and peeled them away. She let them glide down her thighs and calves to the floor.

"Damn." The word came out sounding choked. "You're . . . perfect."

She stood there as he gazed at her hungrily. It was all she could do to keep from diving beneath the covers. But as he continued to study her with those dark eyes, she felt her body respond. Her stomach tensed, and her nipples puckered and hardened. Cooper reached out and stroked one blue-veined breast, and Summer sucked in her breath. He stepped closer and cupped both breasts in his palms, flicking his thumb lightly across the tight, rose-colored nubs. He leaned forward and took one in his mouth, and Summer closed her eyes and gave in to the feel of his warm mouth on her. He nibbled and tugged, and the sensation sent sharp bursts of desire through her belly. He moved to the other nipple, teasing it until it quivered. He pulled her close, crushing her against him as he palmed her hips. He squeezed and kneaded her flesh, then anchored her against him.

"See what you do to me?" he whispered, his voice thick with desire. He reached for her hand and guided it to his painful erection. Summer could literally feel him pulsing inside his jeans. "Touch me," he said.

She fumbled with his belt, her hands made clumsy by desire and anxiety. She unbuttoned his jeans and un-zipped him, then tentatively slipped her hand inside his underwear. He groaned aloud and captured her mouth. His tongue forced her lips open wide.

Summer felt the rigid muscle swell as she closed her

fingers around him. He was big and thick and hard. Her anxiety returned.

Cooper felt her stiffen in his arms. He raised his head slightly. "Relax, babe," he said softly.

She nodded, not trusting herself to speak.

He pulled free and swept the covers aside. Summer climbed beneath the sheets, yanked them to her chin, and stared at the ceiling as he began to undress. "Don't look away," he said. "It's more fun if you watch."

She looked at him as he pulled his shirt from his jeans and unbuttoned it, then tossed it aside. He sat on the edge of the bed, kicked off his boots, and discarded his socks. She watched the powerful play of muscles along his shoulders and back. Finally, he stood and reached into his pockets for a foil pack, tore it open with his teeth, and set it on the night table. He shoved his jeans and underwear past his hips and sturdy legs and stepped out of them. Summer could only stare at the magnificent man before her.

"Well?" he said. "Aren't you going to invite me under the covers?"

She pulled them aside, and he climbed in next to her, scooping her up into his arms. He was big and warm and smelled faintly of soap and male flesh. He looked into her eyes, then took her mouth in a slow, drugging kiss. Once again he coaxed her mouth open with his tongue and tasted the inside. Her own shy tongue greeted him, and he moaned in his throat. He moved one thigh between her own and pressed gently against the honey-colored curls that covered her femininity. The pressure between her legs intensified. Desire coursed through her veins like an awakened river after a thaw. She arched against him instinctively.

Cooper broke the kiss and they both sucked in air. His hands skimmed her body, and he marveled at the silken texture and the generous curves. He gently pulled the covers aside so he could see her, and the sight of her nakedness almost took his breath away. He raised his eyes to hers. "Don't ever try to hide from me."

Summer watched him move over her. Once again his lips touched a nipple, drawing it into his mouth and sucking until she felt a tugging sensation deep within her womb. As his lips paid homage to her breasts, his hands caressed her, stroking her flat stomach and brushing her sensitive inner thigh. Fully aroused, she pressed against his hand. Her own hands skimmed his broad back and shoulders. She fumbled with the leather tie holding his hair back, pulled it free, then plunged her fingers into the thick raven-colored mane. Cooper kissed his way to her stomach and tongued her navel until she squirmed beneath him. She held her breath as he playfully nipped her thighs with his teeth, then buried his mouth in the nest of gold curls. An involuntary shudder racked her body as he dipped his tongue inside.

Cooper thought he'd died and gone to heaven the minute he tasted her. He slid his hands beneath her hips and lifted her slightly. Finally, he pulled his hands free and searched for the sensitive nub with the tip of his tongue. Her soft cry told him he'd found it. He flicked his tongue back and forth, lightly at first, then applied more pressure as she arched higher and higher to meet him.

Her increasing passion was a thing of beauty to watch, like a love song that builds and swells as it nears its crescendo. Her breathing became short, her soft cries a plea for release. Her eyes were glazed with desire as she met his.

Cooper rose up and reached for the foil pack, sitting back on his heels as he carefully fixed the condom in place. He glanced up and found her gaze fastened to his sex. "Tell me you want me."

"I do," she whispered.

He moved between her legs, planting his palms against either side of the mattress. As he probed, she opened herself up to him, and he plunged inside. It was an act of raw possession. Summer cried out, then bit her bottom lip to silence herself.

Panic seized him as her eyes filled with tears. He held himself rigid, afraid to make another move. "Oh, babe, did I hurt you?"

She shook her head even as tears ran down her cheeks. "Don't stop."

He moved against her, slowly at first, taking care not to enter her fully. He gritted his teeth at the way she sheathed him so tightly. Sweat beaded his brow and upper lip as he gazed down at her. Her eyes were closed, her lips wet and softly parted. Her hair fanned the pillow beneath her head, and a thick strand fell across her flushed body. He felt as though he'd explode just watching her. She ran her tongue across her bottom lip, and he jerked involuntarily. She mewed like a kitten, and when she opened her eyes he found them soft with passion. Cautiously, he allowed her to take in more of him.

Desire had left her feeling less inhibited; she ran her hands lightly over his taut hips, then raked her nails against his flesh. Cooper cursed under his breath. His movements quickened, his thrusts grew deeper and more powerful. Summer raised her legs and wrapped them around his waist, and he knew he'd reached the point of no return.

He grasped her hands in his and held them against the mattress as he moved against her. She met each thrust. Finally, their movements became frenzied. What had started out as a beautifully orchestrated dance had turned to need in its most primitive form. Cooper rode her hard, but she gave as good as she got. Her orgasm was powerful to watch; his own was like a rebirth.

Cooper collapsed beside her, his broad chest heaving

from exertion. He glanced at Summer, lying still beside him with her eyes closed. She'd already covered herself with the sheet. "You okay?" he asked, pulling her close, kissing her forehead. He levered himself up slightly and kissed her eyelids as well.

She nodded. "Don't I look like I'm okay?"

"You look like an angel. I could lie here and hold you in my arms forever."

She nuzzled him. "I'd like that. Unfortunately, I need to use the little girls' room. Would you please bring me a bath towel?"

Cooper chuckled at her sudden show of modesty. He climbed from the bed and walked into the bathroom. Summer gazed in feminine appreciation at the wide shoulders and back, the taut hips. He returned a moment later with an oversized bath towel and handed it to her. He saw her glance away from his nakedness. Okay, so maybe the lady needed a little time to get used to him, he told himself. He grabbed his underwear and jeans as Summer hurried out of the room with the towel wrapped around her.

Cooper sat on the edge of the bed and reached for his socks. From the bathroom he could hear the sound of running water. Was she taking a bath? He was half tempted to knock on the door and insist on climbing into the tub with her. He dropped his socks on the bed as he considered joining her. Finally, he decided against it. She was obviously feeling a bit shy with him just then, and it was up to him to show some sensitivity. Not that he had a whole lot of practice in that area, but he was determined to give it his best shot. The last thing he wanted was for her to start feeling guilty over what they'd done. As far as he was concerned, it was the best thing that'd ever happened to him.

As he reached for his socks, he glanced down and felt

his jaw go slack at the sight of the bright red stain on the sheet.

Cooper had pulled the sheets off the bed and put them into a cold wash by the time Summer came out of the bathroom. He was fully dressed, standing at the kitchen counter drinking a glass of water. Through the large opening in the wall she noted the hard line of his jaw. He was not happy. She hurried into the bedroom and dressed. When she stepped out some ten minutes later, there was no indication that she'd spent part of the afternoon in bed with a man.

"Gee, I didn't know it was so late," she said. "I'd better get going—"

"Stop right there," he ordered, slamming the glass on the counter so hard, it made her jump.

The sound of his voice would have stopped a locomotive. Summer did as he said. He left the kitchen and walked toward her. "Why didn't you tell me?" She arched one brow in question. "Don't play dumb with me, Summer, you know damn well what I'm talking about."

She shrugged. "It didn't come up."

He scowled at her. "Oh, I think you had a couple of opportunities to mention it."

The fact that he was so upset hurt her. She had never felt more vulnerable in her life, and all she wanted him to do was take her in his arms and tell her how much he'd enjoyed being with her, how much he cared. She felt her throat close up and knew she was close to tears, but she was bound and determined not to give in to them. "What's wrong, Cooper?" she snapped. "Feeling guilty? Well, don't. At my age being a virgin can be quite embarrassing. Men think there's something wrong with you. Like maybe you're frigid or something."

"We both know you're not that," Cooper said, causing her to blush. "So what is it? You're a normal, healthy woman. Surely you have desires like the rest of us."

"Of course I do," she said sharply. "And just because I've never been intimate with a man doesn't mean I haven't enjoyed some heavy petting in my life. I just didn't want to be—" She paused.

He stepped closer. He was clearly confused. "Was it because you were afraid of getting a disease?"

"That was part of it," she said. "The other reason I put off having intercourse was because I didn't want to risk getting pregnant."

"There are ways to prevent that."

"Nothing is one hundred percent safe. Except for abstinence," she added. She chewed her bottom lip. She was suddenly anxious. "You don't think there's a chance . . . that maybe we weren't careful enough?"

He saw the fear in her eyes. "You're afraid I impregnated you? I seriously doubt it."

"But you don't know," she said. "You couldn't swear on your life."

"I can't swear on my life that I won't run my bike into the back of an eighteen-wheeler tomorrow, Summer." He raked his hands through his hair, feeling more confused than ever. He wanted to kiss her, cuddle her close, and tell her how wonderful it had been. Instead, he was dealing with some irrational side of her that made absolutely no sense. "Do you have some kind of phobia where children are concerned?" he asked, trying to understand. "Are you afraid of childbirth?" He'd heard stories of how some women had suffered through labor. Perhaps Summer had heard similar stories and that's what had her scared.

"I have to go," she said.

He blocked her way. "Not until you tell me what this is all about."

"Dammit, Cooper, do you have to have everything your way? Maybe it's too personal for me to share right now. Have you thought of that?"

"I think what we just shared in the next room was pretty personal," he said.

"For me maybe," she said. "It's probably just another day in the life of Cooper Garrett as far as you're concerned." She hated herself for saying it, for sounding petty and jealous.

"Is that what you think?" he asked.

"You've been trying to get me in the sack since we met."

He nodded. "You're absolutely right. And I'll continue to do so. That doesn't mean I do the same with every woman I meet."

"How do I know that?"

"Because I just said it. That should be proof enough." He studied her for a moment, wondering what kind of battle she was fighting insider her head. "I've been honest with you from the beginning," he said gently, "and I have no reason to start lying to you now. What we just shared—" He held out his hands. "That doesn't come along very often."

"I have to go."

He grabbed her arm. "Are you afraid I'll get you pregnant and dump you?" he asked, trying desperately to understand her.

She pulled free. "Can't you see I don't want to discuss this right now? I have feelings, Cooper, and if you were any kind of gentleman, you'd respect those feelings and give me time to think. You can't just come barreling into my life with both guns, hoping to wear down my resistance." She made for the door.

He started after her, then stopped himself. She was right, he had done nothing but push her in the direction of the bedroom since he'd laid eyes on her, and now he was afraid she would end up hating him for it.

Maybe she already did.

Henrietta was resting in her easy chair with a book when her driver, Axel, tapped on the door. "Am I disturbing you, Mrs. Pettigrew?"

"Of course not. Please come in. Would you like some refreshment?"

"No, thank you, ma'am, I can't stay but a minute," her chauffeur said. "It's about that little matter we discussed the other day."

"And?"

"They promised to put a man on it right away."

"Is this man any good?"

"He's supposed to be one of the best."

"When do they think they'll have something?"

Axel smiled. "It doesn't take long to get information these days," he assured her. "That's the good thing about modern technology. They should be able to give you the whole story in a few days."

"Thank you, Axel. As always, you're right there when I need you."

"You're welcome, Mrs. Pettigrew. I asked them to send the bill to my address once they've tied everything up. That way you won't have to worry about anyone seeing it."

"You always think of everything," she replied. He made for the door. "Axel?"

He stopped and turned. "Yes, ma'am?"

"What if we're too late?"

"Too late?"

"Summer could have already fallen in love with him by now."

NINE

Summer arrived home from work Wednesday with little more than an hour to shower, do her makeup, and dress for the benefit. She was in the process of zipping herself into a slim-fitting black crepe dress with satin collar and sleeves, when the doorbell rang. She stepped into tall satin heels and took the stairs slowly, trying to calm herself as she went. She would have to face Cooper sooner or later. Better to just get it over with. After tonight there would be no need to continue the charade. She paused at the door, took a deep breath, and opened it.

Her knees almost buckled at the sight of him.

A clean-shaven Cooper Garrett stood before her in a perfectly tailored tux. Summer gaped at his white jacket and black trousers. His black shoes shone like a new appliance. He handed her a long, slender box that bore the name of her favorite florist. Still in a daze, she lifted the lid and found a dozen long-stemmed yellow roses inside. "Oh, my!" she said, lifting a hand to her cheek and meeting his dark gaze. "You shouldn't have."

"I wanted to," he said, his voice little more than a whisper. "For many reasons."

Summer almost shivered at the look in his eyes, and she remembered how he'd gazed down at her the day before as they'd made love. "You cut your hair," she said, noting the new conservative style.

She suddenly heard the sound of a motor running and looked past him, where a white stretch limo waited. "That's your friend's car?" she said.

He hesitated. "Not exactly." Cooper couldn't take his eyes off her. He wanted to say to hell with the benefit and spend the evening making love to her. "My, uh, friend works for a limo service. He got me a good deal."

"Oh, Cooper, I wish you hadn't spent so much money," she said, knowing the tux, the roses, and the limo would probably set him back a month's salary. "I insist on splitting the cost."

"Forget it. If I fall short on cash, I'll sell my blood."

She blinked. "What?"

"Just joking," he said. "Are you ready?"

"Yes. But let me put these in water first." She hurried into the kitchen and reached beneath the sink for a large vase. As she stuffed the roses into the container and added cold water, she heard Cooper's footsteps behind her. He slipped his arms around her waist and kissed the nape of her neck. "You didn't return my calls today," he said.

Summer felt her skin prickle as his warm mouth caressed her. The man certainly knew all her pleasure points. "I . . . I had back-to-back appointments all day," she said, her voice cracking. The vase suddenly felt heavy. She set it down and gripped the edge of the counter as he nibbled an earlobe. "We should go," she said halfheartedly.

Cooper turned her around in his arms. His black eyes probed hers. "I think we should clear the air first. I don't know why you got upset yesterday, but I just want you to know what we shared was the best thing that's ever happened to me. I don't want you to have regrets."

"I don't know what to say, Cooper. Everything seems to have happened so fast between us."

"Maybe because it was meant to be. We can't always analyze our feelings."

"Perhaps I'm more cautious than most," she confessed, "but I have my reasons."

He slid his hands up her arms. He could feel her pulling away. Once again he told himself not to push. "I hope one day you'll trust me enough to tell me." He released her, took a step back, and held out his arm. "Shall we go?" He saw the relief in her eyes and knew there were some things she simply wasn't ready to share, and he couldn't blame her because he had the same problem. He suddenly realized they were very much alike when it came to trusting someone. He might come off as a badass, but he was as much afraid of being hurt as she was.

Summer slipped her arm through his, and they made their way into the foyer. She pulled a velvet jacket from the closet and handed it to Cooper, who held it while she slipped it on. She grabbed her satin clutch and exited the condo, pausing briefly for Cooper to lock the door behind them.

Inside the limo, Summer was greeted with soft mood music and chilled champagne. She sipped her drink slowly as the driver took the interstate and headed north to the Pettigrew estate. She tried not to stare at Cooper, but it was next to impossible. He was so stunningly virile that it hurt to tear her gaze away. He took their champagne glasses and set them on the cocktail table that sat between the two seats facing each other. Summer looked up in question.

"I just thought of a better way to kill time until we reach your grandmother's place," he said, slipping his arm along the back of the seat and pulling her closer. He touched a button at his side, and a panel rose from behind the seat opposite them, giving them complete privacy. Summer felt her pulse quicken as he turned his attention to her. "Now then," he said, reaching for her and pulling her into his lap. She glanced around, anxiously at first, but the tinted windows assured her that nobody could see them. "Why don't we play a game?" he said.

She felt breathless as he looked into her eyes. "What kind of game?"

"Tell me what you're wearing underneath your dress."

She chuckled. The man never let up. "Okay, I'll give you a hint. Everything is black."

He placed his hand on her knee and rubbed his thumb back and forth. His black eyes glittered. "Won't work, babe. I need details."

She debated telling him the truth, then decided it couldn't hurt after how they'd spent the previous afternoon. Besides, she had to admit it gave her a delicious thrill to know that she was able to get him all worked up discussing her underwear. "First, I have a confession to make," she said, trying to appear coy. It was so different from the woman she presented at the office. "I have this thing for lingerie."

"Mmm. I like the sound of it already."

His husky voice almost made her shiver. She was unable to break eye contact. It was as though he were hypnotizing her. "Well," she began somewhat breathlessly, "tonight I selected a lace-up bustier and . . . matching panties."

"Details, details," he whispered enticingly.

"Okay. The lace is very delicate and intricate." She felt his palm move upward, sliding ever so slowly beneath the hem of her dress. Her breath caught in the back of her throat. "And over that I'm wearing a black slip," she said.

Cooper closed his eyes. "And silk hose." He inched his hand higher. He reached her thigh and suddenly the silk turned to flesh. He opened his eyes. "Oh, jeez, it's not what I think it is."

She could feel her heart pounding in her ears as the pupils of his eyes dilated. "Did I forget to mention the garter belt?" she said.

The satiny touch of her inner thigh aroused him instantly. Cooper sucked in his breath sharply. "You're a naughty girl for torturing me like this, missy," he said, his voice low and husky. "I'm afraid I have no choice but to punish you." Without another word he pulled her head down and captured her lips, forcing her mouth open with his tongue so that he could taste her. As he took her mouth with a savage intensity, his hand moved higher on her thigh. In a matter of seconds his deft fingers had worked their way inside her panties.

The touch of his fingers sent a shock wave through Summer's body. He dipped one finger inside her, and she was embarrassed to find she was already wet. He searched for the little bud and drew circles around it with his thumb until her body ached for release. The circles grew smaller and smaller, the pressure in her lower belly more intense. She arched against his hand and whimpered as a sensation of white-hot pleasure spiraled through her. She felt it lift her high and carry her to the edge, then, as she slowly floated back, he quickly brought her to a second orgasm. Once she was sated, he pulled his hand free and fixed her dress into place, and Summer curled against his body and closed her eyes.

"You remind me of a soft kitten," he said, pressing his lips against her forehead. "I think I'll keep you."

Summer and Cooper were the perfect picture of propriety as they sat across from Henrietta on the ride to the benefit. Nobody would have suspected what they'd been doing only moments before.

They arrived at the hotel, and their driver parked and hurried around to assist them. Cooper offered his hand to Henrietta, who climbed from the limo looking chic in a wool crepe evening suit with pearl earrings. Summer was next. As the three of them stood together for a moment, they were blinded by flashbulbs. Although the area was roped off, the media snapped pictures and tossed questions in their direction.

Summer happened to glance up at Cooper as they started for the entrance and saw that he was doing his best to avoid having his picture taken. The thought that he might be hiding something suddenly nagged at her. Once again she asked herself, what did she really know about the man? He hadn't shared one detail of his life; if it weren't for Warren, she would know zip.

Summer and Henrietta checked their wraps, and they entered the ballroom a few minutes later, where an orchestra had already begun playing. Henrietta was greeted enthusiastically by a large number of guests who quickly inquired about her health.

A woman named Helen, who was one of Henrietta's closest friends and had helped put the benefit together, chuckled. "We heard you received so many flowers that you ended up sending them to a nursing home," she said.

She spoke to Summer, then glanced in Cooper's direction. "And who is this handsome young devil?"

"Oh, forgive me," Henrietta said. "Helen, I'd like you to meet Summer's friend, Cooper Garrett. Cooper, this is Helen Fry."

"What kind of business are you in, Mr. Garrett?" Helen asked.

He hesitated. "I sell motorcycles."

The woman looked intrigued. "Oh?"

Cooper suddenly glanced around. "Can I get anybody a drink?"

"I wouldn't mind something light," Henrietta said. "Helen, would you join me in a glass of white wine?"

"Certainly, dear."

Cooper excused himself. "I'll help him," Summer told the women, then hurried behind him. She touched the sleeve of his jacket. "Where are you going in such a hurry?"

Cooper motioned to one of the many portable bars set up in the room. "I'm going for drinks."

"I know that," she said, "but why are you rushing? And why did you walk away in the middle of a conversation?"

Cooper stopped at the end of a short line that formed in front of the bar. "Why are you asking all these questions?"

"Because you're acting weird."

He shrugged. "These events make me uncomfortable."

"You didn't have to come. In fact, I tried to talk you out of it, if you remember."

The line moved up. "I came because I wanted to be with you." He tweaked her nose playfully, but his dark eyes were sincere. "Can I get you something to drink?"

She shook her head. "I'm not thirsty right now."

Once they reached the bar, Cooper ordered two glasses of wine and a scotch and water for himself. He handed one of the glasses to Summer, and they crossed the crowded ballroom in search of Henrietta and Helen. Once they handed them their wine, Henrietta told them where their table was. "It's number seven," she said. "Right next to the dance floor."

Not wanting to get caught up in another conversation, Cooper grabbed Summer's hand and led her toward the front of the room. He set his glass on the table and started to pull out her chair when the orchestra began a slow number. "Would you like to dance, Miss Pettigrew?" he said in a pronounced drawl, giving Summer a mock bow.

"Well, but of course, Mr. Garrett," she replied in a nasal tone.

Once more he led the way, and they stepped onto the dance floor, where several other couples had begun to gather. Cooper pulled her into his arms, and their eyes locked in surprise at how perfectly they fit together. "Wow," he said.

"You're holding me too close," she said, hoping no one would notice.

He leaned his head down and whispered in her ear. "That's because I suddenly have the urge to take you to bed."

His warm breath made her shiver. "Be nice, Cooper," she warned, trying to smile as though they were having a normal conversation. She tried to put some distance between them, but she was anchored against him.

"You don't want nice, Summer," he said. "Nice is boring. At least when it comes to us."

"What do you mean?"

"Oh, I don't mind dressing up for your fancy parties now and then if that's what it takes to make you happy. But I think you know what I want in return."

"It always boils down to sex with you, doesn't it?"

"Is that so wrong?"

"That's not all there is to a relationship, Cooper. What about trust and friendship? What about love and devotion? That's the glue that holds a marriage together."

He looked amused. "I didn't realize we were talking

about marriage, Summer. Is that what you want from me?"

Summer felt her cheeks flame, and she stumbled. Cooper caught her easily. "I didn't say that," she replied, irritated that he could provoke her so easily one minute and bring her to ecstasy the next. "Besides, a woman would be a fool to marry a man like you."

"And why is that, love?"

Her stomach fluttered at the endearment. "I know your type, Cooper Garrett. You'll do or say anything to get what you want out of a woman. Then, once you've stolen her heart, you'll grow bored and seek your pleasures elsewhere. Mr. Love-'Em-and-Leave-'Em."

He stopped dancing. "Have I stolen your heart, Summer?"

She was almost tempted to tell him the truth. Not only had he stolen her heart, he'd made her ache for his very touch. Even now, with his lips a heartbeat away, she wanted to taste him, drink him in. She wanted to know his every thought, touch his soul. He'd done more than steal her heart, he'd made her fall in love with him.

"Miss Pettigrew?"

Summer was only vaguely aware that someone was tugging on her sleeve. She glanced to her side and saw Helen Fry's husband standing beside her. She tried to pull herself out of her drugged state. "Hello, Mr. Fry," she managed to say.

"Sorry to interrupt," he said quickly, "but I'm afraid your grandmother is ill."

Summer glanced around frantically. "She's ill? Where is she?"

"We've taken her to the lobby. There's an ambulance on the way."

Without a word Summer hurried from the dance floor and crossed the ballroom. Cooper was beside her.

"Don't panic," he said. "We don't know if it's serious."

"It's her heart. I just know it is."

He grabbed her wrist, bringing her to a dead stop. "Summer—"

"Let me go," she demanded. "I've got to see her."

"You'll scare her to death if you go out there looking like that. You're going to have to calm down first."

Summer felt as though she were hyperventilating. She pressed her hands to her cheeks. "You're right."

"Take a deep breath," he said, rubbing the small of her back in an attempt to calm her down. She did as he said. "Another one," he ordered gently.

She felt some of the stark fear leave her body in a gush of hot air. "I'm okay now." She took his hand and they moved toward the lobby.

Henrietta was lying on a sofa with a coat covering her legs when Summer and Cooper managed to squeeze through the crowd circling her. They could hear the siren of the approaching ambulance. "Back away and give her room to breathe," Cooper shouted.

Summer rushed to her side. "How do you feel?"

"I'm better now," Henrietta said. "I told Helen it was indigestion, I always get it when I have a little wine. She insisted on calling an ambulance, worrywart that she is."

The siren was louder now. The ambulance couldn't have been more than a block away. Cooper leaned forward and scooped Henrietta off the sofa and started for the double doors leading out. "I'm perfectly capable of walking," she protested.

"You're not in charge right now, dear," he said.

The ambulance pulled in front of the entrance, and the paramedics scrambled out and opened the back doors so Cooper could slide Henrietta onto a cot. As one of the men went about checking her vital signs, Summer held her grandmother's hand and explained her heart condition. "May I ride with her to the hospital?" she asked as the other paramedic started to close the doors.

"That's fine."

"I'll meet you there," Cooper said.

In a matter of seconds the ambulance was on its way, its siren wailing loudly.

"I'm so embarrassed," Henrietta said. "I'm sure it's nothing more than indigestion. I don't know why everybody's making such a fuss."

"Please try to relax, ma'am," the attending paramedic said as he checked her blood pressure.

"I can't relax," she said. "My granddaughter has cut off the circulation to my hand."

"Oh, sorry," Summer said, loosening her grip.

"Perhaps you should give *her* something to make her relax," Henrietta told the man. She smiled at Summer. "You and Cooper looked awfully nice on the dance floor tonight. I'm beginning to think it's serious between the two of you." She watched her granddaughter closely for her reaction.

Summer noted her anxious look, and knowing how much the woman wanted her happily married, tried to put her mind at ease. "I suppose you could say that," she said, trying to affect a coy smile when her insides were quaking. "Actually, Cooper has asked me to marry him, and I said yes."

At first Henrietta was speechless. "When did all this come about?" she finally asked.

"While we were dancing," Summer replied. She realized she had just told an enormous lie, and it would take several to cover it up, but she was more concerned with making her grandmother happy. If Henrietta were to die tonight, God forbid, at least she could go in peace, knowing her granddaughter would have someone to look after her. But her grandmother didn't look especially pleased; in fact, her eyes were troubled. "What's wrong?" Summer asked. "I thought you'd be happy for us."

"Of course I'm happy, darling," the woman said. "But sometimes I worry that maybe I pushed you into this relationship."

"Don't be silly," Summer said lightly. "Cooper and I are head over heels in love. Now, I want you to stop worrying about us and concentrate on getting better. I can't imagine trying to plan a wedding without your help."

They arrived at the hospital shortly after, and Henrietta was whisked away into emergency. Summer paced the waiting room while the minutes seemed to drag. Cooper rushed through the door looking harried.

"Sorry it took so long. Traffic was bad. Do you know anything yet?"

She shook her head. "Nothing."

He put his hands on her arms and gazed at her in concern. "How are you doing?"

She glanced away, not wanting him to see how close to tears she was. "I'm okay. I don't think a person can ever be prepared for losing a loved one. I know she's seventy years old, but—" She paused as a lump filled the back of her throat and her eyes stung. "I just can't imagine life without her."

Cooper pulled her into his arms and held her tight as she silently cried. "You want to grab a cup of coffee while we wait?" he asked.

"I can't leave. They might call me."

He squeezed her. "Okay, I'll get us a cup. You sit down, I'll be right back."

When Cooper returned, he handed her a cup of coffee and a pack of cheese crackers.

"You need to eat something," he said. "Neither of us had dinner tonight."

The thought of putting food into her mouth almost

made her gag. She dropped the crackers into her purse and sipped her coffee in silence. She checked her wristwatch. "I wonder what's taking so long?"

"They'll want to check her out completely, babe," Cooper said. "Are you sure you won't eat something?"

"I should have moved back in with her until her health improved," Summer said, ignoring his question. "I can't believe how selfish I've been."

He looked confused. "Selfish? How?"

"After all she's done for me, I should have seen to it personally that she was following doctor's orders. She's all I have. She took me in and raised me because my own parents didn't want me. Her love was unconditional. I remember being so happy as a young child. Then Mrs. Bradshaw came into the picture and things changed. Every time I did something wrong, she'd tell me I was going to grow up just like my mother."

"No wonder you don't like her."

"You figured that out, huh? I was terrified of the woman while I was growing up, but mostly I was afraid she was right. I was afraid I'd grow up like my mother and bear a child out of wedlock and shame my grandmother even worse."

"I'd like to give the old woman a piece of my mind for putting you through that." He took her hand in his and gazed at her palm as though it would point out her future. "Is that why you've been afraid of intimacy?"

More tears. She nodded. "I couldn't bear the thought of bringing an unwanted child into the world, and I wasn't in love with anyone or likely to be married anytime soon. The few times I even came close to making love, I backed out at the last minute. I garnered a reputation as being a tease. One by one, the men stopped calling. My grandmother thought it was because I was a workaholic. If only she knew." Summer wiped her eyes.

"What made you decide to become intimate with me?" he asked, his voice no louder than a whisper.

She gazed at him thoughtfully. "I'm not sure. Maybe I got tired of pretending I didn't need anyone. Yesterday, when you asked me to . . . to make love, my immediate reaction was to withdraw. Once you do it long enough, it becomes a habit. But then you kissed me, and I realized I'd been paying a high price for avoiding being close to someone. Unfortunately, my anxiety returned as soon as my passion cooled," she added on a grim note.

"Perhaps one day you'll be able to let go of it."

"Trust has always been difficult for me," she confessed. "I mean, if I look at it logically, I can understand the reasons for it. Because I was abandoned by my parents, there were times I felt unloved despite all my grandmother did to prove otherwise. And as kind and loving as she was to me, I realized later in life that I hadn't trusted her as I should have. I was afraid if I became a nuisance, she'd leave me too. So I kept a lot from her. I didn't tell her how hateful Mrs. Bradshaw was at times, and I never told her about the kids teasing me for not having parents."

"Kids are cruel," Cooper agreed. "I've been there."

She looked at him. "Warren told me your father walked out when you were just a toddler."

"Yeah. So we caught our share of nasty remarks. I didn't mind it so much for myself, but I used to go crazy when they'd start on my sister, Angie."

"Ms. Pettigrew?"

Summer snapped her head up at the mention of her name. She stood quickly and found herself facing a young female doctor in green surgical garb. "How's my grandmother?" she asked quickly.

"Her EKG was normal. There was absolutely no sign of a heart attack. In fact, she says she's never felt better."

"When can I see her?"

"She should be coming out any minute."

"You mean you're releasing her?"

"I called her doctor. Neither of us saw any reason to admit her."

Summer gave Cooper a wide smile. "Did you hear that? She's okay." She looked at the doctor. "Thank you so much. You don't know how grateful I am for the news."

"I think I do," the doctor said. The doctor left them, promising to send Henrietta right out.

Cooper hugged Summer close. "See? All that worrying for nothing. Why don't you wait here, and I'll have our driver pull up to the emergency exit so your grandmother doesn't have far to walk."

"I'll call the hotel and see if I can have Helen Fry paged. I'm sure she's worried sick."

By the time a beaming Henrietta was wheeled into the waiting room, Summer had placed her call to Helen and Cooper had returned. "See, I told you it was plain old indigestion," the woman said.

Summer chuckled. "Well, I for one was worried sick. We're taking you home so you can rest. I'm even going to spend the night so I can make sure you take care of yourself."

Cooper tried to hide his disappointment. He'd been counting on spending the evening with Summer. But he knew she wouldn't be able to relax until she was certain Henrietta was going to be okay.

They wheeled Henrietta out to the waiting limo and helped her into the car. Summer was exhausted after having spent the evening so worried, and she looked forward to climbing into bed. Tomorrow she would be able to think more clearly where Cooper was concerned, but right now her mind simply wasn't functioning at full capacity.

"Summer gave me the good news," Henrietta said once they were on their way.

Cooper raised a dark eyebrow. "She did?"

"Yes, and even though I agree it was very sudden and I had my doubts at first, I couldn't be happier. I know you'll be a good husband to her."

Cooper sat there for a moment feeling as though someone had pulled the rug out from under him. He glanced at Summer for some sort of cue, but she was doing her level best not to make eye contact with him.

"I know we'd planned to keep it a secret, darling," she said, "but I hope you don't mind my telling Grandmother. She won't tell anyone."

"Nonsense!" Henrietta replied. "I'm going to shout it from the rooftops. In fact, I'm planning your engagement party as we speak. How does Saturday the twentieth sound?"

Summer gaped at her. "That's only ten days from now."

"I've put together bigger events in half that time," Henrietta said proudly. "Besides, with my health being like it is . . ." She let her words trail off as she glanced at Cooper. "I trust you'll have time to find my granddaughter an engagement ring by then. I'll be glad to give you the name of my jeweler and ask that he put it on a payment plan."

Cooper nodded dumbly as he tried to figure out how the whole thing had come about. No doubt Summer had thought her grandmother was dying and told her they were getting married so the woman wouldn't worry about her. Once again Summer had backed herself into a corner. He almost chuckled at the thought. How was she going to pull this one off? He sat up taller in his seat. "I'll start shopping for a ring immediately."

"Have you set a date yet?" Henrietta asked, then

went on excitedly before they could answer. "I hope you don't plan on having a long engagement."

"Oh, no," Cooper said. "We want to get married as soon as we can, don't we, sweetheart?" he said, grinning at Summer, who managed to smile back at him through gritted teeth. "The sooner the better," he added, giving her a hearty wink.

"Well, thank heavens for that," Henrietta said. "I can't tell you how long I've been waiting for this moment."

They pulled up in front of the estate, and the driver parked and came around to help Henrietta out. She kissed Cooper on the cheek once he'd walked both of them to the door. "I hope I didn't spoil your evening," she said.

"Not at all," he insisted. "Just try to get a good night's sleep so you'll feel better tomorrow."

"Who has time for sleep?" Henrietta said. "Summer and I will be up all night making out the guest list for your engagement party. By the way, I'll need your address and phone number so I can contact your mother. I can't wait to meet her." She took Summer by the hand and led her to the door as Mrs. Bradshaw opened it from the other side. "Put on a pot of coffee, Mrs. Bradshaw," Henrietta told her housekeeper. "Summer and I have work to do."

Cooper was forced to stifle his laughter as he watched Summer follow her grandmother inside. No doubt her mind was scrambling for ways to undo the damage. He climbed into the backseat of the limo and leaned back in the seat. Only then did he allow himself the luxury of bursting into loud, hearty guffaws. Sooner or later Summer Pettigrew was going to learn that her little white lies had a habit of blowing up in her face.

TEN

For the next three days Summer managed to avoid seeing Cooper by telling him she was up to her eyebrows in work. She could tell he didn't like it one bit, but he went along with it, albeit grudgingly. She knew she was simply trying to buy time and sort through her feelings, but sooner or later Cooper Garrett was going to demand a showdown.

On Sunday, Summer straightened her apartment, took out the trash, and sat down to work. She had worked most of the night, only to wake up at dawn unable to go back to sleep. She felt as though her brain had been stuffed with cobwebs. As she sipped yet another cup of coffee, she tried to find the file she'd been working on the previous night. She emptied her briefcase, checked beneath the sofa cushions, even looked into her kitchen cabinets, but there was no sign of the file.

The trash! She vaguely remembered tossing a stack of newspapers into a Hefty bag before carrying it out to the Dumpster. Could the file have been under the papers? Could she have inadvertently tossed it in with the rest of the trash? She groaned and went into the kitchen for her flashlight, then headed for the door.

The Dumpsters were tucked inside a tall fence behind the condominiums. As Summer stepped outside her door and started in that direction, the security guard named Jack passed by in his car and waved. She smiled and waved back.

Arriving at the Dumpster, Summer shined the light inside, hoping to find her white garbage bag. There were at least two dozen just like the one she'd tossed in. She sighed and muttered a four-letter word under her breath and, tucking the light beneath her jaw, climbed the metal ladder leading to the opening. She wrinkled her nose as she was assailed by the smell of old food. At the top of the opening, she jumped and landed in a mountain of plastic bags. She swore once more when her flashlight fell into the heap.

Armed with light, Summer began searching through each bag. She almost gagged when she opened one filled with disposable baby diapers and another one containing canned cat food. Finally, after what seemed an eternity, she found a bag stuffed with newspaper. She dug through it, and sure enough, there was her file. She glanced through it to make sure everything was in order, then dropped it outside the opening of the Dumpster. She shined her flashlight about, trying to find the ladder.

There was no ladder. There wasn't even a foothold. Summer stood there for a moment, wondering what to make of the situation. Why would somebody put a ladder on the outside and not the inside? She glanced at the opening. She would have to be an athlete to pull herself up and over to climb out. She searched through the Dumpster for something to stand on. Nothing. She tried stacking a number of bags up the side so she could boost herself up, but the minute she put her full weight on them, her shoe went through the top bag and landed in something mushy.

She grasped the opening and tried to hoist her body up, but her arms weren't strong enough.

There was no other alternative but to cry for help.

She stood close to the opening. "Hello, is anyone out there? Would somebody help me?" she cried out as loud as she could. She waited. "Can anybody hear me?" she yelled, banging on the side of the Dumpster. She waited some more.

Half an hour passed, during which time she called out and banged her fists against the metal as hard as she could. What if nobody threw their trash out today, and she was forced to spend the entire day and night in the Dumpster? What if the temperature were to drop during the night? What if— No, she wouldn't allow herself to think about the possibility of rats or cockroaches.

Wanting to sit down but too terrified to do so, Summer merely stood there, trying to keep herself from crying. There had to be a way out. Finally, too exhausted to care whether a rabid rat bit her on the behind or not, she dropped onto a heap of bags. She pulled her knees up and anchored her chin on top.

And waited.

She dozed.

She was startled awake when she thought she heard the sound of a lawn mower. She blinked several times, trying to get her bearings. No, wait a minute. That was no lawn mower, it was a motorcycle. Was she dreaming? The engine died, and all was silent. "Is anybody out there?" she cried, trying to push herself into a standing position. She heard footsteps. A second later Cooper peered into the opening.

"Well, lookie there," he said. "Somebody has gone and thrown away a perfectly good woman."

She went weak with relief. "Oh, thank God you're

here!" she said, scrambling to get up. "Please help me out of here."

"*Help* you? Did I hear you ask for *help?*" He frowned. "Gee, I don't know. You've pretty much convinced me you don't need anyone. I'd hate to ruin that tough-as-nails image of yours."

"Cooper, that isn't a damn bit funny. I'm terrified of rats and roaches. Just the thought of them—" She paused and shuddered violently.

He shook his head sadly. "Sorry, doll. I think you're going to have to get out of this one on your own. How would you ever live with yourself if you discovered there might be a needy side of you?" He started to climb down the ladder.

"Wait! You're not just going to leave me in here?"

"You'll get out," he said confidently. "If I know you, you'll think of a way."

She burst into tears. "I've already *tried* to get out," she said. "I wouldn't be asking for your help if I were able to."

His look softened. "Okay, I'll help you, babe. Come closer."

She stumbled toward the opening, shining her flashlight in her path so she didn't step on something that might be alive. Once she reached the side, she turned off the flashlight and handed it to Cooper, who laid it on top of the Dumpster.

"I can't wait to hear your explanation of why you're in there," he said. "Were you running low on grocery money?"

She was still crying. "I'm in no mood for jokes, Cooper. Just get me out."

He offered his hands. "Grab my wrists, and I'll pull you up."

"I've already tried to pull myself up. It didn't work."

"That's 'cause you're a wimp, and I'm a big, strong man," he said. "Come on, grab hold."

She closed her hands around his wrists, and he did the same. Without so much as a grunt of effort he pulled her straight up. "Watch your head," he said, trying to get her through the opening. "Now swing one leg over the side . . . there you go."

A moment later Summer was standing on the pavement beside him, feeling utterly ridiculous over the fact she was still crying and he was doing everything in the world to comfort her. "How did you know where to find me?" she asked, glancing up at his rugged face.

"When the security guard called your number to see if you wanted company, he got no answer. We both thought it was strange, since your car was parked right in front of your building. Then he remembered seeing you walking in the direction of the Dumpsters and asked me to have a look. I never imagined I'd find you inside."

Summer reached for her file. "I accidentally threw something important away."

"How long have you been back here?"

"I don't know. At least an hour. I fell asleep."

"Well, you stink something fierce," he said, grinning.

"I stepped in something. I need a shower."

"You also look like you need a nap. How many hours did you sleep last night?"

"Not many. I was restless."

"Have you had breakfast?"

"Just coffee. I haven't had time to buy groceries."

"I figured as much. I stopped by the store on the way. While you take a shower, I'll whip up something."

She was too tired and hungry to argue. She hopped on the back of his bike, and they rode the short distance to her front door, where a single bag of groceries sat. Summer kicked off her shoes and went inside with

Cooper right behind. "I won't be long," she said, climbing the stairs toward her bedroom.

When she emerged from the shower twenty minutes later, she had scrubbed from head to toe and washed her long hair twice. By the time she came downstairs, she found Cooper putting their plates on the table, eggs Benedict of all things, and a small bowl of grapefruit sections. "Have a seat," he told her, then leaned over for a quick sniff. "You smell much better. You ready for a fresh cup of coffee?" he asked.

"Yes, please."

"I tossed your sneakers in the washer."

"Thanks, Cooper." She reached for her napkin and paused as she studied the place setting before her. You would have thought they were having brunch at a fancy hotel the way he'd set the table. Each dish and eating utensil was in its proper place. "Gee, everything looks so nice," she said, wondering where a bike mechanic who wore leather jackets had learned to set such a nice table and prepare a fancy breakfast.

She ate her grapefruit sections first, watching him as she did so. His manners were as impeccable as they'd been the night of her grandmother's dinner party. Something didn't quite jibe.

"Is something wrong?" he asked.

"Huh?" She blinked. "Oh, no. My mind just drifted." She yawned wide.

"You look dead on your feet, Summer. I'll bet none of the other ad executives at Worth are putting in your hours. Why don't you ease up?"

She shrugged. "I don't know."

"Sure you do. We talked about it the other night at the hospital, this crazy need you have to prove yourself. Well, guess what? The only person you really have to please in this world is yourself."

She took a bite of her eggs. "These are delicious," she said.

"Don't change the subject." He leaned forward on his elbows and studied her intently. "How come you haven't gone out on your own?"

"On my own?" Her heart skipped a beat at the thought. "Oh, no, I couldn't—"

"Why? I've seen your work. You know damn well you're good enough."

She hesitated. "I would be taking such a chance," she said.

"That's what life's all about, babe. Taking chances. You're talking to a pro here."

She studied him. "You know what's odd?" she said. "You know everything about me, and I know almost nothing about you."

"You know more about what's going on inside me than most people," he said, then went on to another subject. "After breakfast I want you to take a nap." She opened her mouth to protest. "I insist," he said. "Think how far behind you're going to be if you get sick."

"It's hard for me to relax right now with so much going on. The work at the office and—" She sighed heavily. "My grandmother is driving me crazy with that blasted engagement party. I've tried to convince her to wait, but you know how she is."

"Speaking of engagement parties." He reached for his jacket and dug into one pocket. "You might need this," he said, setting a velvet box before her.

Summer put down her fork and reached for the small box. She opened it and almost gasped at the sight of what had to be one of the biggest diamond rings she'd ever seen. She figured it somewhere between ten and twelve karats. "Oh, Cooper. It's beautiful. And it looks . . . so real."

"What makes you think it's *not* real?" he said.

She met his amused gaze and wondered why he enjoyed teasing her so. "I happen to know what diamonds cost, pal."

"Try it on," Cooper said.

Summer slipped it on her finger. "It's a little loose, but not much."

"I can have it sized by Saturday."

"Don't bother, I'm sure it'll be fine."

Cooper looked concerned. "Well, try not to lose it, okay?"

"If I do, I'll personally replace it. Stop worrying." She finished her breakfast and insisted on cleaning up while Cooper finished his coffee. She chatted about the other accounts she was working on, and he told her about the biker's convention he would be attending soon in Japan.

"Japan?" she said, her heart tumbling at the thought of him going so far away. "Did you get a promotion?"

He shifted in his chair. "Yeah, something like that. I'll probably be over there a couple of weeks."

"Congratulations," she said, noting his discomfort and suspecting he didn't want her to make a big deal of it. He obviously wasn't the sort of man who liked to toot his own horn. Nevertheless, two weeks seemed like a lifetime. Funny how her feelings had changed almost overnight. She'd been trying to think of a way to spend less time with him; now the thought of his being away made her sad. It also made her wish she were in a position to go with him. She couldn't remember the last time she had a vacation.

Cooper was staring at her bare finger. "What'd you do with the ring?" he asked quickly.

"Oh, I took it off while I was rinsing dishes."

"You need to keep it in the box when you're not wearing it," he said. "Otherwise, you might misplace it."

Summer thought he was making a big deal out of a

piece of costume jewelry, but she decided to go along with him. "Sorry, I'll be more careful."

Once he'd returned the ring to its proper place, he pulled her from her chair. "Now, about that nap. Come on. I'll rub your back until you fall asleep."

It was useless to protest. Summer made her way up the stairs with him close behind. He insisted on unplugging the phone in her bedroom. "Climb in," he said once he'd pulled down the comforter. He kicked off his own shoes while waiting for her to do so.

Summer crawled beneath the covers. "I'm telling you, it's useless," she said. "I'm too wired to sleep."

He lay down beside her, remaining on top of the comforter. The last thing he needed to do was snuggle against her warm body and get turned on. "Now, turn over," he said.

She did so. With both of them lying on their sides, Cooper began to rub her tense neck and shoulder muscles and massage her back as well. "You were serious about trying to get me to fall asleep," she said after a few minutes.

"Yeah, why?"

"I thought you were really looking to make love."

"Maybe later. Right now you need rest more than anything."

Summer closed her eyes as his big hands kneaded away all her tension. She *did* feel cherished and protected when he was around. For a woman who'd spent much of her life being in complete control, it felt good to know she could let go.

But letting go also meant giving someone else power over you, risking pain and heartache. As she lay there, she remembered reading from Kahlil Gibran's *The Prophet* how love often caused as much pain as it did happiness. But for those who chose not to take the risk, they chose to live in a seasonless world. Had she been living in such a world?

Summer drifted off to sleep in a matter of minutes. Cooper lay there quietly, listening to her steady breathing. He didn't like to see her push herself so hard. When he was certain she was sleeping soundly, he got up from the bed and made his way downstairs. Trying to kill time until she woke up, he found her Sunday paper on the kitchen counter, still folded. He carried it into the living room and lay down on the sofa, propping his head on several throw pillows.

When Summer opened her eyes sometime later, she saw that she'd slept almost three hours. She felt more rested and relaxed than she had in weeks. She rolled over and found, much to her disappointment, that Cooper was gone. She went into the bathroom, washed her face and brushed her teeth, then ran a brush through her hair. When she came out of the bathroom she found Cooper stretched out on the bed.

"I heard you were up," he said. "I was beginning to think you'd gone into hibernation."

She walked over to the bed and sat down on the edge. "I guess I was more tired than I thought."

"How do you feel now?"

She laughed. "Like I just woke up from a long winter's nap."

He toyed with her hair. "You're going to have to slow down, babe. Why don't you take the rest of the day off? We can go to a movie and have dinner afterward."

Summer glanced at her wristwatch. "It's two o'clock now," she said. "That still gives us a couple of hours."

"What do you want to do until then?"

She smiled, slid closer, and started unbuttoning his shirt. "Does this answer your question?"

The smile he gave her would have melted a frozen creek. "I think I get your drift."

Their gazes locked as they undressed each other. Cooper kissed and stroked her until she became wet and eager for him. His hands trembled as he grappled with a condom, then pulled her on top of him, impaling her slowly in case she was still sore. She cried out softly and sank against his chest, her long hair falling across them like a silken shawl. He cupped her hips in his hands and anchored her against him as he began to thrust, slowly at first, then faster. She climaxed only a moment before him, and they shared a deep kiss as they drifted back to earth in each other's arms.

On Monday, Henrietta called Summer to let her know she'd set Cooper and her up to have their engagement pictures made the next day so they'd be ready to go to the newspaper the following Monday. Summer, who was still on a cloud after having spent the night in Cooper's arms, was forced to do a reality check. Her friends and coworkers would see the picture and naturally ask questions. She had to put a stop to it before she became a laughingstock and scandalized the Pettigrew name.

She finally called Joyce into her office and confessed everything. Her friend and assistant had a dazed look on her face by the time Summer finished.

"How far are you planning to carry this thing?" the woman asked.

Summer shook her head sadly. "Right now I'm so confused, I can face only one day at a time."

"How does Cooper feel about it?"

"I think he's amused that I got myself into this situation to begin with, but I was in such a state of panic at the time. I expected my grandmother's heart to give out right there in that ambulance." She shook her head sadly. "I never thought a few lies could snowball into something like this."

Joyce gazed at her for a moment. "You're in love with him," she said matter-of-factly.

Summer nodded reluctantly, but she didn't look happy about the fact. "Yes, I love him," she confessed, "but believe me, nothing good could come of a relationship with the man. He's not the marrying kind."

"He might surprise you. He was certainly willing to tear Sam Flynn apart on your behalf."

"It's a farce, Joyce. Cooper's agreed to play along until my grandmother's health improves. After that he's off the hook. I just wanted you to know the truth because you'll probably be invited to the engagement party."

"Listen, kid. A man does not agree to something like this unless he has a very good reason. I think Cooper's just as smitten with you as you are with him."

"Smitten is not the word for it," Summer said. "He's made it plain from the beginning that he's more interested in sex than in anything else."

"Ah, so the two of you have been intimate," Joyce said, and the blush on Summer's face confirmed it. She chuckled. "Well, that's certainly a good sign on your part. How was it?"

Summer tried to hide her embarrassment but failed miserably. "It was wonderful, Joyce," she confessed after a moment. "More than I imagined it could be. That's what scares me so much. I mean, Cooper and I are so different."

"Yes, but isn't that what attracted you to him in the first place? The fact he *was* so different from the men you'd dated?"

Summer pondered it. "I suppose that was part of it, but there's something else. I can't really explain it. Sometimes he seems almost . . . primitive in his beliefs on how things should be between a man and woman. I'm intrigued, but at the same time a little frightened over how intense he can be."

"Are you saying he wants to keep you barefoot and pregnant?"

"Not exactly, but I think he expects to be first in my life at all times."

"Which is how it should be," Joyce said. "If you love someone, you automatically place them first. That doesn't mean you can't have a career, friends, and family, but your priorities change once you've met the person you want to spend the rest of your life with. Wouldn't you expect him to place you first?"

"I suppose."

"Well, there you have it. Any more questions Aunt Joyce can help you with?"

Summer chuckled. "I think that about does it for one day. I'll need time to ruminate."

Joyce snapped her finger. "By the way, Max gave me a message for you. Remember that nonprofit organization called The Good Shepherd? They called back. Seems the guy in charge talked to a couple of our competitors but didn't care for their ideas. He wants Worth Advertising to reconsider taking them on. They've managed to come up with a little more money. Max sort of slipped the information under the table to me because he knew you wanted the account. But if Worth happens to find out—"

"I'll make sure Max's name doesn't come up. Listen, Joyce, if I do take the account, I'm going to need your help."

Joyce looked thrilled at the prospect. "You know how long I've waited for a chance like this. Let me get their phone number for you." She started for the door and paused. "What if Mr. Worth *does* find out you went behind his back on this one?"

"I'll have to face that problem if and when it comes up."

Henrietta welcomed private investigator Don Rhodes into her den and asked him to sit. "I believe you've met my driver and close friend, Axel Jones," she said, introducing the two.

"Yes, we've been in touch a couple of times."

Henrietta noted the slim file in Rhodes's hand and shifted uncomfortably in her chair. "And you were able to learn something about Mr. Garrett?"

"Indeed I was. I can sum it up by saying I have good news and bad news." He opened the file as if to read the information, but Henrietta interrupted him. "Mr. Rhodes, would you mind just leaving the file with me so I might look at it in my own good time?"

He looked surprised. Finally, he shrugged and handed her the file. "If that's what you prefer."

"I believe it would be easier this way. You know where to send the bill?"

He nodded, then stood. "Well, if you don't need my services further, I'll be going. Feel free to contact me if you have questions."

"I'll see you out," Axel said. He disappeared for a few minutes while Henrietta stared at the closed file in her lap. When her driver returned, he closed the door once more. "Is something wrong, Mrs. Pettigrew?"

"Yes, something is very much wrong here," she said. "I have no business prying into Mr. Garrett's personal life. I raised my granddaughter to believe everyone on this earth was equal and that a person should not be judged by what kind of work they do or how much they're worth. If Summer loves Cooper and wants to marry him, that's good enough for me." She offered Axel the file. "Please destroy this immediately."

He took it. "Consider it done."

The week passed quickly as Summer worked on various accounts, calling Warren long distance several times to brainstorm ideas about those they shared. With nothing else to do, he sounded only too eager to assist. "I know I haven't been pulling my weight lately," he said, "but that's going to change once I get on my feet again."

"Why the sudden change of heart?" Summer asked.

"I could have lost my life in that accident. While I waited for the ambulance to arrive, all I kept thinking about was how I'd wasted a lot of years chasing skirts and hanging out in singles' bars. Well, I'm going to turn my life around."

Summer remembered what Cooper had said about Warren stealing college tests and paying someone to write his research papers, and she suspected there was some truth to it. Had he begun to feel guilty now that he'd had time to think? "Don't be so hard on yourself, Warren. If I've learned one thing in this life, it's that people can and do change. It sounds like you're ready to do just that."

They talked a few more minutes. Summer told him about losing Sam Flynn as a client and the reasons why, then her decision to take on the Good Shepherd account despite Mr. Worth telling her not to.

"Just be careful," Warren said. "You know how hard it is to keep secrets in that company. Some of the older guys still resent having a woman on board unless she types and takes dictation. Beardsly and Tatum would kill for this kind of information. They'd consider it a real feather in their cap if they could go to Worth with something like this."

She sighed. "Sometimes I think I'd be better off if I went out on my own."

There was dead silence at the other end. "You mean quit Worth Advertising?" he asked at last, sounding surprised.

"At least I could pick and choose my accounts."

"You know, that might not be such a bad idea. As a matter of fact, I might be interested in going in with you. Partners. Fifty-fifty. I think the old creative juices would flow easier if old man Worth weren't always breathing down our necks."

Summer wasn't sure she'd want Warren as her partner, knowing how he worked. Or, rather, how he *didn't* work. He might be ready to change for the better at the moment, but the moment a pretty face showed up he'd forget his promises. "It's just a thought," she said. "I'm not sure I'd be brave enough to give up a regular paycheck and strike out on my own like that."

"You *wouldn't* be on your own," he reminded her. "You'd have me."

"I have to think about it, Warren. I'm not about to make a decision like that without giving it a great deal of thought." They chatted a little longer. By the time they hung up, Warren had convinced her to keep an open mind about them going into business together.

Cooper dropped by most evenings with carry-out or something to cook on the grill. He often listened to Summer's ideas about one project or another and offered suggestions of his own. When Summer told him she was meeting with the staff from The Good Shepherd behind Mr. Worth's back, he seemed genuinely pleased.

Summer found him indispensable, running errands, taking her car in for an oil change, keeping her cupboards stocked and the coffee fresh. "I don't know what I would have done without you this past week," she said one night as he was about to leave.

"Be careful, Ms. Pettigrew," he said. "You sound like a woman who needs a man in her life. Next thing I know, you'll have me swimming moats and slaying dragons."

She averted her gaze. "I was just trying to say thank you for your help," she said, determined not to let him think she was helpless. "I'm not in the market for a knight in shining armor."

He gave her a knowing smile, then kissed her and left. She stood in the doorway several minutes, wondering how he'd managed to insinuate himself so quickly into her life. Later, as she was lying in bed, it occurred to her that Cooper had not pressed for sex all week. Had he lost interest? She realized she'd been worrying about something like that happening all along. He had managed to win her trust to an extent and get her in bed; could it be that he'd lost interest now that he'd accomplished what he'd set out to do?

Her thoughts were troubled as she drifted off to sleep.

On Friday, Summer and Joyce met with the founders of The Good Shepherd, a once-wealthy middle-aged couple by the name of Joe and Marian Smyth, who, unable to make ends meet despite government aid, had contributed their last dime to the needs of the children. With funds running low and more children coming into the facility each month, their situation had become dire. They felt many of the children could be successfully placed with couples who were looking to adopt, but they needed to get the word out.

The home, a sprawling one-story building south of the airport, housed almost forty children, some of whom had spent much of their lives with geriatric patients in various nursing homes before coming to The Good

Shepherd, where they received more attention and stimulation.

After visiting with the children and staff, the Smyths invited Summer and Joyce for a cup of coffee in their office. "Now that you've seen the place, are you sure you want to take us on?" Joe asked.

"I've never been more certain of anything in my life," Summer told them. Joyce echoed her sentiments.

"Naturally, we were thrilled when Worth Advertising agreed to help us," Marian said. "It won't be easy convincing couples to take on a physically or emotionally challenged child. Your company has a reputation of being the very best. I just hope we can afford your services."

Summer shifted in her chair. "Joyce and I won't actually be working on behalf of Worth Advertising," she said. "We'll be handling your account in our spare time at no cost." Joe and Marian exchanged surprised looks. "You'll be getting the same quality you'd expect at Worth, and we'll try every way possible to come up with an inexpensive advertising plan that will offer you the most exposure. It would be better if you contacted me at home instead of the office if you need to discuss your account." She handed Marian her business card. "You can leave a message on my machine, and I'll get back to you as soon as possible."

"Of course," Marian said. "We certainly don't want to do anything to get you into trouble with your job."

"We don't quite know what to say," Joe replied, looking a bit dazed. "I mean, we do have *some* money. We were planning to use it for new playground equipment and a new van for outings."

"I can't think of a better way to spend it," Summer said. "Have you tried to advertise on your own?"

Joe shrugged. "We run a small ad in the newspaper from time to time, but it really hasn't panned out except to capture the attention of every prank caller in the city."

"I know you haven't had much time to think about it," Marian said, "but do you have any ideas?"

Summer didn't hesitate. "There are several avenues I'd like to explore. Give us a few days to think about it," she said. "We'll get back to you as soon as we can."

The Smyths walked them to a small reception area and shook hands. "We appreciate your generosity," Marian said. "These little troopers have come to mean an awful lot to us. We want to see them raised in a loving home."

"We'll do our best," Summer promised. But as she drove away with Joyce beside her, they wondered aloud if people would be able to open their hearts and arms to a child who was in such need.

By ten o'clock Friday evening, Summer was surprised and a little baffled that Cooper hadn't called or come by. All her insecurities sprang to life. She had caught up with her most pressing work and looked forward to a little R&R, but it didn't hold much meaning for her if she had to spend the time alone. Suddenly realizing she hadn't eaten since lunch, she tossed a low-fat frozen dinner into her microwave and ate it while watching a Barbara Walters special. She was in bed by eleven-fifteen with a good mystery novel but couldn't concentrate.

Cooper had been acting strange all week. While he'd been pleasant and helpful, he'd backed off where intimacy was involved. Summer had made an appointment with her gynecologist; in the meantime, she'd selected a form of birth control from her pharmacy that was touted as being highly effective. She planned to use it until she met with her gyn to discuss other alternatives. The small white bag containing her purchase from the drugstore was still in the drawer in her nightstand waiting to be used. She looked at the empty pillow beside her and hated the feelings it gave her. She thought of the secretaries at work who complained about sitting home all weekend waiting for the phone to ring, and she promised herself she would not resort to that. She unplugged the phone, switched off the light, and forced herself to stop thinking about Cooper. Unfortunately, her thoughts could not be turned on and off like a water faucet. She was a long time falling asleep.

Summer awoke the following morning at nine, feeling refreshed. She spent the morning sipping coffee and reading her newspaper. When the phone rang at ten, she grabbed it up and found Cooper on the other end of the line. "I hope I didn't wake you," he said.

"No, I've been up for a while," she told him. She paused, waiting for him to explain why he hadn't stopped by the night before.

"I just wanted to let you know I'll pick you up about seven tonight. You haven't lost the ring, I hope."

"Of course not." He obviously had no intention of telling her where he'd been or what he'd been doing.

"So what's on the agenda for today?" he asked.

"Well, I'm pretty much caught up on everything. I've decided to spend the day goofing off."

"Good for you."

"I might go shopping."

"It's about time you had a little fun. Do you think you can remember how?"

"You make me sound boring."

"You need to cut yourself some slack, that's all. Well, I just wanted to touch base with you. I've got to go back to work now. I'll pick you up at seven."

Summer hung up the phone feeling a bit pensive. He didn't sound as though something were wrong; in fact, he'd been upbeat. But where was the old Cooper who liked to flirt and make off-color innuendos? Perhaps he was trying to prove he could be a gentleman since she'd harped on it so many times. If that was the case, she would have to let him know she preferred the old Cooper.

Did he really wonder if she'd forgotten how to have fun? Maybe he was beginning to get bored with her. Perhaps that's why he hadn't dropped by. She *could* be a stick-in-the-mud at times, especially where her career was concerned. She shouldn't have to keep proving herself to Edwin Worth after all this time, especially since she had landed some of the most lucrative accounts. But each year she watched another ad executive receive a fat bonus check and the coveted gold and walnut plaque that deemed him most valuable employee of the year.

Cooper was right; it wasn't worth it.

Summer reached for her telephone book and called her hairdresser to see if she could get an appointment. The woman had received a cancellation and could take Summer at three o'clock. The manicurist could see her at four-thirty. Summer hurried upstairs for a quick shower, dragged on a pair of light wool slacks and cotton shirt, and was out of the house in less than half an hour.

The parking lot at the mall was already filling up, but Summer managed to find a spot near Saks Fifth Avenue. She spent three hours trying on various suits in spring colors as well as an assortment of evening wear. She breezed through the shoe department and tipped an employee generously to help her carry her belongings to her car. She grabbed a grilled chicken sandwich and coffee from a fast food restaurant and drove to her three o'clock hair appointment.

Summer arrived home with less than an hour to bathe and dress. Luckily, her hair, makeup, and nails were done so she ran a tepid bubble bath of lily of the valley and soaked for twenty minutes. The outfit she'd bought for the evening, a midnight-blue slip dress, hugged her slender figure and drew attention to her new hairstyle. She'd been nervous about cutting the thick mane, but her hair-dresser had convinced her to try a new look. It now hung slightly past her shoulders in generous waves and curls. Summer had also allowed the woman to put in a few highlights which not only lightened it but added body. She selected a simple diamond choker, matching earrings and tennis bracelet, and pronounced herself ready.

The doorbell rang a few minutes after seven, and Summer's stomach fluttered as she considered the surprise she had in store for Cooper. She'd teach *him* to ignore her, by golly. She checked her silk stockings for runs and stepped into satin midnight-blue heels with crossover straps and a rhinestone button. She grabbed her wrap and hurried down the stairs. She opened the door and her heart almost stopped at the sight of him in a gray suit with black silk shirt. Had there ever been any doubt in her mind that she was in love with him? "Hi, stud. Guess what? I'm not wearing panties."

Summer sensed something was wrong the minute the words left her mouth. Not only did Cooper not respond with a sizzling comeback, he gave an embarrassed cough and stepped aside. Behind him, a petite, dark-haired woman in a rose-colored chemise dress and jacket stood there blinking furiously, as though unsure what to do or say next. A simple gold cross hung from a chain around her neck.

"Summer, I'd like you to meet my mother, Vivian Garrett."

ELEVEN

It would have been easier if the earth had split open and swallowed her, but Summer was forced to stand there and shake the woman's hand as though nothing out of the ordinary had occurred. "It's so nice to meet you, Mrs. Garrett," she said, feeling as though her cheeks would burst into flames and singe her new hairstyle.

"I have been very eager to meet the woman who stole my son's heart," Cooper's mother responded politely. "And please call me Vivian."

"We should probably be on our way," Cooper said, motioning toward a black Lincoln Continental. Summer wanted to ask him how he'd come by it, then decided she'd keep quiet for the time being. He helped his mother into the backseat, then escorted Summer to the passenger's side.

"I'm so embarrassed," she muttered before he opened the door. He merely smiled and waited for her to climb in.

Summer did her best to keep conversation flowing as Cooper drove toward her grandmother's house. She turned in her seat. "I understand you and your son have a small farm north of the city," she told Vivian.

The woman smiled. "Yes. We're very proud of it. I've always wanted a place where I could have all the dogs and cats I wanted. Cooper has his horses, of course, but I'm afraid of them. You'll have to visit sometime."

"I'd love to," Summer replied. "I used to ride as a child, but I haven't had much time for it since college." She noted the sudden tensing of Cooper's jaw. Perhaps he didn't want her to visit. After seeing the mansion she'd been raised in, he might not feel comfortable taking her home. Also, he might be embarrassed over the fact he was still living with his mother. She would have to tell him that none of it mattered. Her opinions seemed to have changed overnight.

"By the way, I love your outfit," Summer said, noting the woman had exceptional taste. The dress and jacket had to have cost in the neighborhood of several hundred dollars. She regretted that Vivian had been forced to spend so much on a single evening dress when she suspected the money could have been put to better use. The engagement party was creating hardships for everyone involved.

"Your grandmother sent it," Vivian said. "She called me up, asked my size and coloring, and the next thing I knew I had a new frock for the ball, so to speak. She has exquisite taste."

Summer was relieved that her grandmother had thought of it. "Yes, she does," she said.

If Summer had expected Cooper's mother to be intimidated by the size of her grandmother's estate, the woman looked anything but. Vivian remarked how lovely the place was and asked intelligent questions about the architecture. "You know, I feel I already know your grandmother," she said. "I read about her constantly. She has done so much for this city. I suppose that's why I decided to become more involved with the community once I retired."

"I'm sure Grandmother will be flattered," Summer said.

Henrietta greeted them warmly once they arrived. Wearing a deep emerald-green dress with pearl earrings and necklace, she looked as though she'd never had a sick day in her life. Once Summer introduced her to Vivian, Henrietta took the woman under her wing and began presenting her to friends. Although Summer had recovered somewhat from her embarrassment, she was thankful to have a moment alone with Cooper. He immediately grabbed her hand and led her away from the crowd. A moment later he pulled her into a storage closet and closed the door.

He pulled her against him and skimmed his big hands up the backs of her thighs, past the gartered stockings to where she was completely naked. He cupped her behind. "You little witch," he whispered, his mouth a fraction of an inch from hers. "What do you mean showing up without your bra and panties?"

Summer sucked her breath in sharply as he began drawing delightful circles around her buttocks. "I thought you'd like my new look," she said, her voice little more than a croak. "You're always implying that I'm too conservative."

He took her full bottom lip with his teeth. "Of course I like it. But it tears my guts out when other men look at you. I want you for myself." Even as he spoke, he searched for the warm cleft between her thighs, and his arousal grew to new heights when he found her already damp. His eyes locked with hers. "If a man ever touches you like this, or kisses you here, I'll kill him with my bare hands, so help me."

Summer shivered with the intensity of his gaze, and she knew he spoke the truth. It was frightening to think a man could be that possessive; nevertheless, she could feel her body responding to his words as well as his touch. It was on her lips to tell him she would never be happy with another man after having him, but she remembered how insecure she'd felt the previous night when he hadn't called. "Cooper, I don't think this is the time or place—"

She was hushed when he dipped his finger deep inside her. After that, all logical thinking ceased. She slipped her arms around his neck and let him work his magic. She cried out softly as the pleasure peaked and left her trembling in his arms.

Cooper unfastened his pants, shoved them past his hips, and lifted her in his arms. He entered her swiftly. Summer closed her eyes and gave in to the pleasure of being filled with him. He rocked her slowly until they were both gasping. Her second climax was perfectly in tune with his.

"Let's leave the party," he whispered as he grew soft inside of her. "And go to your place. I want to spend the evening in your bed." He put her down. As he pulled up his underwear and pants, Summer fixed her dress into place and smoothed out the wrinkles.

"We can't leave our own engagement party," she said. "What would people think? I've already made a bad impression on your mother."

"Don't be silly. She's crazy about you." He kissed her. "By the way, I like your hair. I feel like I'm dating a college girl."

"I'm glad I was able to finally get your attention."

He looked bewildered. "What do you mean? You've had my undivided attention since I first laid eyes on you."

"You seemed a little . . . distant this week."

"That's because I knew you were under a lot of pressure. I figured the last thing you needed was some horny guy trying to drag you into the bedroom every fifteen minutes." He smacked her on her bottom. "See, I *can* be a gentleman when the occasion calls for it."

She was instantly relieved. She tossed him a smile over her shoulder. "I've already decided I prefer you just the way you are."

"Good. Because I plan to make up for lost time now that you've caught up with your work. By the time I get finished with you—" He paused and grinned. "I think I'll leave the rest to your imagination."

They stepped out of the closet and almost ran into Henrietta and Vivian. "What on earth are you two doing in the storage closet?" Henrietta asked, then colored fiercely. "Never mind, I think Vivian and I are better off not knowing."

Vivian looked from Summer to Cooper, then glanced at Henrietta. "I can see we're going to have to insist on a brief engagement. They'll hurt themselves sneaking in closets and such." The two women chuckled and hurried away.

"I have to use the little girls' room," Summer whispered. "Why don't you grab a cocktail."

"I'd rather go with you."

She blushed. "Behave yourself."

"I thought you were tired of me pretending to be a gentleman."

"Okay, how about you agree to act like one in public, then once we're alone you can be yourself." She left him and made her way to the half-bath. Inside, she chuckled as she recalled the night she'd squeezed in there with him and demanded to know who he was. He'd looked like the worst hood. Now that she had a better understanding of his past, she could see how it had shaped him. If he came off sounding tough, it was because it had been necessary at one time. But she'd learned he could be thoughtful and caring as well, and she'd discovered brief periods of vulnerability that made her love him all the more. She hoped one day he would trust her enough to tell her about his past.

Summer was washing her hands at the pedestal sink when she felt the ring slip from her finger. She tried to grab it, but missed, and it disappeared down the drain. "Oh, no," she muttered, knowing Cooper wouldn't be pleased. She hurried out, wondering the best way to break the news to him. He'd showed such concern over her losing it, one would have thought it was worth thousands. She found him talking to a man who'd made his fortune in real estate. "Bad news," she said. "My ring fell down the drain."

The easygoing smile he'd worn a moment before turned to shock. "Tell me you're joking."

"I wish I were."

Cooper excused himself from the man he was speaking with and searched for Henrietta. He quickly explained the situation. "Oh, my," she said. "I'll have to close off the downstairs bath and request the guests use the one upstairs until I can get a plumber in. I'll have Mrs. Bradshaw put in a call right away."

Summer arrived to hear the tail end of the conversation. "Why are you going to such a fuss?" she asked. "I told you I'd replace the ring if something happened to it."

He frowned at her. "Maybe it has sentimental value, okay?" he said. "Besides, what would people think if I didn't at least make an attempt to retrieve it?"

"You're right," she said, remembering how her friends had made such a big deal over its size. They'd naturally assume it was a fake if Cooper didn't try to recover it.

Cooper was pacing the floor by the time the plumber arrived, a stocky man in avocado-green bib overalls. He had a dead cigar tucked at the corner of his mouth. "Don't get bent out of shape yet," he told Cooper.

"You'd be surprised how many rings I've pulled from the bottom of drainpipes. Has anyone used the sink since it went down?"

Cooper shook his head. "I personally guarded the door till you could get here."

The plumber first checked the stopper. "Sometimes these things catch 'em before they go down," he said, talking around his stogie. "Unfortunately, that's not the case here. I trust this ring is insured." Cooper didn't reply one way or the other, but he stayed by the man's side while he took the pipes apart. Sure enough, he found the ring. "Well, now, this'n is a whopper," he said, handing it to Cooper. "I don't blame you for being nervous." He went about putting the pipes back together. "Tell your fiancée to have it sized as soon as she can so she won't risk losing it again," he said.

Cooper thanked him and paid the bill. He also tipped the man generously for coming over on his day off. The plumber was so impressed, he gave Cooper his card and told him to call anytime.

Once Cooper had returned the ring to Summer's finger, the guests cheered. "Try to hang on to it," he said.

The evening went exceedingly well despite the ring mishap. A portable bar had been set up in the living room, and the bartender convinced Summer to try one of his special mint juleps. "Make it a light one," she said, knowing she had a low tolerance for alcohol. She sipped the drink slowly as she and Cooper chatted with guests. They were asked the usual questions—where had they met, when was the wedding, and had they decided where they would honeymoon.

Summer told them she and Cooper had not had a chance to work out the details. She noticed how he skirted around some of the questions people posed to him, mostly about his career, and she wondered if he was ashamed of being a motorcycle mechanic. She made a mental note to discuss it with him later. If she'd had reservations about his line of work before, she didn't now.

The furniture had been removed from the oversized sun room at the back of the house, and a three-piece ensemble played mood music. The guests insisted Cooper and Summer dance. As before, it was as though an electric charge had gone off once their bodies touched.

Once most of the guests had left, Cooper assisted his mother and Summer into the Lincoln. They dropped Summer off at her condo first, and she thanked Vivian for attending their party and promised to call her soon. Cooper walked her to the door. "I'd give you a passionate kiss, but we have an audience at the moment."

"I'll take a rain check," she said. "Will I see you tomorrow?"

He hesitated. "I'm probably going to have to work most of the weekend," he said. "Remember the convention I was telling you about? It starts next weekend. I'm trying to get things lined up. Maybe we can have dinner."

She tried not to look disappointed, but she couldn't help but wonder what she'd done with all her time before he'd shown up in her life. "Okay. Just call me."

He kissed her briefly and walked away.

Vivian Garrett gazed at her son thoughtfully as he helped her into the front seat of the Lincoln and drove away. "Summer's a beautiful girl, Cooper," she said. "She's inherited her grandmother's grace and charm."

Cooper nodded, but it wasn't Summer's grace and charm that had him itching to be with her again as soon as possible. "Yes, I think so," he said, realizing his mother was waiting for his answer.

"You've been dishonest with them," she said.

He glanced at her and saw the reproachful look. "I

never lied," he replied. "I just haven't given them all the facts."

"How can you propose marriage to a woman who knows almost nothing about you?"

He stared straight ahead at the road. He'd never meant to include his mother in the charade; in fact, he'd planned to tell her the truth long before she received an invitation to the engagement party. Unfortunately, Henrietta had called her the very next day, before he had a chance to set things straight. His mother had been ecstatic over the news, and even though he knew he was only digging himself deeper into a hole, he hadn't had the heart to ruin it for her. "Summer knows what kind of person I am inside," he said. "But I plan on telling her the truth."

"When?"

"Soon. I promise."

Vivian leaned back in her seat. "I've always believed that truth is the best policy," she said. "You owe it to Summer to tell her everything. It's obvious the girl loves you with all her heart."

Cooper was so stunned by her words that he merely gaped at her. "You really think so?"

Vivian laughed. "Honestly, Cooper. Men can be so dense where women are concerned."

Summer overslept on Monday, no doubt a result of having forgotten to set her alarm the previous night before she fell asleep in Cooper's arms. A quick glance at the other side of the bed told her he'd obviously left during the night. With a sinking heart, she raced into the shower.

Edwin Worth's weekly meeting was well under way when Summer slipped through the door as unobtrusively as she could and took the first empty seat. She opened her briefcase and reached inside for her pad of notes. When it was her turn to speak, Worth brushed her aside. "I'll see you in my office right after the meeting," he said, and motioned for the man on her right to speak.

Summer could feel all eyes on her as she tried to maintain her professionalism despite the fact that Worth had just spoken to her as if she were a naughty child. Although she wasn't in a hurry to face Worth, she couldn't wait for the meeting to end. Once it was over, she closed her briefcase and started down the hall toward the penthouse, where she knew Max would give her a small briefing if he had a chance. Unfortunately, it didn't happen that way. Worth was snapping orders as fast as he could, and Max was scribbling furiously on his steno pad.

"Hold all my calls," Worth said, then motioned Summer into his office. As he took a seat behind his desk, he indicated a chair on the other side.

"You're full of surprises, Miss Pettigrew," Worth said, leaning back in his seat and studying her thoughtfully.

Miss Pettigrew? Summer knew she was in hot water now. "How is that, Mr. Worth?" she asked politely.

"I read about your engagement in the morning paper, and I'm embarrassed to say I wasn't even aware you were seeing anyone."

Summer relaxed slightly. So that was it. But why should Worth care one way or the other about her personal life? "It happened rather suddenly," she said. "You might say it was one of those whirlwind romances."

"You're obviously feeling very secure financially to be marrying a man with as much money as your own family."

She blinked several times. "I beg your pardon?"

"That's the only reason I can think of that you would lose your enthusiasm over your job."

Summer's mind was still spinning over what he's said

about her marrying a man with money. He obviously didn't know Cooper was a bike mechanic. "I'm afraid there's been some sort of misunderstanding here," she said. "My, er, fiancé is not wealthy."

Edwin Worth's face became red. "Don't add insult to injury by lying to me, Miss Pettigrew." He reached for the folded newspaper and tossed it at her. Summer immediately recognized the engagement picture she and Cooper had posed for the previous week. She scanned the write-up. It gave a brief history of who she was, where she'd attended college, and what kind of work she was in. When it got to Cooper, the article referred to him as an overnight multimillionaire who'd barely graduated high school but managed to rise out of the slums by designing a motorcycle that had garnered respect among his competitors such as Harley-Davidson and the Japanese manufacturers. His bike, the New Breed, cost less to build but maintained the high-quality standards set by other companies. He was listed in the top one hundred of the Fortune 500; the article went on to describe the many charities he contributed to, mostly trying to change the face of Atlanta's projects. Summer was stunned speechless.

She looked at Worth. "Are you sure we're talking about the same Cooper Garrett?" she asked dumbly.

"Dark-haired fellow. Wears a suit only when it's absolutely necessary. Looks like he might rob the family silver if he had the chance. I've run into him at various business functions."

Summer felt her cheeks flame. She laid the newspaper on the desk. "I'm afraid I don't know him as well as I thought I did."

Worth waved the matter aside. "That's not really the issue here. I ran into Sam Flynn at the Atlanta Athletic Club yesterday, and I asked him if he was happy with our services. He said he had gone to another firm. Said the last time he was here some goon tried to rough him up. Please tell me that was a gross exaggeration."

"Did he mention the fact he'd made a pass at me?"

Worth eyed her steadily. "Come now, Miss Pettigrew, you're a grown woman. Surely you've had that sort of thing happen before. As an employee of Worth Advertising, I would have expected you to handle it with more grace and dignity. You have not only embarrassed our firm, you caused us to lose what could easily have been our biggest account this year."

Summer opened her mouth to reply, but he cut her off.

"Furthermore, you went behind my back and took on the Good Shepherd account after I specifically told you not to."

She straightened her shoulders. "I told you from the beginning how much the Good Shepherd account meant to me, Mr. Worth. I also told you it would not affect my other work, and it hasn't. I work on it at home."

"You also work at home on your regular accounts, so it's interfering no matter which way you look at it."

"I'm probably one of very few who takes work home," she replied. "I would think what I do on my own time is up to me."

"Not when you sacrifice the quality and integrity of your other accounts. You're paid very well. You don't need to do freelance work."

"I'm not doing it for the money—"

"I refuse to argue with you, Miss Pettigrew. I won't permit my clients to be *roughed up*, nor will I allow you to keep a client that will not generate profit and take your focus off your other accounts. Have your girl write a nice letter to the people at Good Shepherd, telling them you simply can't handle more work at this time."

"Mr. Worth—"

"Also, I expect a full letter of apology to Mr. Flynn."

He checked his calendar. "As of today, I'm putting you on sixty days' probation, during which time you will not take on any new accounts. This should give you time to get caught up on all your work and prove yourself to this company."

Summer forced herself to stand despite the trembling in her knees. "I thought I'd already proven myself to this company," she said coolly. "I'm a professional, Mr. Worth, and I refuse to put up with the Sam Flynns of this world. As far as the Good Shepherd account, we have a verbal agreement, and that's good enough for me. I have no intention of giving it up."

He looked surprised. "Then you and I have nothing further to say to each other."

"Except for me to tell you I quit." Summer turned and made for the door. She glanced over her shoulder before opening it. "I'll have my office cleaned out by the end of the day, and I'll see that *my girl* delivers all my files to *your boy*."

Max looked up from his desk as she stepped out of Worth's office. "Well?"

"I'm outta here."

Max looked stunned. "He fired you?"

"I quit. Look, I don't want to get you into trouble."

"It's okay," Max whispered, pointing at the square buttons at the bottom of the phone. One was presently lit up. "He's on a call. What are you going to do now?"

"I don't know," she said, feeling miserable. "I should call Warren."

"Oh, blast it, I forgot to tell you. Warren called first thing this morning. He asked to speak to Mr. Worth. Which I thought strange, since Warren's not one of Mr. Worth's favorite people."

"I didn't know that," Summer said.

"Face it, Summer. Everyone knows Warren spends more time at the coffee machine flirting with secretaries than he does on his work. Joyce has told me how you've covered for him. Just don't be surprised if Warren doesn't come back from his personal leave, if you get my drift."

Summer couldn't mask her surprise. "Why didn't you tell me?"

He shrugged. "I know the two of you are close friends." The light blinked off on the switchboard. "Worthless is off the phone," he said, using the name he called his boss when he was angry with him. "Why don't we talk later? Let's meet at Crazy Albert's for a drink after work."

Summer nodded and hurried to the other side of the building. Joyce glanced up and frowned at the look on her face. "What happened to *you?*"

Summer filled her in as the woman followed her into her office. "I'm quitting with you," she said.

Summer spun around to face her. "You can't do that! You need your job."

"The only reason I tolerate this place is because of you," she said. "Besides, you know I'll never go anywhere. Worth sees me as a secretary and nothing more."

"Think about it carefully, Joyce," she warned. "I don't want my leaving to hurt you. Now, we've got a busy day ahead of us," she said, pulling her degree from the wall. "See if you can find some empty boxes. I plan to be packed and out by the end of the day."

Joyce started for the door. "Have you seen the newspaper?"

Summer almost flinched. She didn't want to discuss Cooper at the moment. "Yes."

"Did you know he had more money than the U.S. Treasury?"

She looked thoughtful. "Are you still seeing that guy with the phone company? Larry what's-his-name?"

"Larry Johnson." Joyce nodded. "We've decided to date exclusively."

"Think he can pull up an address on an unlisted number for me?"

"Are you kidding? He thinks you're the best thing since white bread for giving him all your Atlanta Hawks tickets. I'll call him."

Summer waited until Joyce closed the door before slumping in her chair and covering her face with her hands. Joyce buzzed her.

"Your grandmother's on line one."

Summer picked up the phone. "Hi."

"Have you read the morning paper yet?" Henrietta asked.

"Mr. Worth showed it to me first thing this morning."

"Did you know Cooper was loaded?"

"I hadn't a clue."

"I'm so embarrassed. I sent his mother that dress she wore to the engagement party because I was afraid she couldn't afford one. Do you think I insulted her?"

"No, Vivian knows how good-hearted you are. Besides, if that skunk of a son of hers had been honest from the beginning—"

"Are you angry with him?"

"What do you think?"

"Well, I hope you won't call off the wedding."

Summer closed her eyes. "Grandmother, you and I are going to have to have a talk."

"Of course, dear. Let's have dinner tomorrow night."

Summer said good-bye and hung up as Joyce came through the door with several empty boxes.

Cooper stared at the phone on his desk and wondered if he should try reaching Summer again. His mother had shown him their engagement picture and the article as soon as he'd awakened that morning. "You have no choice but to tell her the truth now," she'd said. But each time he called her office, her assistant informed him Ms. Pettigrew was tied up and couldn't take calls.

He didn't have to be a genius to know she was mad. And she had every right to be.

Why had he allowed her to believe he was struggling to get by, when, in fact, he'd amassed a fortune in the past few years? He supposed in the beginning he'd done it because he thought she was one of those society chicks who thought she was too good for him.

That was before he realized there were rich people who had hearts of gold. Henrietta and her granddaughter were prime examples. And he'd been a jerk for pretending to be something he wasn't. Perhaps Summer *was* too good for the likes of him. She had lied to protect a loved one, but he'd done it out of spite.

It was nearing five o'clock when Joyce and Summer carried the last of her boxes to her car. The other employees had given her curious stares all day, but several of her coworkers had stopped by to wish her well and say how much they regretted seeing her go. Much to her surprise, Beardsly and Tatum were among them, and even more surprising, they seemed sincere. She'd been deeply touched. "I'm meeting Max at Crazy Albert's for a drink after work," Summer told Joyce. "Care to join us?"

"Sure. But only if we can run Worth into the ground like a dog."

"Try to look at the bright side," Summer said. "I received some excellent training while I was here. I shouldn't have any trouble finding another job."

"You should go out on your own," Joyce told her. They were still discussing the pros and cons of such a move as they took the elevator to the top floor and headed toward their offices. The phone rang and Joyce snatched it up. "Oh, hi, sweetie," she said. "You got addresses?" She scribbled something on a sheet of paper. "Okay, I'll see you later. Thanks, hon."

Joyce glanced down at the paper in her hand. "Okay, let's see what we've got here. Seems your intended has a horse farm about forty-five minutes north of the city called Ashley Estates. Also, a small cabin on Lake Lanier, and a three-bedroom condo at Windsor Condominiums. Larry talked to one of the guys that recently installed extra lines at the farm. Said Cooper spends most of his time there, but likes having the condo and lake house for business associates. Also, believe it or not, Cooper actually had the century-old home renovated for his mother, but she refuses to live in such grandeur and keeps an apartment in the servants' quarters." She handed Summer the sheet of paper. "Here are the addresses. Just don't tell anyone where you got them."

Summer nodded and started for her office. "I'll see you at Crazy Albert's," she said. "Right now I just want to be alone." Joyce nodded as though she understood. Summer closed her door and locked it, then sat behind her desk, gazing out at the Atlanta skyline as she allowed the hurt to seep in. She had kept it at bay all day, knowing if she allowed herself to give in, she would never accomplish what needed doing. She could no longer keep her emotions under control. Cooper had made a fool of her. He had listened to her secrets and fears but had refused to share vital information about himself. He'd allowed her to think he was struggling to keep his head above water, and she had gone and fallen in love with him and discovered it didn't matter what he did for a living.

Why, if it hadn't been for Warren, she would never even have known about Cooper's troubled past. She tapped her nails against her desk. So, why hadn't Warren told her the rest? The part about Cooper turning his life around and making a success out of himself.

She wiped angry tears from her face and dialed Warren's number in Florida. She was still determined to maintain her control until she'd taken care of everything. He sounded glad to hear from her. "I have several questions for you," she said tersely.

"Uh-oh, what'd I do?"

"First question, why didn't you tell me the truth about Cooper?"

He hesitated. "You mean about the money."

"You're a genius, Warren."

"Hey, it really didn't cross my mind in the beginning. I mean, who would've figured the two of you would ever see each other again after that first night."

"What about later? When you knew how I felt about him?"

He sighed. "I'm sorry, Summer, I should have told you. But when I realized the two of you were getting involved, I suppose I got jealous. I figured if you thought Cooper was a down-and-out biker with no future, you'd lose interest. I think I secretly hoped it would make you appreciate me more."

She told herself not to feel sorry for him. "Okay, next question. Why didn't you tell me you'd been fired?"

"I was wondering how long it would take the news to leak. Worth was keeping it under wraps until I broke the news to my family, which I still haven't done, by the way."

"You didn't answer my question."

"I wasn't exactly proud of the fact," he said defensively. He was quiet for a moment. "I never told you this, but he walked in on my presentation with Gridlock Tires the day your grandmother was rushed to the hospital. I guess he could tell I didn't have a clue as to what I was talking about. Why do you think they never called back?

"Anyway, Worth summoned me into his office the Friday I was supposed to show up at your grandmother's and pretend we were a couple. He fired me, and a couple of hours later I got into that accident. I called Worth right away because I thought he'd give me a break and hire me back. Some break. He had Max send flowers." He paused. "You said you had several questions."

"Yes." Summer took a deep breath. "I want to know why you called Worth this morning and told him about my losing Sam Flynn's account and that I'd taken on the Good Shepherd account."

He didn't answer for so long that Summer thought he wasn't going to. When he finally did, he sounded sad. "You should've figured that one out for yourself, Summer. I've been riding your coattails for a long time. I was hoping you and I could go into business together, but I knew you were afraid of the risks involved in going out on your own. I figured if Worth fired you, you'd have no choice." He paused. "I haven't stopped feeling guilty since I made the call. I'm sorry for being such a selfish bastard."

"So am I, Warren. I thought you were my friend, but it's all beginning to come together now. Here I was, fresh out of college, and you were the only one who looked happy to have me at Worth Advertising. Of course, that was to get me in bed, but I was too naive to realize it at first. I thought we were buddies. Then, when you insisted I work with you on various accounts, I was flattered. At least *somebody* in the company thought I had talent. I suppose you felt if you couldn't get me in the sack, you could use me in another way, and you did."

"If you're accusing me of dumping most of the workload on you, I've already confessed to that," he said.

"And that's not all. You convinced me I wasn't well liked in the company, that most of the men didn't respect my work. I no longer believe that. As a matter of fact, I don't believe anything you have to say to me."

"So where does this leave us?"

Her eyes burned. "Our friendship is over. Don't call me, don't visit, don't even bother to send me a card on my birthday." She hung up and buried her face in her hands. Finally, she cried.

Joyce and Max already had a table and were on their second drink by the time Summer arrived at Crazy Albert's. "Sorry I'm late," she said, having spent the time trying to fix her face after shedding her share of tears. She ordered a virgin strawberry daiquiri. As the waitress hurried off to fill her order, Joyce reached across the table and squeezed her hand. "You should have let them put rum in it. You look like you could use it."

"I need a clear head," she told her friend.

"Max and I have been talking," Joyce said. "We agree you should strike out on your own. We've even decided to go with you for a lot less money if we have to."

Summer felt her jaw drop. "I can't afford to go out on my own without some sort of client base. Besides, do you have any idea what it'd cost to set up an office?"

"We've already talked about it," Max said. "My uncle manages several office buildings near town. He could probably cut you a deal on a lease."

"With your advertising skills you could build up a solid client list in no time," Joyce said.

"Why would you guys be willing to take salary cuts?"

"I would do it so I never had to work for Worth again," Max said.

"And I'd go with you so I could become more involved in the advertising field," Joyce replied. "You know as well as I do that Worth has no plans to advance my career. I might as well tear up my degree when I get it."

Summer listened thoughtfully. What they were suggesting would take a lot of money. Although her savings account was healthy, she knew it would last only months if she weren't bringing in steady income. She thought about the various trust funds Henrietta had set up for her over the years. She had intended to use part of the money to buy a house when she married and the rest would go to her children's education. But here she was, pushing thirty, and she was without husband *or* child.

The thought of going out on her own frightened her. It was like walking a tightrope with no net. What if her business failed? What if Joyce and Max quit perfectly good jobs only to end up in the unemployment line? What if—" She mentally chided herself. She'd been living with *what-if*s all her life. It wasn't until that dirty, rotten, lying dog Cooper had pointed out her remarkable talent that she'd begun to believe in herself.

"Okay, here's the deal," she said, leaning forward. "I'm not agreeing to anything as of yet. I want each of you to continue working your present job until I can get an idea of what it's going to cost to launch a new business." She looked at Max. "Talk to your uncle and see what he has. Joyce and I will each need our own office, plus a conference room. A small kitchenette and rest room would be nice, but if it's too expensive, we'll just have to share with the other businesses until we can afford better."

"I'm getting my own office?" Joyce said, looking hopeful.

"You'll need one if you're planning to be my assistant. As time goes by, I hope you'll agree on a full partnership."

Joyce was speechless, a rarity with her.

Max whipped out a small notepad and started scribbling. "I'll need to check into the cost of office furniture," he told Summer. "You want me to look at new or used?"

Summer didn't hesitate. "New. And make sure it's nice. In order to be successful we need to look successful. We'll also need several computers, a copier, and fax machine and—" She didn't finish the sentence. "Oh, never mind. You know more about that sort of thing than I do. You handle it."

Max beamed with pleasure that she was leaving it up to him. "The two of you will need business cards," he said. "You'll want to pass them out every chance you get. While I'm at it, I'll compare prices with office suppliers."

"What do you want me to do?" Joyce said.

"Is your brother still involved in photography?"

"It's his favorite hobby."

"I'd like to talk to him about coming with us to The Good Shepherd this Saturday and taking pictures of the children while you and I visit with the kids and interview staff. I think he'll be able to put more emotion into the pictures than we would. Also, I'll give you some cash. Go by one of the department stores and buy coloring books and crayons and those wooden puzzles children like to work."

"Do you know the children's ages?"

"Not off the top of my head. You'll need to call Marian or Joe."

"Maybe Henrietta could convince some of her friends to become involved," Joyce said. "You know how she feels about children."

"Why didn't I think of that sooner?" Summer said. They discussed their ideas for another hour before Summer excused herself, saying she had an errand to run. Max and Joyce promised to be in touch.

The drive to Windsor Condominiums was fifteen minutes from Crazy Albert's. It was at least thirty stories of mirrored glass and reminded Summer of the building in the movie *Sliver*. The parking garage was located below, and the entire building was surrounded by a tall wrought-iron fence. A security guard admitted guests and owners while another guard walked a massive German shepherd who stopped every now and then to sniff at the shrubbery. Summer pulled up to the security gate, and the guard nodded politely.

"Could you tell me if Mr. Cooper Garrett is home?" she said, still certain there was some mistake.

The guard scratched his jaw and looked through a list of names. "Yes, he arrived home an hour ago. Would you like me to ring him for you?"

Summer glanced at her watch. "Actually, I'm late for another appointment. I'll be back later." The guard smiled and nodded as she turned her car around and headed toward the main road. She stopped for gas at one of the many truck stops along the interstate and bought a map and a pair of binoculars.

She studied the map for a good five minutes, then took the interstate north. It took more than an hour and several wrong turns before she found the right road. She traveled a couple of miles farther and found herself sitting at the entrance to Ashley Estates. The house was set far back from the road. She reached for the binoculars.

The house was an old but large colonial with round pillars and wings jutting out on either side and cozy porches sprouting here and there. The property surrounding it was vast; horses and cattle grazed beneath the fading sun. A pristine white fence ran along the front of the property as far as the eye could see.

Summer tossed the binoculars aside and gripped the steering wheel tightly as anger raged through her. Oh, what a jolly time Cooper must have had with her, pretending to be a struggling bike mechanic who'd known nothing but hard times. She could feel her throat closing up with emotion as she slammed the gears in reverse and sped away.

Cooper was sitting on his bike in front of her condo when she returned. Her anger grew to new heights. He winced at the look on her face. "Can we talk?"

She spun around and faced him. "It's too late for that," she said. "I have absolutely nothing to say to you." She stabbed her key in her lock.

"I'm sorry I didn't tell you the first night we met," he said. "But I sort of got the impression you thought you were too good for me."

"So you decided to make me look like a fool."

"No. I guess I was trying to see if it mattered to you one way or the other what I did for a living. I was beginning to think it didn't matter in the least."

She glared at him. It hadn't mattered, but she'd sooner bite her tongue off than tell him as much. "Go away, Cooper. I don't want to see you or listen to any more of your lies."

"I don't see how you can point a finger at me, when you've lied about our relationship all along."

"You don't get it, do you?" she said. "I don't have to answer to you. Thanks to you, I'm without a job."

"Worth fired you?" he said in disbelief.

"I quit before he had the chance."

"But that's great, babe," he said. "You can go out on your own now."

She almost flinched at the endearment, and she knew she was very close to tears. "What I decide to do with my career is none of your concern." She opened her door and stepped inside her condo. "I want you to leave. I'm going to call the security guards and tell them not to allow you on the property again." She slammed the door in his face and locked it. It wasn't until she heard him pull away on his bike a few minutes later that she allowed the tears to fall.

❧━━━━━━━━❧

By the end of the week Cooper knew she meant business. It wasn't just a matter of her getting over being mad at him, she wanted him out of her life. She refused to take his calls, and security wouldn't let him anywhere near the premises. On Friday he visited Henrietta. A pleasant, middle-aged woman answered the door and asked him to wait in the foyer while she notified Mrs. Pettigrew. Henrietta hurried down the hall a moment later with her arms outstretched, obviously delighted to see him.

She introduced them, and the woman offered to take Cooper's jacket. "Gladys, would you bring us fresh coffee?" she asked, then led Cooper to her private den.

He waited until Henrietta invited him to sit. "What happened to Mrs. Bradshaw?"

"Oh, I got tired of looking at that sour puss of hers. Summer was right, the woman wasn't happy. I regret that I kept her on all these years, especially since I've come to believe she was hard on my granddaughter at times. But I had my attorney set up retirement funds for my employees, so she'll be okay. Gladys is a delight. Not only is she an excellent housekeeper, she's sort of a companion as well. She takes walks with me in the afternoon, and she just started teaching me to play chess." They chatted a few minutes more about the nonessentials, giving the new housekeeper time to bring their coffee.

Once Gladys arrived with a tray, she poured two cups of coffee and left them. Cooper noted several cookies on a plate and reached for one.

"They're low-fat," Henrietta said proudly, "but you can't tell the difference."

"You're right, I can't." He sipped his coffee in silence.

Henrietta shifted in her chair. "Before you say anything, I think you should know, Summer has told me the truth. I know everything."

Cooper felt a sense of deep shame. "I'm sorry, Henrietta."

She smiled with effort. "I'm afraid I'm just as guilty as the two of you. I faked the severity of my illness."

"You mean you don't have heart trouble?"

"I have angina. It's common in people my age and can be controlled with diet, exercise, and proper medication. My doctor assures me my old ticker still has a ways to go."

"That's wonderful news."

Henrietta nodded but was quiet for a moment. "I'm so ashamed of myself for allowing Summer to think it was worse than it was, but I never thought she'd go to such extremes."

"She loves you very much."

The woman's eyes misted. "I just want to see her happy. I look at Mrs. Bradford, who has never been married and doesn't have children or grandchildren, and I see a very lonely and bitter woman."

This time it was Cooper's turn to look thoughtful. "Henrietta, I've gone and fallen in love with your granddaughter."

She reached over and captured his hand and squeezed it. "I know. And she loves you, though she'd never admit it."

"I'm afraid I've lost her."

Henrietta was silent. Worry etched deep lines around her eyes and mouth. "If only she weren't so stubborn. I think deep inside she's afraid of being abandoned again, so she's convinced herself she doesn't need anyone."

Cooper drained his coffee. "Well, I just wanted to see you and say good-bye."

She looked startled. "Where are you going?"

"To a biker's convention in Japan. After that I'm going to visit a number of European stores I recently opened. I leave tomorrow night."

Henrietta nodded. "Yes, I read about this New Breed bike of yours. Someday you'll have to tell me how it all came about."

"Simple. I was tired of living in poverty and watching my mother work her fingers to the bone to keep us fed. But the only thing I ever really knew anything about was bikes."

"How long will you be gone?"

"I don't know. There doesn't seem to be any reason for me to rush back. Summer made it perfectly plain she never wants to see me again."

Henrietta's brows puckered as she considered the problem at hand. "Wait a minute," she said. "I just think I might know of a way to change her mind."

Max stirred the paint, dipped a paintbrush in it, and swiped it across the wall. "What do you think?" He turned to Summer and Joyce.

Summer tried to rouse herself out of her stupor and sound excited, but it took quite an effort considering her depressed mood. "I like it," she replied. "It's very close to teal, but softer. And it'll look great next to those white leather sofas Joyce picked out." She paused and looked from Max to Joyce. "But everybody has to agree on it. We're a team, remember?"

Max and Joyce looked flattered to be included in the decision making. Both had already given their notices at Worth Advertising and would sign on with Southern Advertising in a week. Although Summer was a little nervous at the thought of being responsible for their welfare, she knew she'd do everything in her power to see the business succeeded.

Joyce and Max agreed it was the perfect color. "All I

have to do is call the paint store and ask them to mix up a few more cans," Max said. "I've already bought the brushes, rollers, and drop cloths."

Summer suspected it would be healthier for her to keep busy than to sit home brooding over a broken heart. Besides, the sooner they got it done, the better, since they planned to open for business in two weeks. She had been working steadily on an advertising plan to draw clients. "Okay," she said. "Max, if you'll go for the paint, Joyce and I will get started in here. Just tell them to put everything on my credit card since I'm sure we'll have more expenditures." Max's uncle had found them a great deal on a suite of offices in a prime location and had agreed to waive the stiff deposit if they made repairs, painted the walls, and had the carpets cleaned. Since Summer was trying to be cautious with her money, she'd been only too willing to comply.

Max reached into his pocket for his car keys. "I'll grab sandwiches and cold drinks from the deli while I'm out," he said.

Summer nodded. "Just remember to get a receipt for everything."

Max started for the door just as someone pushed it open from the other side. All three stared in silence as Cooper Garrett stepped into the room. Summer felt her heart turn over in her chest at the sight of him.

"Am I interrupting something?" he asked, his black eyes narrowing slightly at the sight of Max. He pried his gaze off the man and focused on Summer, but he couldn't help but wonder who the guy was. Then he reminded himself he was jumping to conclusions, a habit he was trying to break.

"Yes, as a matter of fact, you are," Summer replied coolly. "What are you doing here and how did you know where to find me?"

Joyce looked at Max. "On second thought, I'd better

go with you to help carry the paint cans." They slipped out the door without another word.

Summer tore open a cellophane bag containing a thick drop cloth. "I'm very busy, Cooper," she said. "Besides, I asked you to stay away from me." She refused to look at him as she spoke, knowing it would only make it harder for her to be firm with him. Already she could feel a frightening current racing through her, but then, her body had always betrayed her where the man was concerned. She refused to give in to it, focusing instead on how he'd used and humiliated her. Why it had surprised her as much as it did was the real question. She'd expected as much from the beginning. But he'd torn down all her defenses with his smooth talk and his kisses, and she had nobody but herself to blame for falling for it.

"I'm not here for personal reasons," he said, trying to sound as professionally detached as Henrietta had warned him to be. Summer needed new advertising accounts, and he meant to hire her if that's what it took to stay in touch with her. Perhaps as time went on he could convince her how sorry he was for not being honest with her. "I have a business matter I'd like to discuss with you," he added.

She shot him a dark look. "I can't imagine us having *anything* to discuss, much less business."

"May I sit?" he asked, indicating a chair.

"No, you may not. Just say what's on your mind and leave."

One corner of his mouth twisted in frustration. "Boy, you don't cut a guy any slack, do you?"

"Not when it comes to men who enjoy making absolute fools of women. And using them," she added. Not only was she deeply hurt by Cooper, she was still sore as a bad tooth over what Warren had done. Never again would she let herself be put in such a situation.

"I never used you," he said. "I may have kept things

from you, but what we had between us was real. It's just easier for you to believe the worst of me because you don't think you deserve to be happy. That's your choice to make, of course, but I refuse to take all the blame."

"Don't try to analyze me, Cooper," she said coolly, giving no indication of the painful feelings he was dredging up. "Either get on with your business or leave."

He sighed. "Okay, here it is. My accountant is working on my taxes," he said. "Several of my stores didn't fare so well in the last fiscal year."

She shrugged. 'What's that got to do with me?"

"I obviously need to advertise."

She laughed mirthlessly. "Oh, no, you don't. I am *not* going to let myself get involved with you personally *or* professionally. Forget it, Cooper."

"This would be the perfect opportunity for you, Summer. I have three stores in Atlanta alone and dozens more nationwide. My bikes are some of the best machinery money can buy, but I'm having to compete with companies like Harley-Davidson and the Japanese manufacturers."

"Go tell somebody who cares," she quipped once she'd laid the drop cloth in place. "I'm not interested."

"Listen," he said, his voice smooth but insistent. "I'm leaving the country, so you won't even have to deal with me if you don't want to. You can go straight through my secretary."

"Oh, boy, that should be a riot. Let's see if I remember how to spell bimbo."

He frowned. "She happens to be happily married, with teenagers. You'd have full creative control, and an unlimited budget," he added. When she still didn't look convinced, he went on. "I would think with you just getting started, this would sound appealing."

She paused and thought of Max and Joyce, who would be joining her full-time. All she had going right now was the Good Shepherd account, and since she was doing the work for free, she presently had no money coming in. Still, she didn't know if she could handle the emotional strain of working with Cooper, even if their contact was minimal. She'd suffered enough over him the past few days. She considered it. "I'd insist on a contract stating in writing everything you just said," she replied. "Plus, I'd need a retainer. If you break the contract, you'd automatically forfeit it."

"That sounds fair." He pulled a checkbook from his back pocket. "Name your price."

She went as high as she dared, but he didn't so much as flinch. He simply wrote out the check and handed it to her, along with his business card. She laid them on her desk. "I'll have Max type up the contract as soon as he gets back. You can come by later to sign it."

"Who's Max?"

"My secretary."

"You mean the guy who was just here?" he asked, trying to mask his relief.

She didn't answer him. Instead, she went back to work. "Have a pleasant trip, Cooper," she said. "I'll have Max contact your secretary if I need something."

He stood there for a few seconds, grim-faced but determined not to make a move toward her and risk losing what ground he'd managed to win back. He thought of the plane he would be catching later, and the thousands of miles that would separate him from her. He wanted to take her in his arms and kiss her until neither of them could think straight, but she had accused him of bullying his way through life all along. If he hoped to win her back, it would have to be under her terms.

Of course, she had to *want* him back. That was the clincher.

TWELVE

Two weeks later, the *Atlanta Journal-Constitution* did a full-page story on Joe and Marian Smyth, founders of The Good Shepherd. It hadn't mattered to Summer that she'd had to involve her grandmother in rousing the newspaper's interest; whatever it took, she was willing. The paper was willing to donate space twice a month for the cause. Of course, once Henrietta became involved, things began to happen. In a few short days, toys and clothes were delivered to the facility, as well as cribs, playpens, hospital beds. Henrietta even asked for a list of the items they needed. The staff was overrun with phone calls from readers eager to donate money, and a volunteer group who was more than willing to assist. Marian and Joe wept with happiness.

An editor from the *Journal* also interviewed a fourteen-year-old boy named Sammy who'd lost his family in a car accident and had become paralyzed from the waist down. Although Summer had asked that the newspaper concentrate on the positive aspects of each child, she knew she had absolutely no editorial control. Fortunately, the article turned out to be quite uplifting. There were pictures of Sammy and several other wheelchair-bound children playing a new form of soccer, and of Sammy scraping plates in the cafeteria to show that he was perfectly capable of keeping up with his chores. Sammy's teachers were interviewed, and they bragged about how bright the boy was and how he refused to let the disability stand in his way. By the end of the week, there were numerous calls from couples interested in adopting the boy.

Although Summer had promised herself to remain professionally detached where the children were concerned, it wasn't always easy. Finally, she stopped fighting it. How could she not give love to and receive love from children who were in such need? She thought of the seasonless world Gibran had written about in his book. Is that what she wanted? Was it better to play it safe and escape the pain that often rode on the coattails of love? Of course, playing it safe meant never knowing the full measure of joy and happiness. You could not experience one without the other. If you hoped to soar to heights of ecstasy, you had to be prepared to fall to the lowest depths as well.

Summer suddenly felt like the world's worst hypocrite. Here she was, asking couples to open up their hearts and homes to children with handicaps, some of them so bad the child would never make it to adulthood, and yet she herself was afraid to take the same risk. While she'd spent a good deal of her childhood feeling unloved because her parents had abandoned her, she should have spent more time counting her blessings. Not only had her grandmother taken her in and given her unconditional love, she'd seen that her granddaughter was raised with all the advantages. Summer realized she'd been selfish in longing for more, when there were so many children worse off.

Warren had written a letter of apology to Summer.

She'd read it, then set it aside to read again at a later date. Perhaps in time she could forgive him, but right now she felt very vulnerable. Some of her ex-coworkers at Worth Advertising had recently referred clients to her, small accounts that Edwin Worth was not interested in taking on. She was thrilled to have them. She met Henrietta for lunch one day and assured her worried grandmother that business was picking up.

"You know, if you need money—"

"I'm fine, stop worrying about me." Summer reached for her hand and squeezed it.

"How's Cooper?" Henrietta asked, changing the subject.

Some of the light went out of Summer's eyes. She shrugged. "I wouldn't know. I haven't had a reason to call him or his secretary."

"Oh, sweetie," she said, shaking her head sadly. "How long are you going to punish the poor guy?"

Summer looked away. Pride alone would not allow her to let her grandmother see how hurt she still was over Cooper's deception. "I'm not punishing him," she said. "I'm merely taking care of myself. The guy should wear a label across his forehead that says WARNING! DANGEROUS TO THE HEART."

"Maybe he feels the same about you." When Summer didn't respond, Henrietta went on. "Have you started working on his account yet?"

She tried to suppress a smile. She'd started planning his ad the day Cooper had handed her his check. "You might say that."

Henrietta studied her. "You're holding out on me, Summer Pettigrew. What is it?"

"You'll have to wait like everybody else to find out."

"And when will that be?"

"Not much longer, if everything goes as planned. I've worked around the clock in order to launch his ad as soon as possible." Even now she wondered how she'd managed to get everything done and still devote time to the Good Shepherd account and the new clients. Of course, Joyce and Max had proven themselves invaluable the past month, skipping lunch hours and working overtime in order to get the job done.

"Why are you rushing Cooper's ad?"

"I want everything to be in place by the time he returns to the United States. So far I've been lucky. Cooper hasn't seemed in a hurry to return home."

"Why should he? The love of his life dumped him like a hot potato."

Summer offered her a coy smile. "Yes, well, he ain't seen nothing yet."

Cooper had tried to sleep during the ten-hour flight over the Atlantic, but his thoughts wouldn't give him the rest his body required. After four weeks traveling from one country to the next, he was impatient to get back on American soil and try to convince Summer to listen to him once and for all. For weeks he had mentally practiced what he would say as he'd visited his European stores and outlined a five-year plan with his managers. The conference had been an overwhelming success; New Breed bikes were giving competitors a run for their money. So why wasn't he excited?

The answer was quite simple. Hopes and dreams meant nothing when there was no one to share them with.

Cooper landed at the Atlanta airport shortly before seven A.M. Feeling tired and disgruntled after the all-night flight, he waited for his bags and flagged a taxi. He'd already planned his move. First, he'd swing by his condo for a quick shower, then drive to Summer's office and insist she see him, even if he had to use what she referred to as his caveman tactics.

Cooper leaned his head back in the seat and closed his eyes but discovered the futility of it since the cab-driver seemed to be in a talkative mood. He mumbled his responses as he gazed out the window at the passing scenery through gritty eyes. The taxi came to a stop at a red light and Cooper found himself staring at a billboard he hadn't seen before. At first he thought it was his tired mind playing games, then realized with a jolt that it was real.

It was an advertisement for New Breed motorcycles. The bike was black leather and chrome, massive in size, and a thing of great beauty as far as Cooper was concerned. But it wasn't the bike that captured his stunned attention, it was the woman in the skimpy, fire-engine-red string bikini straddling it. Summer smiled back at him provocatively, giving him a come-hither look that sent his pulse skyrocketing. Beneath the bike were the words NEW BREED BIKES ARE RED HOT!

The driver grinned at Cooper from his rearview mirror. "Ah, you like that sign, huh? They been popping up like crazy the past few days."

"You mean there are more?" Cooper said, a sinking sensation in his stomach.

"Oh, yes. This chick is plastered on billboards all over the city. I don't know who she is, but she certainly gets *my* motor running first thing in the morning."

Cooper was tempted to slug the driver, but realized it wasn't his fault. A man would have to be a blind eunuch not to get excited by the temptress and the powerful machine. If this was Summer's idea of a joke, he didn't think it was a damn bit funny. "I want to see the others."

The cabbie shrugged and made a U-turn. Ten minutes later Cooper was staring at another sign. This time Summer was dressed in black leather that clung to her like a second skin, emphasizing her breasts in a way that made the blood rush to certain areas of Cooper's body. Her hair seemed to be flying in the breeze, she had a wild, untamed look to her that spoke volumes. Beneath the picture in bold red colors someone had painted RIDE A NEW BREED. NOTHING FEELS BETTER THAN LEATHER. He almost groaned aloud.

The third sign showed Summer leaning against a bike in a skin-tight denim skirt that showed more thigh than anything Cooper had ever seen on a woman. A bustier was loosely tied in front, showing plenty of cleavage. Eyes closed, lips wet and slightly parted, she seemed to be in a state of full arousal. He gritted his teeth as he read the words HUG THE CURVES WITH A NEW BREED. He felt his gut tighten. She'd done it on purpose, the little witch! She knew he didn't like men looking at her, and she had gone and rubbed his nose in the fact that she could and would do as she damn well pleased.

"There's a couple of more along the interstate," the cabbie said. "She's curled up with a jaguar in one of them, and it says something about these bikes bringing out the animal in us. But the one causing the most excitement is the one she had taken with Fabio, that male model."

"She actually had her picture taken with a man?" Cooper said, feeling his temper rise.

"Yes, this Fabio guy is wearing cut-off jeans and nothing else, and there's a lot of oil on his body. She's wearing the shortest shorts I've ever seen on a woman, and she's completely bare in front."

"Bare?" Cooper croaked.

"Yeah, but you can't see nothing 'cause she's hugging Fabio. You want me to drive you by it?"

Cooper shook his head. His blood was boiling, his ears roared. "No, I've seen enough. And I've changed my mind where I want to go. I have another address in mind." He gave it to the driver, and the man nodded. Cooper was silent the rest of the way, his thoughts running in a deadly direction.

They pulled up in front of Summer's condominium complex shortly before eight o'clock. The guard immediately turned him away, but Cooper pulled out a one-hundred-dollar bill. He was determined to see her even if it meant spending every dime he had.

The guard hesitated, although his eyes never wavered from the cash. "Ms. Pettigrew specifically asked us not to let you in."

Cooper gave him a beguiling smile as he added another hundred dollars to the offering. "She was just mad at the time," he said. "We had a lovers' spat. Now that both of us have had time to cool off, I think we'll be able to work things out." He smiled at the guard reassuringly, trying to hide his true intention, which was to wring her neck.

"Tell you what," the guard said, leaning in the window. "If she starts a ruckus with my boss, I'll just tell him I was in the men's room and didn't see nobody come through."

"Sounds good to me," Cooper said, stuffing the bills in the man's shirt pocket before the cabdriver pulled into the complex. Cooper paid his fare, tipped the driver well, and climbed out of the taxi. He hurried toward Summer's condo.

"Hey, what about your luggage?" the cabbie said.

"Just leave it on the sidewalk for now." Cooper told him. He paused, took a deep calming breath, and raised his hand to knock.

The door opened before he had a chance, and a startled Summer jumped back. She had obviously been ready to walk out the door, because she carried her purse and briefcase. "What are *you* doing here?" she demanded, her heart lurching wildly at the sight of him. "And how did you get past the security guard?"

"I bribed him."

"Liar. They don't accept bribes."

"Okay, I hid in the bushes and waited until he disappeared into the men's room, then I sneaked in."

"That sounds more your style. Now, if you'll excuse me, I'm on my way out." She tried to push past him.

"Not so fast," he said, backing her inside once more. He closed the door and locked it behind him. "First, we talk."

"I have nothing to say to you," she said, trying to focus her attention on anything but the man. He'd lost weight, and there were dark circles under his eyes. She hoped it meant he'd suffered as much as she had.

"Oh, I think you do," he said with gritted teeth. "I demand a full explanation behind those tawdry-looking signs."

"Tawdry? I happen to think they're quite tasteful. I tried to make them sexy *and* classy."

"You look like a woman who charges for sex."

"That's your opinion."

"It's my account."

"You gave me creative control, remember? It's all in the contract."

His eyes glittered with pent-up rage. "I was not aware you'd planned on being the model and giving every man in Atlanta a free show. You're wasting your time in advertising, babe. You should be giving girlie shows downtown for traveling salesmen."

She was getting angry now. "Have you been home yet?"

"No, I came straight from the airport." His eyes narrowed into black slits. "Don't tell me I have another surprise waiting."

"I'm wearing a fig leaf," she said proudly. "I had

them erect the sign so that it's the first thing you see when you wake up each morning."

He was so angry, he wanted to shake her. Instead, he raked both hands through his hair. He had never felt more frustration. "Do you realize everybody in this town is going to recognize you?"

"So? You're the one who said I needed to loosen up. Frankly, I think I look pretty good up there."

His look was menacing as he pointed a finger in her face. "You did this on purpose, Summer," he said, his tone edged with almost uncontrollable rage. "You know how I am when it comes to—" He stopped. "I go crazy when men look at you. If this is how you decided to get back at me, you've won. I know dirty fighting when I see it. But if you think I'm going to sit by and let everybody gawk at the woman I love, you can forget it. Those billboards are coming down first thing in the morning, and I don't care if I have to personally take care of it." He started for the door.

Summer stared at his wide shoulders as he made to leave. The thought of him going away again was more than she could bare. "Cooper, wait—"

"I don't care how much money I lose." He reached for the doorknob.

Summer rushed ahead, blocking his way. "What did you say?"

He glowered at her. "I said, I don't care how much money I lose—"

"No, before that, you big clod."

This time he almost shouted the words. "I said I won't have people gawking at the woman I love. Satisfied? All I've done the past month is think of you. I can't eat or sleep, hell, I can't even concentrate on business. I made up my mind I was going to convince you to marry me no matter what, but then I saw those god-awful signs, and I realized you don't give a damn about me; otherwise, you'd never have done something like that." He glanced away, afraid to let her see how torn up he was over the whole thing. His bottom lip trembled, but the hardening of his jaw told her he was not going to let her get to him. "You were the best thing that ever happened to me," he said. "I felt I was a better person when I was with you. I may have let you down, but you let me down too."

Summer saw the misery in his eyes and was immediately ashamed of what she'd done, not to mention the money she'd spent doing it. "I'm sorry, Cooper," she said, her eyes stinging. "I was so angry and hurt at the time, I guess I wasn't thinking straight. Not to mention humiliated. I bared my body and soul to you, but you obviously didn't trust me enough to reciprocate."

"It was wrong of me," he said, staring at the floor. "When people accuse you all your life of not being good enough, it doesn't go away that easily. I had to know you cared enough to accept me the way I appeared to be." He shook his head. "I never for one instant thought it was possible for someone like you to love someone like me."

Her eyes glistened with tears. "But I do."

He looked at her, studying her green eyes closely for signs of doubt. They were soft and full of love, and for a moment he couldn't believe the emotions were directed at him. He took a tentative step toward her. "If you really feel that way, then have the signs taken down. Call me jealous or possessive or whatever, but the only one who gets to watch my wife prance around in string bikinis and fig leaves is me."

Her heart skipped a beat. "Are you proposing?"

He shrugged. "Yeah, I guess that's what it boils down to." He held his breath for her answer. He'd laid himself wide open this time, put his heart on the line like never before. She had the power to break it or make him the happiest man in the world. It was almost frightening to know she had so much control over him.

Summer stepped closer and curled her arms around his waist. His look remained guarded, but she promised herself one day he would not feel the need to protect himself. "I would love to be your wife," she said, and saw a flicker of relief cross his face. "As for the billboards, I couldn't care less what you do with them. I did it only to get a rise out of you."

"You got a rise out of me all right," he said, grasping her hips and forcing her against him so she felt for herself that he was already hard. "Me and every other red-blooded male."

"I hope you don't expect me to wear burlap sacks just to keep you from being jealous."

His look sobered. "The truth is, I sort of get turned on watching men look at you as long as they know up front you're mine. Just do me a favor and save the revealing stuff for the bedroom. Does that sound fair?"

She nodded. "I already have a half dozen models lined up for the ads, so you can take the others down as soon as you like. As for what I wear in public, I'll agree to dress like a lady and save the kinky stuff for you. Speaking of which—" She paused and undid the top button of his shirt, then nuzzled the curls at his throat. He sighed and closed his eyes, and she took great delight in knowing he wanted her. She would see that he never stopped. "Now that we understand each other, perhaps you'd be interested in seeing my new fig leaf collection. I'm sure my new business partner won't mind taking over for me today."

He opened his eyes, and the black irises impaled her. "Oh, babe. I can't think of a better way to spend the day."

Bestselling Historical Women's Fiction

❧ AMANDA QUICK ❧

____28354-5 SEDUCTION . . . $6.50/$8.99 Canada

____28932-2 SCANDAL . . . . $6.50/$8.99

____28594-7 SURRENDER . . . . $6.50/$8.99

____29325-7 RENDEZVOUS . . . . $6.50/$8.99

____29315-X RECKLESS . . . . $6.50/$8.99

____29316-8 RAVISHED . . . . $6.50/$8.99

____29317-6 DANGEROUS . . . . $6.50/$8.99

____56506-0 DECEPTION . . . . $6.50/$8.99

____56153-7 DESIRE . . . . $6.50/$8.99

____56940-6 MISTRESS . . . . $6.50/$8.99

____57159-1 MYSTIQUE . . . . $6.50/$7.99

____09355-X MISCHIEF . . . . $22.95/$25.95

❧ IRIS JOHANSEN ❧

____29871-2 LAST BRIDGE HOME . . . $4.50/$5.50

____29604-3 THE GOLDEN

                 BARBARIAN . . . . $4.99/$5.99

____29244-7 REAP THE WIND . . . . . . $5.99/$7.50

____29032-0 STORM WINDS . . . . $4.99/$5.99

Ask for these books at your local bookstore or use this page to order.

Please send me the books I have checked above. I am enclosing $____ (add $2.50 to cover postage and handling). Send check or money order, no cash or C.O.D.'s, please.

Name _____

Address _____

City/State/Zip _____

Send order to: Bantam Books, Dept. FN 16, 2451 S. Wolf Rd., Des Plaines, IL 60018
Allow four to six weeks for delivery.

Prices and availability subject to change without notice.   FN 16 11/96

Bestselling Historical Women's Fiction

❧ IRIS JOHANSEN ❧

____28855-5 THE WIND DANCER . . .$5.99/$6.99

____29968-9 THE TIGER PRINCE . . .$5.99/$6.99

____29944-1 THE MAGNIFICENT

ROGUE . . . .$5.99/$6.99

____29945-X BELOVED SCOUNDREL .$5.99/$6.99

____29946-8 MIDNIGHT WARRIOR . .$5.99/$6.99

____29947-6 DARK RIDER . . . .$5.99/$7.99

____56990-2 LION'S BRIDE . . . .$5.99/$7.99

____09714-8 THE UGLY

DUCKLING . . . .$19.95/$24.95

❧ TERESA MEDEIROS ❧

____29407-5 HEATHER AND VELVET .$5.99/$7.50

____29409-1 ONCE AN ANGEL . . . . . .$5.99/$6.50

____29408-3 A WHISPER OF ROSES .$5.50/$6.50

____56332-7 THIEF OF HEARTS . . . . .$5.50/$6.99

____56333-5 FAIREST OF THEM ALL .$5.99/$7.50

____56334-3 BREATH OF MAGIC . . . .$5.99/$7.99

____57623-2 SHADOWS AND LACE . . .$5.99/$7.99

Ask for these books at your local bookstore or use this page to order.

Please send me the books I have checked above. I am enclosing $_____ (add $2.50 to cover postage and handling). Send check or money order, no cash or C.O.D.'s, please.

Name _____

Address _____

City/State/Zip _____

Send order to: Bantam Books, Dept. FN 16, 2451 S. Wolf Rd., Des Plaines, IL 60018
Allow four to six weeks for delivery.
Prices and availability subject to change without notice.   FN 16 1